About the Author

Amber Zierath lives in Alberta, Canada. She writes a monthly column of fictional stories told from the point of view of animals living in the Canadian wilderness. When she isn't writing, you can find her with the horses; riding bareback in the mountains, caring for and learning from them, and working with beginner horseback riders. *Horse Karma* is her first novel. For more information, visit: www.amberzierath.com.

Horse Karma

Amber Zierath

Horse Karma

Olympia Publishers
London

www.olympiapublishers.com
OLYMPIA PAPERBACK EDITION

A CIP catalogue record for this title is
available from the British Library.

ISBN: 978-1-80074-759-3

First Published in 2023

Olympia Publishers
Tallis House
2 Tallis Street
London
EC4Y 0AB

Printed in Great Britain

Dedication

I dedicate this book to Vickie Tait – an amazing horsewoman, person, and the ultimate teacher of horse karma.

Acknowledgements

The road to publishing this novel was long and not without challenges. Through it all, I was fortunate to have much love and support. Thank you to my dad, Sig Zierath, for always believing in me and offering countless manuscript reads and proofreading. Dad, you've been my constant cheerleader, and I'm blessed to be your daughter. Thank you, Erika Zierath, my sister, for reading my work and offering blunt and honest advice – genuinely grateful. Thank you to my kids, Riley, Kiyomi and Kyra, for their patience while I hid away with my computer for many hours to write. Thank you again to Kiyomi and Kyra, also massive horse lovers, for reading and offering editorial advice for this book. Thank you, Bob, for being a great friend and supporter of my work. Thank you to the entire Eagle Feather Riding community, both human and equine, for the lessons, stories shared and overwhelming love and support over the years. All of you, whether or not you may realize it, have contributed to this novel in some way.

/horse *noun* /hors/ – a large plant-eating domesticated mammal with solid hoofs and a flowing mane and tail, used for riding, racing, and to carry and pull loads.

/karma *noun* /kar-ma/ – the cosmic principle according to which each being is rewarded or punished according to that being's deeds. The force created by a being's actions that some believe causes good or bad things to happen to that being.

Chapter 1

Although I'm unable to speak, there's a lot I'd like to say. Since I can't use words, I've had to adapt to be heard. From a young age, I discovered that the most effective way of conveying my thoughts and opinions to others is by biting their butt.

I can't take credit for thinking of this strategy. My mama began teaching me this lesson shortly after I was born. Nipping my rump seems to be Mama's preferred style of parenting. If she and I are enjoying a stroll, but Mama insists I'm moving in the wrong direction, she'll bite my backside to make me fall in line. Whenever I'm filled with excited energy and need to run and kick around our home, she'll dig her teeth into my tender flesh once she's had enough of my shenanigans. On days when I may need to have a mid-afternoon nap, but she wants me to get up and get moving, she'll wake me by pinching my rear with her teeth.

Even though it may seem it, Mama isn't a harsh parent. There are moments aside from the biting when she grooms me gently or settles in for a cuddle. Mama always watches over me to make sure I'm safe, sometimes she'll follow me around so dang close it's smothering. Truthfully, it's a good thing she decided to parent me with biting because I'm often being bitten on my backend by several of the others we live with. In fact, some have taken the hair clean off my hide with their teeth. Honestly, that's just the way we do things around my home, and it's a good thing Mama prepared me for it.

The reality is, however, that our lifestyle has my rear taking bites often. If I'm drinking water and one of my older brothers is too impatient to wait until I'm through, they'll lunge at me, and give me a bite that sends me quickly getting out of the way. Or, if I'm eating something particularly tasty and one of my aunts or uncles thinks they should have it instead, they'll charge for me with their teeth and pinch my rump, forcing me to move on.

It may appear to some that my family likes to pick on me. At one point in my life, I did feel that way. Before I truly learned that biting was a normal form of communication for fellas like me, I often took it personally and wondered why they'd want to harm a kind-hearted soul such as myself. I thought perhaps they were jealous. I'll admit, I'm one dang good-looking guy. My long blonde hair is wavy, and the golden tone of my summer body is enviable. It's been said by several that I'll make a mighty fine breeder someday, and that all my little ones will be excellent specimens. They've also said, in front of the others, that I could be a prized commodity for sale with the right grooming. So, some may in fact be jealous of how fine and stellar I am. Honestly, I think us horses just enjoy getting our point across by sinking our teeth into each other's rumps.

It'd be much easier if we could use words like humans do. The way they can ramble on and on fascinates me. Perhaps I'm wrong, but I've never seen the humans around my place bite one another on the backside when they're trying to communicate. Although the humans who live here, Justin and Mara, do spend a lot of time inside a house and on occasion I've heard the oddest noises – maybe they do bite each other from time to time.

Thankfully, the humans don't bite me or the other horses either. Instead, they mostly use words to direct us. The word they use most often with me is, Saturn. They've said it's my name. If the humans say it, I know to approach and pay attention to whatever command they're keen on me obeying. At times, they'll use new words and new commands with me. New words are most difficult to understand in the beginning. If I don't get the human's meaning as quickly as they'd like, they'll use a small whip and slap it on various parts of my body, to try and drive their message home deeper. Truthfully, that little whip hurts more than any of the horse bites I've taken. If I could tell the humans that, I would.

There are a few other messages I'd like to deliver to my caregivers, too. Things like, my favorite place to be brushed and rubbed is on the top left corner of my neck. Also, there are some days when I'm too tired to train or learn new things – I'd love it if, on occasion, we could just hang out, snuggle and be together. When you're grooming me with the yellow brush, the one with the coarse green bristles, it scratches and pulls my hair – I'd like to be groomed with something softer, please. I'd like to tell my humans how wonderful it would be if they could feed me more food, more often. I'm feeling a little skinny and would love the kind of plump body horses all envy. Also, on the topic of food, dandelions are delicious. Have you tried them? Please don't cut them with your machine and throw them away. I'll gladly eat them all for you.

You should also know that if you're picking my feet and I pull a leg away, I'm not trying to be a brat. Sometimes I can't keep my balance and I just need a quick break before we can try again. Forcing me to do something may make you feel better, but it eats away at my soul a little. Small plastic bags are the scariest thing in the entire universe – you may not think so, but trust me, they're horrifying. I know it upsets you when I make a mess of my hair by rolling around in the mud. But it feels incredible, and I have a hunch the mud improves the appearance of my hair, so, you're welcome.

Even in the times when I'm feeling hurt or saddened by you, I'll still try and show you as much love as I can. It occurs to me that perhaps you've not been shown enough love and may not fully understand what it is. I have a solution for that. Although you're always teaching me new things, perhaps I can teach you something, too. My theory is if I show you my love, even in the times when you may hurt me, perhaps you'll learn what it looks like.

Chapter 2

A warm breeze tussles my long hair as I lift my head and sing a quick song. I'm a dang good singer. With the sun peaking up over the horizon, the world is preparing to awaken. Birds flutter above and create a harmonious melody like an organized choir. Being a bird must be incredible, seeing as how they're always making such joyous sounds.

I sing along for a few beats but stop. I'm feeling excessively warm. It's only early in the day, but I'm already sweating. This past winter, I seemed to grow a lot more hair. I mean, I've grown a bunch of hair everywhere. Which was great in the colder months when the air bit at me and made me shiver. Now that the air is warming a little more each day, I no longer need such a thick layer on my body. Hopefully, I'll shed my winter coat fast.

With the start of spring the grass is green and growing, sharing the earth with clover and, my favorite, dandelions. Summer foliage is delicious and there'll soon be plenty of it and life will be sweeter.

As the sun climbs higher into the sky and I dream of grass and clover, my tummy rumbles. It must be time for breakfast. I lower my head and pull at whatever small pieces of grass I can grip with my teeth. But there's not enough to satisfy my growing-boy appetite.

The energy amongst us horses pick up once we hear a familiar noise in the distance. It's the engine of the tractor sputtering and roaring to life. This usually means someone is preparing to deliver us hay. I'm honestly sick of eating hay after that being our main option during the winter, but I'll eat it anyway. Only until the grass is more abundant.

I'm caressed by the morning air as I trot from one end of my paddock to the next. I'm hoping to get a better view of the tractor coming with our food. I stop at a fence post and look. If I arch my neck a certain way, I can see the corner of the hay barn and exhaust rising from the tractor.

Today, however, I see something different. The birds all scatter and stop singing. The exhaust from the tractor shifts from grey to black. Then, there's a vibrant yellow and orange light that mimics the sun.

"Fire!" shouts a human from the hay barn. "Come quick! Fire!"

A shiver rushes against my spine. Some of the other horses run and buck in the opposite direction of the barn. My eyes grow wide and there's a hard thump within my ribcage. A sensation ripples across my skin, one that tells me I should consider running away.

"Fire," is yelled out by several others nearby.

My feet shuffle backward. There's danger and I want to find protection. Yellow and orange flames grow larger than the barn, and an intense heat pushes from it. Grey pieces, soft like butterfly wings, fall from the sky and blanket the ground. I move as the intensity is too much for me and turn to run away.

Chapter 3

There's nothing left of my home. All that remains are my fellow horses and the white wooden fences that corral and keep us here.

After the noisy red trucks left, the humans left, too. Then, after another full day and night, a black truck rolls up the driveway and stops along the fence. Justin and Mara climb out of the truck before looking at the blackened rubble where buildings once stood. I can sense their anxiety and sadness.

At this point, the other horses and I are restless and dang hungry. Thankfully, Justin and Mara don't waste any time with feeding us. Once there's a bowl of food in front of me, I eat too fast, making my tummy ache a little, but at least I'm full again. With my hunger satisfied, I can finally think. What's next for us? What will happen now that our home is gone?

Crickets living in the tall grass near the pond begin to hum as daylight fades. There's much uncertainty coming from both the humans and horses. It makes me uncomfortable and worrisome.

A few stars glimmer above, and I stare. I've always been fascinated by stars for some reason. Seems to me there's inexplicable magic held within those glittery specks of light. At times, I consider they may grant wishes, or something. Right now, I wish I could be in a peaceful home surrounded by love and joy instead of sadness.

Several large trucks and horse trailers shake the ground and create billows of dust as they move up our dirt driveway. I've never seen so many in a row like that before.

Justin approaches the trucks after they stop while Mara stands with her arms crossed looking at us horses. A man wearing a large brown hat that shades his face climbs out of the first truck and carries some papers in his hands. Justin and Mara aren't happy and look worried. Then, Justin and the man with the large hat walk toward us.

"I'll load all the younger ones into the smaller horse trailer," says the man from the truck. His face is wrinkled and there's a roughness to his voice.

He and Justin move around, pointing at us horses, one by one. Then, they walk to join a small circle of other humans who've gathered before us. The wrinkled man gives them all instructions before everyone scatters to different trailers. Each one grabs a halter and rope before scattering amongst us horses.

The wrinkled man comes to my paddock holding a plain brown halter. I prefer the beautifully beaded one I usually wear. I suppose it was destroyed in the fire along with everything else. Justin moves around the paddocks, helping the strange humans as they scurry about, but Mara doesn't. Instead, she stands near the horse trailers with her back turned to us. Her shoulders are shaking, and she keeps looking up at the sky.

Once the wrinkled man places a halter onto my head, he guides me out of my paddock and toward a horse trailer. As we move along the gravel road, one I've walked on at least a hundred times, the rocks feel sharper somehow. Almost as if they're trying to warn me about something.

I'm led to a large silver horse trailer with black decals on it. The door to the back of it is open, and the wrinkled man moves me toward it. Instead of following him, I stop dead in my tracks and plant my feet firmly into the ground. I draw in a long, deep breath through my nostrils, hoping to get a sense of why this deranged old man would want me to get inside the trailer. There's the scent of other horses, but none of which I recognize from my home. Nothing seems right about the thing.

A sharp tug on my lead rope jerks my head forward. I take one step closer to the horse trailer, then stop again. My eyes widen and each thump of my heart shakes my ribcage. I've never been inside a horse trailer before, and I've never met this old man before – I'm terrified.

"Get in there, boy," says the old man, clucking his tongue and yanking on the rope again as he steps inside the trailer.

"That guy has never been trailered before," says Mara. "Go easy with him, please."

"Well, first time for everything," says the old man. "I ain't got time to go easy, lady. The auction starts in a few hours."

The man yanks at my lead rope again. I lose my balance and pain pushes down my neck and back. I move forward again, and once I've run out of space to stall, I lift my front feet, one at a time, and enter the horse trailer.

"See," says the old man. "They'll do anything if you force them to."

Every part of me wants to run out of this horse trailer and get away from the wrinkled man. All I feel I can do in this moment is try and communicate with some of my other family members. Maybe one of them will know what's going on and can reassure me that everything will be okay. Lifting my head close to the small, open window in front of me, I sing loudly. Some of the other horses sing back, but they all sound loud and frantic, which doesn't ease me. I sing back and knock the side of the trailer with my foot.

"Stop doing that!" shouts the man, banging his fist on the outside of the trailer. My body jumps as the sound of his fist echoes off the sides of the metal walls, making my heartbeat even faster. I've only been inside this horse trailer a short time, but I already hate it.

My nerves calm slightly when another horse my size is loaded into the trailer next to me, a chestnut fella named Chuck. We're separated by a long metal barricade, but at least he's there. At least I have a piece of familiarity in this strange place.

Three more horses are loaded into the trailer before there's a loud bang and it gets darker. Us horses all call out loudly. Just when I don't think any of us can feel more scared, the wheels of the truck and trailer begin to move. My eyes are wide open, and I look out the small window in front of me as we move away from my home.

Chapter 4

This place is loud. There are human voices, horse sounds and odd noises coming from every direction. Sadly, among the human sounds, I don't hear Justin or Mara. My heart is beating fast, and I'm soaked with sweat. I call out to my family, but no one responds. Or maybe they do, but I just can't hear them.

A loud thud at the back of our horse trailer makes me pause and look. The back door opens wide, and the wrinkled man appears. He takes the other horses off the trailer, one by one, until it's finally my turn.

"Don't give me any grief, boy," says the wrinkled man, tugging hard on my lead rope. I don't want my neck to hurt more than it already does, so I move obligingly with him.

My feet meet wood chips once I'm out of the trailer. I try and find the sky, but instead, only see a tall ceiling and large bright lights. I must be inside the largest barn in the world, and I'm surrounded by at least a million horses, or so. Humans of all shapes, sizes and colors walk around and stop occasionally to look at a horse within a pen. My nostrils flare rapidly, trying to take in all the new smells in this place.

There are a bunch of round pens set up, all full of horses. The wrinkled man leads me toward one and I see some horses from my home already there. Before I join them, the wrinkled old man puts something sticky onto my hip. I want to scratch at it, but I'm immediately led into the pen with the others.

Even though we've all lived together our entire lives, each

of us behaves like the other is a threat. As much as our tiny pen allows, we buck, kick, and bite one another on the butt and neck. After several minutes of this, I push myself into a safer position against the cool metal of the round pen and watch the rest of my pen mates continue to behave like ding-dongs.

Then, Chuck, the chestnut fellow from my old home, moves in next to me. Instead of giving into my fears and chasing him off, I allow him to stay. It's nice to be still and feel close to someone again, especially within the chaos of this new place. After a time, the others also begin to settle. Feeling somewhat safe again, I take another gander around.

My eye catches the look of something I like. In a round pen not too far from ours are a bunch of ladies. There's one, not much bigger than I am, with hair dark as night and eyes that sparkle like the brightest star. I can't take my eyes off her, she's stunning. Although I'm a gelding, I haven't lost the lure of a pretty lady. Chuck looks in her direction, too. He must see the same vision of beauty that I do. I wonder if she's into blondes like me or red heads like him?

The loud voice of a human speaking fast, like a yipping coyote, shakes me from my stare. I wish it would stop, but it goes on and on, and on. As the voice speaks, horses leave their round pens, one by one. Then, the wrinkled man comes to my pen and removes horses in the same manner.

I'm the third to go. My legs shake with each step. Where is the wrinkled man leading me? Will I need to defend myself against other horses when we arrive? I hope he's taking me to food.

The wrinkled man and I walk through a small corridor before arriving in a new space within the large building. Instead of being surrounded by the million other horses, I'm the only one there.

The wrinkled old man stays with me, firmly holding onto my lead rope close to my head. He and I stand in the middle of a large round pen. On one side, there are rows of humans sitting still and looking at me. Then, the man sounding like a yipping coyote speaks loudly again.

"Here we have a two-year-old Palomino male named Saturn," says the coyote man.

My ears perk up with hearing my name. After that, nothing else the coyote man says makes any dang sense. While he speaks quickly, the wrinkled man leads me around in a bunch of circles in front of the watching humans. Then, the talking and our walking stops.

"Sold," says the coyote man.

What does sold mean? The wrinkled man leads me out of the round pen. I want to go back and be with the other horses I arrived with. Instead, I'm led in an entirely new direction.

Chapter 5

My new home is nothing like my old one. After a long ride in a small horse trailer, the backdoor swings open and my new owner steps into view. His name is Spencer, and his face has no wrinkles like the man who took me from my home. His jeans are tight enough to show off his skinny legs, and his shirt is too big for his scrawny shoulders. Our hair is similar in color, but the stubble on his face is brown.

"Welcome home, little buddy," says Spencer, stepping up into the horse trailer and taking hold of my lead rope.

My feet meet gravel once they come off the trailer. The sun is already crouching down to make room in the sky for the moon. What I see first is the enormous rocks the sun is ducking behind. They're off in the distance and must be the largest things in the entire world. Closer to me are trees spread out; spiked green ones and some with leaves on top.

There isn't a barn anywhere that I can see, just a tiny human home. Spencer gently tugs on my lead rope, which I appreciate rather than hard yanking, so I move for him. We walk along a gravel road for a minute or two before stopping at a gate. It leads to a small square paddock with a rickety old wooden shelter and just enough room for a horse or two. Spencer opens the gate and leads me into the paddock.

"I know the place isn't much yet," says Spencer in a low voice. "But heck, I'm only twenty-one and I've got big plans. I used most of my savings to buy this plot here of ten acres, put my single wide mobile home on it, and did all the fencing and your horse shelter myself with scraps I salvaged."

The horse shelter shakes a little when the breeze picks up. Made from scraps, indeed. In fact, there's scrap metal, wood and all kinds of garbage strewn everywhere. An old truck is parked close to one section of my fence. A tractor that may be older than dirt is lined up along another section with some of its rusty pieces pushing through the fence and into my space. Along the ground on one side are stacks of old metal pipe, fence posts and sheet metal.

The breeze pushes against my face and offers up something new I'm keen to investigate. It's the smell of another horse. Another dude, as far as I can tell, but I'm guessing much older than me.

"Shadow!" yells Spencer as he removes my halter and closes the gate to my paddock.

"Shadow!" shouts Spencer again, then looks toward a cluster of trees beyond the fence of my pen.

From the trees emerges a black and grey horse whose twice my size. Shadow's mane whips in the wind as he runs majestically toward Spencer's call. Just before he reaches us, he sings out like a dang rockstar.

Shadow stops along the fence separating his space from mine. Spencer climbs up onto the top wooden rung and sits there between us. Shadow leans his nose over the fence and pushes it close to my neck. I'm terrified of this hulky dude, but my legs won't move me out of his way, so I just stand there frozen.

"Heck," says Spencer. "I know you two are meant to be separated for two-weeks, but I just don't have the set-up for it. I'm sure it'll be fine. You look healthy enough to me, little buddy."

Shadow remains close, and I feel his warm breath as he smells me. Then, he howls out like someone just kicked him in the ribs, hard. As far as I can tell, Spencer's boot is nowhere near him, and neither is anything else that could've hurt him. He's making all that noise because of me.

I decide to test Shadow a little. I'd like to smell him, too. Boldly, I push my nose through the space between the top two fence rungs and get close to Shadow's barrel. I smell him once, twice, then the old coot howls again, like I've just bit him aggressively. But I didn't bite the dang guy, not even a little.

"You two will get along just fine in no time," says Spencer, laughing a little and smiling.

Shadow moves away from Spencer and me, his long, black tail swaying as he trots in the direction opposite to us. After moving a short distance, he stops within an open space in the middle of his paddock. Then looks at me, bucks his back legs and twists around before trotting back toward us again. Shadow's trying to show me his best moves. I guess I'd better go ahead and show him what I've got.

I step back from the fence and quickly run opposite to Spencer and Shadow. My neck arch's back and around, so I can look to make sure they're watching. When all eyes are on me, I move my behind and prepare to kick back. But before I can show off my awesome skills, I trip on a stick and fall to the ground. Spencer laughs so loud that it obliterates any other sounds around us. I've never been so humiliated in my life.

When I scramble back up to my feet and Spencer stops laughing, he jumps down from the fence and uses both hands to shift his tight jeans. "I'll go and get you two some grub," he says, scratching Shadow on the neck. "I need you to show the little man how things work around here, Shadow. Even though he's young, I aim to train him into the best roping horse the rodeo has ever seen. Some day, we'll win the big money at the Calgary Stampede and build a big old house and warm barn for you boys. Yes, sir, we're going to be rodeo rich some day. But Saturn doesn't sound like the right name for a superstar rodeo horse."

Spencer leaves Shadow and walks over to me. He looks into my eyes and rubs at the space above my nose. "You're a golden boy, and I like gold," says Spencer. "And I aim to make you the fastest horse in rodeo so we can win some gold. Ah heck, I've got it. Your new name is, Golden Flash. Flash for short."

Chapter 6

Although Shadow and I are separated, I stay close to the fence between us. I'm glad to see that Shadow doesn't move off too far from me either, even though he could disappear into the woods within his space. It helps to have another horse close by, even if we hardly know each other.

As the sky blackens for night, a shiver rushes over my body. The air is warm, but I still feel chilled. It's the first time I've ever been alone and away from the small herd of horses I've known since birth. Usually, there was always a warm body to press up against in my old home. Besides, it wasn't only about having bodies close to stay warm. It was more about knowing someone was around if trouble came near.

How far away is my family? I lift my head up high and point it toward the sky. After taking a long, deep breath, I sing as loud as I can, then pause. I wait for a response, but all is quiet. I lift my head and sing again, this time, louder than the last, but I hear nothing in response.

A glimmer from above catches my eye, so I look up. Stars freckle the sky and the familiarity of knowing them eases me just a little. I stare at a single star and with each passing second, it appears to get brighter and brighter. My heart aches and another shiver rushes over my body. With my gaze fixed on the star, I wish to be surrounded by love, so I'll feel better. Perhaps Spencer will do that for me.

Bright lights and the sound of an engine comes down the

gravel road and toward Spencer's home. As it gets closer, loud music adds to the mix of noise. The door to Spencer's home opens and he rushes out. A large, red truck stops in front of Spencer and the driver's side door opens. With the music still playing loudly, a young man steps out and into the lights of the truck.

He's much taller than Spencer and three times larger around. His hair is short, brown, and messy on the top. He and Spencer shake hands, laugh, and speak – but I can't hear what they're saying because the music is so dang loud.

"Turn the music off and come meet my new horse," says Spencer.

The visitor shakes his head in agreement, turns the music off in his truck but leaves the lights on. Then, he grabs two brown bottles filled with liquid, hands one to Spencer, and the pair of them walk toward me.

I'm eager for the company, so I run over to the fence in their direction. Maybe the brown liquid in the bottles is more food for me. I'm still hungry, even though Spencer fed me a bowl of food and a small portion of hay.

"Kyle," says Spencer to his friend, twisting a cap off the brown bottle and pointing it toward me. "This is my new fella, Golden Flash."

Kyle makes a noise sounding like a cross between a grunt and laugh which seems to offend Spencer.

"This is your new roping horse?" asks Kyle. "Are you kidding me? How old is he?"

Spencer leans his arms on the rickety wooden fence and looks me up and down. I can tell he's upset, so I move in close and nudge him with my nose, just to let him know I'm here if he needs anything.

"I know, I know," says Spencer, scratching my forelock with his hand. "He's just two-years-old now, but I figure since I got him young, I can train him fresh and groom him to be exactly the kind of roping horse I want. No bad habits, just trained the way I like."

"Roping horses aren't any good until at least ten years old," says Kyle. "You're going to feed and train this guy for the next eight years before you even use him? This guy will end up being a waste of time and money. Sell him and find a horse that's useful to you now."

Something about Kyle's words and mannerisms makes my tummy curl in an uncomfortable way. I'd like to bite him on the butt and move him off Spencer, but I can't reach through the fence, and I've learned not to bite a human. Too dang bad.

"There was a five-year-old at the 1974 NFR who went on to be a star," says Spencer. "Shadow and I can start now by showing Flash the ropes and what not. I can start by saddling him up and getting him used to me being on his back and soon after, train him for roping."

"You think Shadow has enough hustle left in him to wait another five plus years for this guy to be ready?"

"Shadow's only nineteen," says Spencer. "He'll be good for another five years. Once rodeo season is over for the year, I'll have plenty of time to start training him through the fall and winter. Besides, I only paid a grand for this little palomino. Good roping horses cost at least ten times as much. If I train Golden Flash here well enough, I can sell him for that price and make a nice profit if nothing else. Maybe even for more if he and I win some events."

Did Spencer just say sell? I hadn't known what the word meant until today. I haven't even been here a full night, and

Spencer is already talking about selling me? I don't want another new home.

I push myself in closer to Spencer. I nuzzle my head and try to hug him. Maybe if I love him enough, he'll never want to let me go.

"Looks to me like your new horse would be better suited to kid's pony rides," says Kyle, emptying the liquid from his brown bottle. "He's a giant softy. You might be better off saddle training him, then selling him for a slight profit."

"Shut up," says Spencer, throwing a fist into the side of Kyle's shoulder. Kyle flinches, but smiles and seems unbothered.

The pair of them laugh and walk toward Spencer's home. I replay their conversation in my mind, focusing on the words useful and sell. Would he honestly only train me to sell me?

Chapter 7

The sun has been up for hours, but there's no sign of Spencer or Kyle. They played loud music well into the night while laughing and talking. I'm not sure how long it's been since my last meal, and my tummy is growling with intensity. But as I search my small pen for anything edible, it turns up bare.

I walk over to the fence separating Shadow and me. He's in a better space than I am. At least his area has bits of grass growing in some spots. Luckier still, he has a billion trees around him with bark he can chew on to satisfy his hunger, if he were desperate like I am now.

Shadow notices me lurking and approaches. The old dude smells my neck again and this time, instead of hollering, he does nothing. I suppose this means we can be friends now. I decide I'll need to carefully study the old man, knowing that I need to be as good of a horse as him, so Spencer thinks I'm useful and won't sell me.

If Shadow is that impressive, I'll need to be exactly like him. He bends down and sniffs at the ground. To mimic him, I bend down and sniff the ground also. Then, Shadow walks over to the water trough we share through the fence. Although I'm not thirsty, I also walk over to the water trough. Shadow takes a drink. I take a drink. He walks away from the water. I walk away from the water. Nothing too impressive so far, but I'll press on and keep copying his actions.

Then, Shadow turns himself around so he's facing away from me and has his backside pointed in my direction instead. I'd like to turn around, too, but then I won't be able to see what he'll do next, so I pause and watch. He takes a few steps backward. I take a few steps backward. Shadow continues to move until his butt touches a post of the wooden fence that separates us.

Curiosity consumes me, so I watch the old dude. Shadow sways his backend from side to side along the fence. Scratching noises come with each movement as the fence bends and cracks a little. Shadow arches his neck with delight as he continues having his moment with the fence. If I'm being honest, he looks like a dang ding-dong.

Because I vowed to mimic this weirdo, I turn myself around and back into the fence a few posts down from Shadow. I move my butt from side to side, and I'm overwhelmed by an indescribable feeling.

Each movement my butt makes against the fence scratches at places my scrawny neck can never reach. All the bug bites back there and hair shed I can't grab at on my behind, are suddenly soothed with each rub. It feels awesome. I guess Shadow isn't an idiot after all. In fact, he's a dang genius.

"Morning, boys," shouts Spencer, walking out of his home and toward us.

Shadow stops scratching and sings out in response to Spencer's voice. I follow Shadow's lead and present Spencer my best singing voice, too. Then, I sing again, only louder once I realize Spencer is bringing us food.

I dive my face into the bowl of food the second Spencer puts it down on the ground. Once that's gone, I move onto the meager helping of hay he's laid out for me.

"You guys look like you're getting along fine," says Spencer. "Another day or two, and I'll put you together in the larger pen. Then, we need to get to training you, Golden Flash. No training today though, boys. Ah heck, maybe tomorrow."

Chapter 8

Spencer says the phrase 'maybe tomorrow' often. He always attaches other words to it like – errands to run, people to see, a small job to do, or something of the like.

Each morning since I've arrived, Spencer walks out of his home to feed Shadow and me. He spends a bit of time with us and explains how we're all going to do big things in life, win big money and make this place first class. We just gotta train – maybe tomorrow.

After several weeks of hearing 'maybe tomorrow' Spencer says something new. "Today is the day, boys," he says, after delivering our daily bowl of feed. "Eat up 'cause, we have some training to do."

Always hungry, Shadow and I gobble up our food. "Let's get your halters on," says Spencer. He walks toward us with his hands full of ropes and such. Shadow lowers his head to allow his halter to be placed on his head. Still mimicking Shadow, I lower my head once Spencer comes close and allow him to place my halter onto my head, too.

"Good boy, Golden Flash," he says. My chest puffs a little with pride at hearing him say I'm good. Wanting him to know he's a good boy, too, I nuzzle my head close to his chest and lick his shirt.

Spencer laughs and smiles. "Ah heck, you're a funny little fella, Flash. Come on, boys. Hey, Shadow, let's introduce Flash to Bessy."

Spencer opens a gate and leads Shadow and me through it. While Shadow follows Spencer with calm and decorum, I can't seem to keep myself still. I'm too excited about the training to walk calmly. My backside skitters from side to side, and I toss my head in all directions to get a good look at everything. We walk until we arrive at a pen on the other side of Spencer's home. The thing is this pen has a creature in it.

My nostrils flare searching for a scent as I try and figure out what the heck that dang creature is. It's all black and has horns on its head. I don't imagine anything with horns is going to be nice. This notion makes my legs scoot and skitter even more. I tug on the lead rope within Spencer's hand, hoping he'll realize he's leading us to danger. That horned beast could probably eat the three of us up in one gulp.

"It's okay, little buddy," says Spencer, leaning his head closer to mine. "I see it, and it's okay. Shadow isn't afraid, I'm not afraid, so you don't need to be afraid."

I stop dead in my tracks, nostrils flaring and my eyes on the horned beast. My heart pounds in my chest, and I'm so scared that I need to pee. I assume the position, but because I'm still frightened, my legs wobble and shift as I go. Now, I've gone and wet myself. More dang humiliation.

Thankfully, the creature is closed off and it hasn't moved or made a sound since we've approached it. Maybe it's not as scary as I thought. At least we're safe over here on this side of the fence.

Spencer leads us to the gate within the fence housing the creature and, to my mortification, he opens it. My legs scramble to move my feet backward. The farther I can get away from the horned beast, the better.

In one swift motion, Spencer unclasps Shadow's lead rope

from his halter and says, "Shadow, go and stand next to Bessy."

Shadow trots off into the round pen, my legs scramble with more intensity forcing Spencer to use two hands with my lead rope. Then, he lets go with one hand, raises it, and smacks me across the nose. The sting from the strike is intense and instant.

"That's enough fussing, Flash," shouts Spencer.

I want to stop, but I'm still scared of the horned beast. Even more scared with Spencer hitting me like there's something terribly wrong. My legs scramble more, and I toss my head around a few times. Then, Spencer strikes me on the nose again. This time, harder than the first.

"Ah heck, enough!" he shouts. "Stop fussing."

The sting forces me to stop moving as it dominates my attention. My nostrils flare and I look into Spencer's eyes. I can see that he's angry with me. Although I'm hurting from the hitting, I don't want him to be angry or worse, think I'm a terrible horse and want to sell me and send me away. But I don't think it's right that he's hitting me either.

"That's better," says Spencer, pulling me into the round pen and closer to the horned beast.

Once we're nearer to it, Shadow stands next to the monster, still and strong. He's not upset, scared nor fussing like I am. This slows my heart rate a little and I ease up to follow Spencer with more grace.

"It's not alive or real, Flash," says Spencer, moving to stand beside it. "It's just a dummy, to practice my roping."

I move myself a little closer to the dummy, and sniff. It smells like a plastic bag. This lowers my heart rate a little more, even though I hate plastic bags.

"You'd best get used to it, Flash," says Spencer. "You're going to be spending a lot of time with this dummy for training.

Heck, real cows, too, once I can win some more money and buy them."

My nose is throbbing now, but I try and ignore it. At least Spencer isn't mad at me anymore. Like he says, I'd better get used to being around dummies. Whether I like it or not.

Spencer had Shadow and me working with the dummy until nightfall. We were led back to our paddock only by the light of the stars and a crescent moon. Once Shadow and I were securely back in our space, Spencer left us without saying a word.

It would have been nice to have some encouragement or love from the guy after working so hard for him today. My nose still pulsates with a sting from where Spencer hit me earlier. Although it physically hurts, the events scarred my heart more.

A bright star hanging close to a cluster of others grabs my attention. The way it's shimmering makes me think it's waving at me, beckoning me. I stare at it and focus all my attention onto its magnificent light. Then, I wish to be smothered by tons of human love. Just as the wish enters my mind, the star blazes through the sky, leaving a tail of glitter behind it. I follow it with my eyes until it completely leaves my sight.

Chapter 9

After feeding me, Spencer places my halter onto my head and leads me back to the round pen with Bessy the dummy. Shadow isn't coming along this time as he's already a master roping horse. I, on the other hand, still have much to learn.

Once in the round pen, Spencer holds my lead rope and has me run around in circles. He calls it lunging. We work hard and long enough for the sun to shift from one edge of the sky to the next. When my lungs are burning and I'm not sure I can move anymore, he tells me to stop. I do as he asks on cue and wait for my next command. With a tight grip still on my lead rope, Spencer leads me over to the dummy where another rope rests around the plastic horns. This one is different to my lead rope; white and coiled up into itself. Spencer grabs it with one hand and holds it.

I haven't had any training with this coiled rope, but Spencer uses it for rodeo. Still holding it with one hand, he moves it closer to my face. This rope and I haven't been properly introduced, and I'm hesitant, but not as much as when I first met Bessy. Spencer lifts the rope closer to my face, and I flinch, tossing my head away from it.

"You're all right now, Flash," says Spencer, shaking the rope a little. "You need to be a champion roping horse, so I can't have you scared of ropes."

I sniff the rope and stare at it with wide eyes. I can tell it means me no harm, so I stay put and let Spencer keep it close to my face. Then, Spencer moves his hand with the rope quickly and taps it against my neck. This sends a jolt through my heart and scares the heck out of me. I kick my back legs and toss my head.

"Stop it!" shouts Spencer, using his hand with the rope to strike me on the nose.

It hurts mighty bad to be struck with a rope, so I stop to try and collect myself. Why do I have to be so dang scared of everything? Why do I keep disappointing Spencer? Worse, why does he keep hitting me?

"It's just a rope, Flash," says Spencer with intensity in his eyes and voice. "Stay put and don't make me regret buying you. I'll send you back to auction, sell you and buy a horse that can actually be useful."

I don't want Spencer to take me back to auction. I don't want him to sell me and send me away. I don't mean to keep messing up. I lower my head, nuzzle close to Spencer, and allow him to tap the scary rope all over my body.

Once the ground was covered with a blanket of snow, we didn't train. Spencer doesn't like the cold, so he mostly stayed inside his home. Thankfully, I got to be with Shadow every day. During the coldest nights of winter, I was grateful for his company. To keep warm, he and I stayed huddled together beneath the rickety old shelter within our enclosure. As far as winter goes, that's about all we did, beside eat, and scratch our butts against fence posts.

But now, the air is warming by the day, and I'm excited for the arrival of spring and all the yummy green things it'll bring me to eat. Droplets of melting snow drip from the roof of our shelter. Any day now and winter will be officially over.

Spencer walks toward us with pep in his step. He's holding mine and Shadow's food bowls, so we walk over to the fence to meet him. My eyes grow wide, and I nicker as Spencer brings us both a heaping portion of food, much more than he would normally bring us.

"Eat up, boys," says Spencer. "We've got some exciting things going on today."

I'm not too interested in what exciting things Spencer is going on about because all I want is to get all the food from the bowl and into my belly before anyone else can try and get to it. As I eat, Spencer is busy with the wheelbarrow he normally uses to bring us hay. Instead of laying hay out once and putting the wheelbarrow away, he goes for another load, then another. Spencer was right, this is one heck of an exciting day.

With my bowl licked clean, I move over to the hay. I haven't seen this much laying out on the ground since I lived in my last home. Shadow takes a few bites before Spencer approaches him with his halter. I keep eating, hoping to gobble up a bunch before my halter is placed onto my head, too.

Instead, Spencer leads only Shadow out of the gate, then closes it behind him. "Shadow and I are going to a training clinic a few hours away," he says. I keep eating hay as Spencer loads Shadow into the horse trailer already hitched to his truck. "We'll be gone for three days and two nights. Don't go eating that hay all at once."

I ignore him and keep eating only lifting my head once to watch Spencer and Shadow drive off and leave me on my own.

Chapter 10

I stand at the gate for quite a time, waiting and watching for Spencer and Shadow to come home. Once the sun climbs to its highest point in the sky, I get bored and decide to move on. My hay pile is about a quarter gone, and my belly feels full, but I can't resist it and stop for another few bites. As I chew, I'm distracted by a noise within the trees, nothing scary, but it makes me curious enough to want to check it out.

I walk slowly on the uneven ground, now a combination of thawed snow, ice, mud, and hard earth, and enter the grove of trees in the back of the pen. The noise intensifies and I realize that it's more like a cluster of soft sounds uniting to create something louder. It comes from all around and although I search for the source, there's nothing else here besides me and the trees. Then, a drop of water, splatters onto my nose and makes the same sound.

When I lift my head to look at the clouds, there's only bright blue sky, nothing to indicate a rainstorm is afoot. Droplets of water spill from leaves and branches and create the noise. Although I'm glad there's not any danger, I'm also a little disappointed to find it's only the snow melting. I'm so dang bored without Shadow and Spencer. I hoped the noise would bring a little excitement to occupy my time.

After a long, uneventful walk through the same trees I pass every day, I mosey on back to the front gate to see if Spencer and Shadow are home yet. They're not. I draw in a deep breath, then sigh heavily through my nose. When are those guys going to get back? They said a few days, but what the heck does that even mean? I don't like being here alone. And it's getting darker which means it'll be nightfall soon.

My feet slip on the ground as the air cools and hardens the day's melt back into ice. I step carefully and steady my balance as I move. The wind picks up the corner of a piece of sheet metal laying within the pile of junk at the end of my paddock. Since I've got nothing better to do, I decide to investigate it.

I step, slip, step a few more times, then slip again until I'm at the flapping piece of metal. My head moves along with it as it flaps up, then down, then up again until this all bores me, too. With my head lowered, I walk around to the other side of the junk pile and sniff.

Something shimmers with the moonlight and catches my attention. I move to get closer and check it out. As I step, my foot doesn't connect with the ground properly as it meets a patch of ice. My heart drops within my chest as I scramble to balance myself, but I can't steady my feet.

The stars blur as my body lunges forward. Metal crashes as my head collides with the pile first. Then, there's a sharp, stabbing pain in my chest above my front leg. I cry out, as loud as my voice can muster. My cry echoes into the night sky until fading into the expansive solitude.

I'm stuck in position, so I jerk my head and push my feet into the slippery ground. When this tactic fails to help me regain my stance, I squirm my mid-section, then flail my head and claw at the ground with my feet. Each movement induces more pain, and I continue to cry out. I wish someone were here.

After several grueling attempts to stand, I pause to catch my breath. Warm liquid leaks from the front of my chest where it struck the metal, then down my leg. My nostrils flare and each pump of my heart thuds against my chest and in my ears. There's a glimmer above me that beckons me to look. It's the sparkle of an early evening star, pushing through the last of dusk to be seen. I cry out again and sing in the best voice I can muster.

The star shines brighter, then flickers, like it's trying to communicate with me. It gives me a boost of energy, a rush of adrenaline. I take a deep breath then all at once, jerk my head back and move my feet onto the ground and hoist myself up.

A sharp pain consumes me as I pull backward onto my feet and away from the pile of junk. I slip and struggle to use one of my front legs but still manage to get myself into the shelter. Each breath I take feels difficult, and the warm liquid blankets my chest only to freeze shortly after with the night air.

My chest and leg throb and when I try to put pressure on it, I wince with pain. I sing out loudly again, but still, there's no reply. I feel uneasy about the night and what the light of morning will bring.

Chapter 11

My eyes blink wearily as the sun rises above the trees. I'm glad to see daylight. A shiver rushes across my spine, a chill from my wet chest. I take a few labored steps out of the shelter and expose myself to the dull rays of the sun. Soon, it'll be at full strength and should heat me through.

Although the hay pile isn't far from me, it hurts too much to walk, so I ignore the growl within my belly. I turn my head to look toward the front gate and over at Spencer's home. There's still no sign of either he or Shadow. When will they return? I need them.

After another long, cold night and almost full day, I finally hear an engine encroaching. With weary eyes and the weakness of hunger, I turn my head to look. My eyes widen when the front grill of Spencer's truck and the top end of the horse trailer come into view.

I lift my head and sing loudly, then take one limped step toward the gate. Intense pain surges through my body, but I force myself to step again and again, until I'm closer to the gate and completely visible to Spencer.

He drives the truck in a semi-circle, then backs the trailer all the way into the gate of my paddock. Once he steps out from the driver's side, I take another couple of painful steps in his direction and sing out as loud as I can.

I'm pleased to hear Shadow sing back to me, he must have missed me, too. Spencer is whistling as he walks toward the back of the trailer. Then, I see him, and he looks at me.

"Holy heck, Golden Flash," says Spencer, removing his large-brimmed hat and rushing toward me with wide eyes. Shadow uses a foot to knock on the side of the horse trailer, singing out to Spencer and me, like he's begging to get out.

I take another limped step forward before Spencer is in front of me. He bends down and gently places his hands onto my swollen chest. When he lifts his hands and looks, they're covered in red.

"What happened to you, little man?" says Spencer in a whisper.

Then, he scrambles to his feet and rushes over to the horse trailer. He opens the gate then the back door to the trailer and lets Shadow climb out and into our paddock. I take another limped step toward my friend as he trots over to me. Shadow sniffs my chest, then calls out loudly. Before I can respond to Shadow's cry, Spencer is at my side with a halter and lead rope.

He quickly halters me, then slowly guides me over to the horse trailer. I follow as best as I can. Shadow remains at my side, nickering and whinnying the entire way. He sounds distressed, so I nicker and whinny in my most loving and positive way, trying to reassure my friend that I'll be okay. I want him to know that I'm not leaving him.

It takes some time, but I manage to get into the horse trailer and stand in position. Shadow is still carrying on, so I use what little strength I have and sing to him.

Don't worry, Shadow. I'll be okay and we'll be back together soon.

Chapter 12

My legs want to give out by the time Spencer finally stops the horse trailer. He makes noise getting out of the truck before speaking to someone.

"Thanks for meeting me," says Spencer. "I'm worried, he looks bad."

"What happened?" asks a new voice; a beautiful tone that's soft and sweet.

"I don't know," says Spencer, opening the back door of the trailer. "Shadow and I were out, and when I came home, I found him like this."

A beautiful young woman with long raven hair and tanned skin approaches the trailer. She smells of other animals, some I recognize and some I don't. Her energy radiates love and kindness, making me want to nuzzle in close to her.

Spencer rushes into the horse trailer and grabs my lead rope. He gently pulls on it and guides me toward the exit. Once I'm on the edge and know I need to jump down off the thing, I pause. Pain throbs within my chest, and it's going to hurt like heck to climb out.

"Awe, darlin, you look like you're really hurting," says the young woman. "Let me get him something for the pain. That should help him come out."

"Sure," says Spencer, offering her a look. There's a twinkle in his eye when he looks at the young woman. It reminds me of the look I gave the beautiful female horse I saw at the auction when I wished I could get closer to her.

"Thanks for your help, Lorraine," says Spencer when the young woman comes back.

"No problem," she says.

Lorraine has put on a pair of clear plastic gloves. She's holding something long and narrow filled with liquid. She looks at me, smiles, and stands close. Her eyes are deep brown, soft and kind.

"Easy, darlin," she says, her voice gentle and sweet. She softly places one hand near my injured chest before looking at me again. "Easy, sweet boy. I'm going to give you something for the pain."

She lowers her head, close enough for me to lower mine next to her. She giggles as I smell the skin on the back of her neck. Then, there's a sharp pinch near my wound that causes me to flinch.

"I know, darlin," says Lorraine. "Easy, now. This will help you feel better."

She wasn't kidding. In no time at all, my wound feels warm, then almost as if it isn't there at all. Not only that, but my head also feels light and airy, like I'm suddenly floating up in the clouds.

Lorraine takes the lead rope from Spencer, then carefully motions for me to follow her. Heck, I'll follow this beautiful darlin anywhere. Man, I'm feeling dang good right about now. My knees wobble a little, but almost painlessly, I climb down and off the horse trailer.

Spencer and Lorraine walk side by side and talk as they lead me into a large metal barn with bright lights. Other animal and human noises come from inside, but I can't tell what any of them are at this point. Whatever Lorraine has given me for the pain blurs my vision.

"I'll need to do some x-rays and tests," says Lorraine to Spencer, her voice sounding like a distant echo, as she leads me into a small box stall. "It could take time."

"Do whatever you need, Lorraine," says Spencer with a smile. "Awe, heck, I love this little guy, and I want you to spare no expense. Give him whatever he needs."

Spencer loves me? That's all I've ever wanted from him. Now that I understand that I'm sure things will be different once we return home.

"Are you sure?" asks Lorraine. "Would you like me to call you and get permission first? He could need surgery."

"You just do whatever it takes," says Spencer. "Call me anytime you like, I don't mind. But do whatever you think he needs. No permission necessary."

"Okay. I'll call you when I have more information."

Spencer nods his head and smiles at Lorraine before moving over to me. He scratches my head and leans in close. "You're in good hands, Flash. I'll be back to pick you up just as soon as you're healed."

My eyes blink heavily, and Spencer walks away leaving me with Lorraine.

Chapter 13

My insides feel like soft mud after a summer's rain; warm and smooth. Each time I attempt to open my eyes, they seem to fight back, pushing me to close them and drift off to sleep. Dreams fill my mind as I rest. At first, I'm flying through fluffy white clouds with a cluster of black birds. Then, most suddenly, I'm running through a field of tall, lush grass at top speed and feel like the fastest horse in the world. Again, the scene rapidly shifts to me standing in the same field of grass, but this time, I'm eating as quickly as my teeth can rip the greens from the earth.

"Golden Flash," says a beautiful voice in the distance.

Still in my dream state, I lift my head to look for the source of the voice. There's nothing around but me, some birds, and a few butterflies. Weird. Maybe it's the birds, singing my name as they fly overhead, admiring the magnificent creature that I am. Must be. I lower my head down to eat more grass when I hear it again. This time, my dream vision disappears, and all is black.

"Golden Flash," says a female as a hand strokes my neck.

My eyes open to a bright light. I blink a bunch, then see the silhouette of a woman. Then, she says my name again. I've heard that voice before, but because it still feels a bit unfamiliar to me, I scramble onto my wobbly legs from where I was laying and stand.

"Good boy, Golden Flash," says the female.

The room is spinning, and my vision is blurred, but after gaining my bearings, I find the female with the voice again and realize, it's the nice woman I met earlier named Lorraine. She continues to stroke my neck, and I allow it, lowering my head a bit in case she wants to scratch behind my ears, too. Then, she bends down in front of me and gently touches my chest.

"You did very well with the surgery, darlin," says Lorraine. "It wasn't anything too major, I just cleaned it up and sewed you back together. But you were left for so long without care that I'm not sure how well you'll heal."

I lower my head and put my nose next to Lorraine. Then, out of nowhere, a giant sneeze blasts from my nostrils and onto Lorraine's face. She jumps to her feet, so I toss my head and step back, in case I've angered her.

To my surprise, she laughs and wipes the side of her face with the back of her hand. This eases me, and I take a step toward her so she can go back to stroking my neck and scratching my ears. Before she can get back to pampering me, a buzzing sound comes from behind her. She reaches her hand around to her backside and brings a phone around and looks at the screen.

"What do you know, Golden Flash," says Lorraine, smiling at me. "It's your human, Spencer."

My ears perk at the sound of his name, and I nicker. I love Spencer and Shadow so much, and I just want to get back home to them.

"Hey, Spencer," says Lorraine into her phone. "I'm good, how are you?"

I step closer, limping, and can hear Spencer's voice, faintly through the phone pressed next to Lorraine's ear. I whinny to say, 'I love you', hoping he'll hear it and maybe Shadow will, too. Lorraine smiles and laughs under her breath then strokes the soft space just above my eyes.

"Yes, that was your boy," says Lorraine. "The surgery went

well, and I cleaned the wound and put him back together as best as I could."

Lorraine pauses and her forehead wrinkles as she listens to Spencer speak.

"Well, unfortunately there was some damage to the muscle just above his right leg," says Lorraine, her energy shifting slightly to sadness. "I repaired what I could, but I'm afraid there may always be damage in that area. It's still too soon to tell, but there's a possibility his gait and balance will always be off."

Lorraine pauses to listen to Spencer again, then, she sighs heavily and frowns.

"I don't know that he'll ever be the runner you need for a roping horse, Spencer," she says. "I'm really sorry. I could be wrong, but the way his injury sits around that leg, I'd guess he'll need to spend his life as more of a leisure horse. And I have to say, this boy is so loving and there's just something so special about him, you know?"

I lean in closer to Lorraine, fully relaxed by the way she's been rubbing my head. A loud sigh escapes through my nose, and I feel sleepy again.

"He's good to go if you can give him a space to heal and stay dry for a few days," says Lorraine. "When do you think you'll come and get him?"

Lorraine listens, her eyebrows raise, then she looks at me and smiles.

"Great," she says. "Golden Flash and I will see you then. Okay, have a good night. Bye for now."

Lorraine reaches her arm around to her backside and slides her phone back into a pocket. Then, she uses both hands to rub each side of my neck before finally, getting to scratching behind my ears.

"Good news, darlin," she says. "That was Spencer and he said he's coming to pick you up – maybe tomorrow."

Those words, maybe tomorrow, repeat in my mind several times. I've heard Spencer say them too often. I only hope this time he really means it.

Chapter 14

One of the best things about being with Lorraine in her clinic is the food. That girl has made me some of the best dang meals I've ever tasted. And the portions are bigger than what I get at home. Heck, she also gives me as much hay as I can eat, so I never feel hungry.

It's officially the tomorrow that Spencer said he'd come and fetch me, and I'm waiting as patiently as possible for him to get here. Although being in a small pen, like the one Lorraine has me in, should bore me, there's a lot of interesting stuff around here. When I'm not eating, I like to look through the metal bars of my space at some of the other critters in this place.

For example, someone has just brought in their dummy. They've placed it in a stall across from mine, and I've decided to keep my eye on it. She's black and white with a giant belly and milking buttons the size of my head. This dummy looks nothing like the one Spencer has at home.

Lorraine and a woman named Julie, who also works in the clinic, enter the back area where we animals are and approach the dummy.

"This beautiful darlin is pregnant with triplets," Lorraine says to Julie.

"Wow," says Julie. "Isn't that pretty rare?"

"It is rare," says Lorraine. "What's even rarer about this mama is that it's her first pregnancy and she's a bit immature to even be having a calf, let alone three. That's why she's here. Her owner has planned a c-section for her in hopes all three babes and mama will be safer that way."

"Shall we get to it then?" asks Julie. "I'll prep for the c-section."

Lorraine and Julie hustle around the place like bees collecting pollen. Then, they enter the dummy's pen and cover it with a large blue sheet. After a few more preparations, like magic, Lorraine and Julie rub and tickle that cow's belly and make three more dummies appear in the pen. It's one of the most incredible things I've ever seen in my life.

After all the excitement, Lorraine and Julie disappear again. And instead of things returning to normal, instead of the area of my temporary home being quiet and peaceful again, all those dang dummies start mooing just about every second. I figure I ought to lodge a complaint with the management by raising a fuss, but instead, I pause when hearing a new noise.

"Right over here," says Lorraine, walking through the door separating us animals from the human section at the front of the clinic. "And doing really well. I'm so pleased with how the procedure went."

My heart flutters, hoping Spencer is following Lorraine through the door to come and get me. I can't wait to get home and see Shadow. I especially can't wait to have some peace and quiet away from all these noisy babies. But instead of Lorraine bringing Spencer through the door, she escorts a man so wrinkled that he must be older than dirt. They both stop in front of the pen housing the dummies and smile.

"That's just wonderful," says the old man to Lorraine. "And they're all healthy?"

"They're all perfectly healthy," says Lorraine. "I'd like to keep them all here until Friday if that's okay. Just to keep an eye on mama's incision."

"Sounds good to me," says the old man.

Lorraine and the old man shake hands before he walks back through the door leading to the human side. The dummies moo a little louder as Lorraine takes a moment to look at each one. Once she's finished, she turns and walks toward me.

"Hey, darlin," she says with a long look on her face. "Spencer hasn't shown up yet, and I'm getting ready to close. I'm sorry, looks like you won't be going home today. But maybe tomorrow."

Lorraine uses a pitchfork to pick up some hay from one end of the room then brings it over to me. I take a few bites just as the lights overhead go out for the night.

Chapter 15

I am never having kids. Those dang babies and their mama cried and fussed all night. I didn't get a wink of sleep. If there were any way I could get myself closer to them, I'd give them all a firm bite in the butt to make them hush up.

The morning sun illuminates the room, and I can see my roommates more clearly. The little babes drink from their mama's milk buttons, making noises with their mouths as milk dribbles from the sides of their smiles. My tummy growls with hunger as they fill their bellies, but there's a more intense feeling within me – sadness. I wish I had someone to snuggle up with like the babies and their mama all do.

I pick at small specks of hay strewn across the floor of my pen. Then, Lorraine walks through the door with a large bowl of my morning grub. This settles my nerves, a little. At least with her arrival and the sun coming up, it means that it's finally morning. Which means Spencer should be on his way to pick me up and take me to my peaceful, quiet home, and to Shadow.

"Good morning, darlin," says Lorraine, placing my food down in front of me. "How are you today?"

She rubs my neck as I eat. I nicker and grunt, hoping she'll understand that I didn't get any sleep with all those dummies around and that today, I am not feeling fine. I'm cranky and tired.

Soon after I've finished my meal, the large animal door at the back of the building lifts to create an opening to the outside. Warm air wafts through and tickles my face. From where I stand, it seems like spring has fully taken hold outside. Which suits me fine. That means the green grass will be up and ready for me to eat before too long.

A trailer backs up close to the opening of the large animal door. I get excited and even though I'm still limping, I pace my pen a bunch of times with anticipation. It must be Spencer with the horse trailer to collect me. I sing out my best song, as loud as I can, just to let him know how much I love him and how thrilled I am to be going home to see Shadow.

Once the trailer is in place, Lorraine walks around to the far side of the thing. Doors of a truck close and humans mumble. Is it my human? I lift my head and sing out again, louder than before, letting him know I am ready to go home.

My heart plummets within my chest when Lorraine walks around to the back of the trailer with a human who isn't Spencer. It's a woman with black hair to her shoulders and a nervousness in her walk. I sing out again, this time, it isn't a happy tune.

Lorraine and the other woman open the back door to the trailer and step inside. Both speak softly to the animal inside as feet and hooves shuffle. Soon, they are leading the strangest creature I've ever seen in my life.

It's covered in short, curly hair, like it's wearing a fuzzy coat, and is about the size of a young colt. Its belly is round and the animal walks extra slow. Lorraine pauses for a moment with the wild thing in front of my pen, allowing it to take a break from walking. From this position, I can see its face well, and it has eyelashes so long, they look like butterfly wings. I nicker softly, sensing this animal is in distress. Maybe there's something I can do to help it?

"It's okay, darlin," Lorraine says softly to me. "This is Delila, and she's a llama. You've probably never seen an animal like her before."

"Beautiful horse," says the other woman to Lorraine.

"He is so beautiful, both inside and out," says Lorraine. "Golden Flash here is a very special boy."

"How old is he?" asks the woman.

"He's three," says Lorraine.

Knowing they're talking about me; I get closer to the openings of the metal bars that make my pen and stick my nose out as far as possible. My nostrils flare as I get a good whiff of this llama creature. Delila makes a noise, like a goose and cow crying all at once. Her singing voice is quite terrible, frankly, so I pull in a deep breath and sing loudly for her. Just to show her how it's done.

Once my magnificent song is complete, I pause and wait for Delila and the humans to praise me. Instead, a large glob of wet slime lands between my eyes and rolls down toward my nose. I step back and shake my head before pushing my nose back over to the slats to rub the goo away.

Lorraine and the woman laugh hysterically. But I don't think it's funny at all, so I use my foot to dig at the wood chips covering the cement floor.

"Awe, poor Golden Flash," says Lorraine, still chuckling. "Delila does like to spit, as llamas do."

The woman, still chuckling, too says, "Sorry, little guy. She does get ornery at times. Especially when she's on the verge of having a baby."

I stop rubbing my nose and lift my head, perking my ears and widening my eyes. Did that woman just say baby? Is that rude, obnoxious, spitting creature going to have a baby in here? We don't need more kids in this dang place. Awe heck, this is terrible.

"Let's get her into her space before this baby arrives right here in front of Golden Flash's box stall," says Lorraine.

The ladies lead Delila away from me and I call out again, protesting the fact that there's going to be another dang kid in here. But neither of them listens. They ignore me and lead the llama into a spot only two down from mine.

Where is Spencer? When the heck will I get to go home?

Chapter 16

Another night passes, and still no Spencer. I pace my stall, with an improved limp, and call out as much as I can, hoping my human will hear me from wherever he is.

Lorraine feeds me my breakfast, then goes about her day treating patients. First, it's a dog, which I don't mind much. Then, someone brings in a large bird which Lorraine calls an ostrich. Near the end of the day, I'm thrilled to watch the mama dummy and her three babies all loaded up onto a trailer and taken away – good riddance to those chatter boxes.

Before Lorraine follows her routine and shuts the lights out for the night, she comes to my pen and joins me. First, she uses a soft brush and grooms me all over. It's nice to feel that kind of human touch again. Then, she takes a long look at my injury, poking and prodding around it a bunch. She sighs loudly, then holds my head in her hands.

"Okay, darlin," she says, leaning in and kissing my nose. "I've tried all week to get in touch with Spencer. He's no longer answering his phone or calling me back."

I nicker and step closer to Lorraine.

"It's the weekend, and I don't feel right leaving you inside any longer," she says. "I really thought you'd be home by now, but here we are."

Lorraine walks back over to the gate of my pen, and I follow, not ready for her to leave me just yet. Instead of leaving, though, she reaches through a small opening of the gate and brings in a lead rope and halter.

"Let's get this halter on you," she says, reaching around my neck to place it onto my head. "Then, I'm going to take you to a larger pen outside. You'll have a shelter and more room to move. No running yet, but you'll be able to stretch your legs better."

Once Lorraine has finished, she opens the gate for my stall all the way and leads me out. We walk together toward the large animal door before she pushes a small button to open it. My knees buckle a little as the noise of the door startles me, but Lorraine strokes my neck and tells me it'll be okay.

I'm surprised to see the sky is black and littered with stars. The fresh air feels good on my body, and it's nice to fill my lungs with it.

Lorraine and I walk around to the side of the clinic, escorted by the song of frogs in a nearby creek. My feet crunch against the gravel road until we reach a section behind the clinic with a large paddock. At the end of the paddock is a small shelter, much more solid than the one I'm used to, and painted a clean white.

"You'll be the only horse out here," says Lorraine, opening the gate to my paddock and leading me through. "But at least you'll be outside, and this will be better for you until we find Spencer."

After Lorraine removes my halter, I lower my head, and walk slowly and sniff. There's been other horses here before me, but like she said, none are here now. Limping and cautiously proceeding, I move over to the shelter and check it out. It'll be nice enough to keep the wind and rain off me. It'd be much better if Shadow were here, though.

On the other side of the shelter is a nice pile of hay, which I take a bite of before continuing my investigation. There's a trough with clean water, which I decide to sample, too. After a long drink, Lorraine walks through the gate and onto the other side of the fence.

I sing her a song and walk over. She rubs my neck and smiles. "You'll be better in here for now, darlin. I'll be back in a couple of days. Trent works here on the weekends, so he'll make sure you're still fed until I get back."

She rubs my head one more time and walks away. I sing out again, hoping it'll entice her to come back, but she doesn't. I hope she does come back eventually.

Once Lorraine is completely out of my sight, I admire the sky. A bright star flickers and catches my attention. Instead of simply admiring its brilliance, I begin to think about how lonely I am. I wish I weren't alone out here. I sing aloud to the star and wait for something, maybe an answer or a sign. But the only response comes from the frogs.

Chapter 17

Lorraine forgot to tell me that Trent is a dang giant. He's as tall as the roof of my shelter, but skinny as a fence post. Perhaps he isn't as tall as I might think, though. His hair is fuzzy and full, like a white dandelion head, but brown like dark mud after it rains. So, maybe his hair makes him taller than he really is.

Trent doesn't say much to me. I don't suppose I'd hear him anyway with his music playing so loud. He parks his small pick-up truck close to my pen and leaves the door open as he works. The entire truck rattles and vibrates as the music plays. Typically, I love a good song; but whoever is singing Trent's music sounds angry and like they need a hug or some food.

"Here's breakfast," says Trent, then whistling like I need prompting to come and eat.

I limp over to my bowl of food and eat as Trent uses a pitchfork to pick up all the manure packages, I put out for him. Once he's finished with that, he uses the same pitchfork to lay out more hay for me. It would be nice if he used two different tools for the two jobs, but I'll eat the hay anyway.

"Looks like you got hurt bad," he says, picking up my empty food bowl and looking at my injury.

I limp closer to him and push my head over the side of the fence, hoping for a neck rub. Trent loads his tools into the back of his truck and pays me no mind.

"I'll be back tomorrow morning," he says before getting into the driver's side of his truck. "See ya."

This is the extent of mine and Trent's relationship for the next several weeks. I'm always so glad to see Lorraine on the days opposite to him because at least she brushes me and picks my feet. Lorraine has stopped talking about Spencer, even though I still look for his truck and trailer each day. And not much changes around here aside from the new animals coming in for Lorraine's help. I've seen all kinds, but what I'd really love to see is another horse.

Heat ripples from the ground, creating an orb effect that distorts objects in the distance. The mid-afternoon sun is so dang hot it's making me sleepy. That's why, when Lorraine walks toward me with a horse at her side, I worry I'm hallucinating.

My eyes widen and I rush toward the fence closest to Lorraine and the other horse. I flare my nostrils wide and pull in a long breath of air. That most certainly is another horse. I'm not imagining things, and now, I can hardly contain my excitement. I trot from one end of my pen to the next, adding an artistic buck of my behind and flipping my magnificent hair. Every few steps, I sing loudly, a welcoming diddy with pep.

"Good morning, darlin," says Lorraine, smiling and looking at me.

I nicker and sing aloud again. It makes Lorraine laugh. The other guy, though, just stares at me like I'm a ding-dong.

Lorraine and the other horse stop at the metal gate of a paddock two away from mine. I sing and stare at them, wondering what the heck is wrong with the spot directly next to mine. It'll be difficult for us to snuggle or groom one another if we're separated by another full paddock.

"Sorry, darlins," says Lorraine, leading the other horse into the paddock. "We must keep you separated, just as a health precaution."

I flare my nostrils and take in as much of the scent of the newbie. It's a dude, which is okay by me, I guess. It might be nice to have a lady friend around to eventually canoodle with. But it looks like I'll have to just make small talk with this guy.

I sing loudly and prance around in a few circles. Lorraine smiles and chuckles. "Wow, Golden Flash, you sure are happy to have someone else around, aren't you? I don't blame you, darlin."

I respond with a quick call out and a nicker. Lorraine opens the gate for the other horse's paddock, then moves to stand midway between us. She leans over the metal fencing, smiles, and watches.

With my insides still full of excitement, I trot around in a few more circles and whip my head to shake out my mane. Once I stop performing, I pause and look at the other horse to give it a chance to show me what he's made of. But the new guy is quiet and docile and not showing me any of his moves. I suppose I might have intimidated him by showing off mine so well.

I rush over to the fence of my paddock that's closest to the new horse and reach my neck over as far as I can. I desperately want to feel close to another horse. Even if this is as close as I'll get to it. The new guy shuffles his feet as he turns away from me, walks directly into the shelter and pushes his bay and white painted rump in my direction. How rude is this guy?

"This is Tex," says Lorraine. "Tex, this is Golden Flash."

I nicker and call out again but still hear nothing from Tex.

"Poor Tex is still drowsy from the medicine I had to give him," says Lorraine, walking closer to me and rubbing my neck. "He had some colic but is feeling much better now."

Realizing I won't be getting any attention from Tex, forget

him anyway, I shift my attention to Lorraine instead. She walks toward me and reaches her arms through my fencing. Using both hands, she rubs my neck. I lower my head in close and give her all the love I've got until she's called to leave me again.

With Lorraine gone, I wander around my paddock for a few minutes until I'm bored again. The only new source of entertainment for me around here is the new guy. Even though he doesn't seem keen on me, I figure I just need to show him how interesting I can be.

I reach my neck over the top of the fence again, as close to Tex's stall as I can get it, and stare. Not a lot of folks are aware that I am excellent at staring. I can stand still in one spot for a long time and stare the heck out of something or someone. So, I do. My eyes remain locked on Tex as he stands in his stall. Just to let him know I'm a fun guy to be around, I nicker, over and over, and add a short song in from time to time. Then, something awesome happens.

Tex shifts his body, so his head is facing me. His eyes find mine and we just sit and stare at one another. His long, black hair flips over his eyes, but he doesn't make a move otherwise. I nicker again and again until finally, he nickers back.

This really gets me excited. I show him so by running and bucking my back legs. It's so nice to have some horse company again.

Chapter 18

With a pile of fresh hay in the corner of my paddock, I shift my attention to that instead of trying to impress Tex. He's not too keen on me yet, but it may just take more time.

While chewing a mouthful of hay, I study the sky. The stars are out and especially vibrant tonight. I sigh heavily as I finish chewing and notice the same star I had been focused on the night before. It appears to wave and something occurs to me.

I quickly glance over at Tex then back up to the star. When I was looking at the star last night, I kept wishing that I weren't alone. I glance back over at Tex then to the star again. Did my new horse companion come to be here because I wished for it?

Suddenly, Tex storms out of his shelter and moves quickly in my direction. It scares the heck out of me, and I jump and run around a little. It takes me a few laps to realize that Tex isn't running away from anything, and there's no present danger. So, I pause and watch the ding-dong to see what he's up to.

Turns out Tex has some awesome moves of his own. Maybe he comes more alive in the nighttime. Still watching the guy, I lower my head and grab a mouthful of hay. While I chew, I watch.

He starts with a few gallops around his enclosure, whipping his hair like a flag flapping in the wind. I nicker and sing out, encouraging him to show me more, so he does. Stopping hard and fast from his gallop, Tex lifts his front legs up a little off the ground, then gallops off again. After a few hind leg bucks, he gallops before stopping in front of me on the other side of the fences that separate us.

I lean my head over my fence, flare my nostrils, and nicker to tell him I mean no harm. He leans his head over his fence and takes a good whiff of my manly scent.

Tex lifts his head and sings a long, loud song. I'm impressed, as he has one heck of a good singing voice but not as good as mine. It's interesting how each horse I meet has a unique voice and tune of song all their own. Just like the sound of a human's voice is unlike another, horses seem to, too.

After singing a few great hits, Tex leans his neck closely into one of the fenceposts then rubs his head and neck all over it. His eyes are closed, and he sighs a little with delight.

I lower my head and get close to one of my fenceposts and mimic Tex. As I rub my head and neck, I can't believe how dang good it feels.

Tex nickers and leans his head over the fence, as though he's asking me if I liked my neck rub. I nicker back and lean my head over the fence, hoping he'll understand that I surely did, darlin. We stare at one another for a few seconds before I nicker again, wanting him to know how glad I am that he's here. His eyes widen and he nickers, as though with a response to say, he's glad to meet me.

We continue to exchange pleasantries back and forth, a kind of communication between us like old friends. If Spencer isn't coming back to get me, and if I'm not going to have Shadow with me anymore, I figure I can be content with this life if I have Lorraine's love and Tex nearby.

Chapter 19

Tex and I got to talking most of the night. We paused for a while to sleep some, but otherwise, we both had a lot to say. It would have been nice to have Tex closer, but after spending so much time alone, I'm not going to get picky.

Birds from the nearby trees begin to sing, the little darlins keen to awaken the world. It's the start of a new day and that means new possibilities with my new friend. I'm not sure how long Lorraine will keep us separated. There's a larger paddock on the other side of mine that could keep both Tex and me well enough together. With Tex here, I have all that I need – a friend, food, water, shelter, and love.

After taking a long drink from my water trough, I sigh long and loud then turn around to look at my new friend. What will he do next? My heart kicks up its pace as Tex turns his backend into the fence and scratches his butt against the metal. I knew this guy and I became fast friends for a reason. We seem to almost be the same horse.

I turn myself around and give my butt a good scratching, too. Then, although the day was already great, in my opinion, it got even better. Tex and me nicker and whinny as we watch Lorraine walk toward us with our bowls of morning grub.

"Good morning, darlins," says Lorraine once she's closer to us.

She smiles and places our bowls within each of our own paddocks. Then, she throws a hearty helping of hay down for each of us, too. Before Lorraine turns to leave us, she reaches into her pockets and feeds each of us a long, colorful carrot. I crunch and gobble the thing down, nodding my head with delight as its sweetness fills my mouth.

Once the carrot is gone, I dive into my food bowl and realize there's something about today that feels different, but special. The food tastes extra good, the birds singing in the sky sounds more beautiful and the sun seems a heck of a lot brighter. Yup, I can already tell this is going to be one of the greatest dang days.

"I'm glad to see you looking so much better today, Tex," says Lorraine, rubbing the side of his neck and watching him closely as he eats. "You're eating so well."

I nicker and lift my head, looking in Lorraine's direction. I'm eating well today, where's my neck rub? As though Lorraine can hear my thoughts, she smiles and giggles before moving toward me to rub my neck, too.

"You've never been this happy, Golden Flash," says Lorraine in a whisper. "Proof that horses love to be with other horses. I suppose it might be time to consider a new home for you."

Lorraine speaks, but I'm too invested in my food and neck rub to process the words. I'm surrounded by love, and that's how I'd like things to stay.

The day is warm and humid, so Tex and I just hang out and eat. Then, not too long before the sun is meant to set, Tex's energy picks up. I feel it, so my energy picks up, too. My friend paces his paddock, trotting and whinnying as he does. I mimic him and look around for whatever the heck he's fussing on about.

Is there a coyote nearby? Did he see a plastic bag? I hate those dang things. Does he see another horse coming to join us in the other paddock opposite to me? That would be the best thing ever – this establishment could use a bunch more horses as far as I'm concerned. Tex's energy heightens even further, so mine does, too. Does he see a wild animal, maybe a cougar?

From around the corner of the Vet building walks Lorraine and a middle-aged woman. The woman is wearing blue jeans and a bright purple and yellow floral shirt. When the pair of ladies get close, I see the woman has short hair full of tight brown curls, and her face is decorated with bright colors. She flashes Tex a half smile then reaches her hand over the fence of his paddock and rubs the front of his face. Tex relaxes and leans into the woman.

"He looks much better," says the woman.

"He is so much better, Ruth," says Lorraine to the woman. "His belly was certainly twisted, but it didn't take much to fix things up."

"That's good news," says Ruth. "Ready to get home now, Tex?"

Home? What the heck is that woman talking about? Tex already is home. He's meant to be here, with me. I become anxious and feel the need to stir things up a little. My feet move into a trot, and I whip my head and sing as loudly as I can. Then, I stop at the fence line separating Tex and me and reach my head over as far as I can.

Tex doesn't move, in fact, he's acting like he doesn't even notice me at all. What the heck is his dang problem? Aren't I his new best friend like he is mine?

"Who's that?" asks Ruth, moving away from Tex and toward me.

Finally, someone is paying attention to me. Come over here and rub my neck, darlin. Lorraine and Ruth pause in front of my paddock. I lean in close to them both. Lorraine reaches and rubs my neck. Ruth stands at a bit of a distance with her hands at her side and only stares.

"This is Golden Flash," says Lorraine. "He's been here for almost three months, poor guy."

"Golden Flash," says Ruth. "That name is a mouthful. Been here that long? What's going on with him?"

"He's Spencer Cook's horse," says Lorraine. "He's sweet as anything, and only three-years old. He was injured while Spencer was out of town. Although his wound site looks garish, he's healed up really well and seems fine."

"Spencer Cook, hey," says Ruth before flashing Lorraine and awkward smile. "You hear what happened to him?"

"No," says Lorraine. "I've been calling him every day for months to come and pick up his horse, but the guy never responds."

"Well, I heard he's gone to try the rodeo circuit in the States," says Ruth. "He left town with his other horse and is free-loading off someone down south. I don't think that kid will ever come back here."

"Ah, man," says Lorraine, sighing heavily and stroking my neck. "What am I supposed to do with this guy?"

"Seems to me he's your horse now."

"I can't keep him forever. It wouldn't be fair. I just don't have the time he deserves, or the space for a full-time horse. What about you, Ruth? Need another horse for your Outfitting business?"

"Well, we are super busy these days, but I wouldn't pay money for that horse. Not when I know he's had an injury so close to his leg. And look at him when he walks, he's pigeon toed. If he's disabled, then he'd be useless to me."

Ruth's words sting my heart. My eyes soften, I lower my head and sigh. Am I disabled? Sure, my walk is a little funny, but I don't feel too different. Is the reason why Spencer never came back for me because I'm now a useless horse?

"I promise you," says Lorraine, turning to look toward Ruth. "He's sound and can still walk, trot and I've even seen him canter. Besides, Tex seems to really like him."

"Has he been broke?" asks Ruth. "Ever been saddled or bridled?"

"I don't know. I kind of doubt it, though."

"Not broke, injured, he was Spencer Cook's horse so probably full of bad habits. Sounds to me you've got a real dud of a horse on your hands. Not worth nothing if you ask me. Besides, I'm so busy with summer clients, I don't have any spare time to train him and use him this season. He'd be freeloading off me and not working. My horses must all be working if I need to pay money for feeding them."

My head lowers close to the ground as the ladies speak about me. All this time, I really thought I was a magnificent and amazing horse. How can one accident, which wasn't even my fault, make me useless in the eyes of others? It doesn't seem fair. How can they know I'm disabled for sure without even giving me a chance? Do they know how hard I'll work in exchange for some love?

"I don't know," says Lorraine. "Something about him tells me he's special. He seems fine to me."

"Like I said," says Ruth, bending down onto her hunkers to look at my lower body. "I'd never pay money for a horse whose been injured the way this one has. He may be okay now, but what if he turns up lame as he finishes growing. Spencer likely left him here because he knows, as do I, that this horse is now disabled and defective."

"What am I going to do with him if people think he's defective?" says Lorraine.

"Put him on a truck for the slaughterhouse," says Ruth. "Or I can take him off your hands, no charge for me, though, and we can wait and see what kind of horse he turns out to be."

"I'll need to think about it," says Lorraine. "I'll try Spencer one more time, but if he doesn't answer, I'll need to re-think Golden Flash's future."

Chapter 20

I'm consumed by sadness watching Ruth and Lorraine take Tex away from his paddock to load into a horse trailer.

What started as one of the best days of my life, ended as one of the worst. My heart sinks each time Ruth describes me – disabled, defective, dud, worth nothing, useless, slaughterhouse.

Once Ruth begins to drive the truck taking away my new friend, Tex, I drag my feet and walk over to the water trough nestled next to my shelter. Before taking a drink, I pause to look at my reflection within the water. Maybe Ruth is right. As I study my features, they appear different to me now. My face no longer looks as perfect as yesterday and my shoulders are uneven and hunched due to my injury. Perhaps I am a defective horse after all.

As the sun begins to set, a strong wind picks up and gives me a chill. But I don't care enough to move into my shelter. My reflection within the water has me frozen in place. I keep searching for something that might make me feel like I am a worthy horse instead of a dud. Each time I've found something remarkable about myself, one of Ruth's words repeats in my head and alters my impression of it.

Perhaps I'm meant to always be alone. Even though I have so much love to give, maybe I'm not meant to give it. Maybe it's time I accept that.

Even though Lorraine is calling me from behind, I don't turn around. Now that the sun is out, I'm sure she's just coming to me with my food dish. Eating my food is usually the highlight of my day, but I'm not hungry just now.

"Golden Flash," calls Lorraine, her voice getting closer. "Hey, darlin. Come on over here."

I sigh loudly before reluctantly turning around to face her. Once she's at the fence, I'm surprised to notice she isn't brining my food, but rather, holding my halter. My ears perk up a bit at this change in my routine.

"Your life is changing today, sweet boy," says Lorraine, as I stop in front of her.

Her face is expressionless, but I feel a heaviness emanating from her. An energy that's both sad and anxious. What's going on?

Lorraine climbs over the fence and walks toward me. Then, she reaches up and places my halter onto my head. "I want you to know that I did everything I could to try and reach Spencer. But he just hasn't responded."

A tear rolls down her face, but she quickly wipes it away with the back of her hand. I keep my head low and drag my feet as she leads me toward the gate and opens it. We walk beyond my paddock and toward the Vet building in awkward silence.

"I'm sorry, darlin," says Lorraine. "I wish I could keep you with me, but I just can't. You're an incredibly special boy, but it wouldn't be fair to keep you locked up in that small paddock forever. I barely even know how to ride. And I don't know that I have the time to learn or even spend time with you at all."

As we walk closer to the Vet building, red lights move from around the corner and toward us. I recognize immediately that they're attached to a horse trailer. My head lowers further and each step I take feels shaky. Is this horse trailer for me?

“The solution I’ve come up with may not be the most ideal,” says Lorraine, sniffling and lowering her head. “I wish you could have a forever home with someone who can give you as much love as you have to give. But this was all I could come up with for you. My hands are tied, and this was the best solution as far as I could see.”

Lorraine holds onto my lead rope before opening the back door of the horse trailer. She takes a deep breath, looks over at me, then walks onto the trailer. I resist and stand firm in my stance, not wanting to get inside and leave Lorraine. Another tear rolls down her face, and it makes me want to be close to her and make sure she’s okay. So, I walk onto the trailer and nuzzle in close and give her as much love as I can so it might make her feel better.

“You’re such a sweet boy,” says Lorraine, leading me to the end of the trailer before clicking a barrier in place behind me.

I’m stuck in this position. I can’t move my body to turn toward her.

“Good-bye, Golden Flash,” says Lorraine from behind me.

I sing her one of my songs, whinny, and nicker. My heart feels like a giant boulder, sinking fast within my defective body. But instead of Lorraine responding to my calls, the door of the horse trailer closes with a loud thud.

Then, the trailer moves. Where is this thing taking me? Will I ever see Lorraine again? What does she mean by solution?

Chapter 21

Raindrops fall onto my face when I lift my head to look through the small windows of the horse trailer. I keep flaring my nostrils for scents to offer hints about where I might be going, but the rain keeps snuffing them out. I guess I'll just have to wait and see once this rig stops.

There's a small pile of hay before me, so I take a bite here and there before glancing through the window again. We pass by a bunch of buildings, all huddled together tightly. Many cars and trucks line the roads and several drive by in the opposite direction, too. This scenery goes on for a while before the buildings are replaced by small houses, then those are replaced by open fields with a house or barn popping up sporadically.

Large trucks and cars whip past us at speeds faster than I've ever seen any horse move. We drive for quite a time before the open fields are replaced by large trees plump with thickly needled branches. At first, there's only a few of them, but then, there's enough to make a crowded forest.

Keeping my eyes fixed as we drive; I hope to find clues as to where I might be going. Thankfully, the rain has stopped, and more smells are coming to me from the air. There's the scent of fresh trees, squirrels, and dirt. Nothing too exciting.

The truck and trailer shift position to a point where I'm struggling to keep myself upright. Good thing there's a barrier behind my butt, keeping me standing as we move. The engine of the truck becomes louder as we slowly inch our way up over some of the tree's tops and closer to the sky. Then, the scenery shifts so dang dramatically, I can hardly believe my eyes.

Massive cragged rocks with hats made of white snow emerge like magic. I've seen these things before, they've always been in the distance from my home with Spencer. They appeared so huge from that perspective, but now, I'm sure they must be the largest things in the world.

I admire the view of the rocked giants for a while before large trees block them from my sight. It's a little disappointing to only see trees again, but I only take a second to dwell on that. Now, something new has gripped my attention. The smell of other horses.

My nostrils grow huge as I pull in the scents. If I'm correct, there's boys and girls where I'm going. Holy heck, maybe I'll find a pretty darlin to canoodle with. The pace of my heart quickens as the trees open to spaces of grass surrounded by wooden fencing. The soft beats of my heart turn into hard thuds when the other horses come into view.

They're all too busy eating grass to pay any attention to me within the trailer, so I decide I'd better announce my arrival to them as loud as possible. I take a long, deep breath, and summon my best singing voice to show off my skills. But I'm too excited, and it shows through the cracked, awkward song I pelt out instead. Not off to a great start.

The truck and trailer pull-up to a building made with a bunch of tree trunks stacked on their sides and stuck together. I nicker and whinny, over and over, until finally, the back door of the trailer opens. Cranking my neck, I move my head as far as I can to try and see which human is coming to get me. But because of the barrier holding me in place, I still can't see.

Footsteps made by heavy boots move on the metal floor

behind me before the barrier is unlocked and I have more mobility. I suck in my gut and turn myself around to find a sour-faced human. The one who's taken me away from Lorraine is none other than Ruth.

Chapter 22

What does a woman who thinks I'm defective and disabled want with me? As though she can hear my thoughts, she answers my question.

"You're extremely lucky to be here, Golden Flash," says Ruth, leading me toward the opening of the horse trailer. "I don't have a use for you, yet, but one of my older horses has come up lame and may not recover, so I told Lorraine I'd take you in and see if your useful or not."

My head lowers as Ruth speaks. What if I'm not useful? What will she do with me then?

Once Ruth and I step off the back of the trailer, I'm surprised by the sight of the place. There are horses within large paddocks everywhere. Some of them don't notice me and continue to graze while a few perk up and begin to sing and prance around. There aren't as many horses here as when I lived with Justin and Mara, but many more than my homes with Spencer or Lorraine. Nestled a short distance beyond the large wooden building I stand in front of now are several little cabins, each one with windows, a door, and a smokestack emerging from their tops.

Instead of letting myself get excited by the grandeur of it all, I lower my head and look at the ground again. Ruth has made it perfectly clear that she may not keep me. Because this is already my fourth home in three years, and no one seems to want me, I'm guessing I won't be here for long anyway.

"This place has been in my family for more than a hundred years," says Ruth, leading me away from the horse trailer and closer to one of the paddocks. "I'm the third generation to own it. There's thirty horses on three hundred and sixty mixed acres."

I walk alongside Ruth as she speaks. Other horses call out and fuss with my presence, but I keep my head low, just the same as my spirits. Then, a young man approaches with a smile full of crooked teeth and odd metal things on them. He's not too tall, average, and has brown and red hair with a freckled face. He pulls his gloves from his hands and tucks them into the back pocket of his blue jeans before dusting off his grey plaid shirt.

"This is the new guy?" asks the young man. "He's limping a little still, huh?"

"Yip, just a little," says Ruth. "But we'll give him a trial run and see if he can keep up with the others. Otherwise, we'll send him to auction. I've got nothing to lose but some feed as I didn't pay a cent for him."

"What's his name?" asks the young man, rubbing my back with his hand.

It's comforting to have someone showing me a little love. But still, I won't allow myself to get too attached.

"His name is Golden Flash," says Ruth. "Too much of a mouthful. So, we'll call him Ranger from now on."

"Ranger, yip, that's a good name," says the young man. "Where do you want him?"

"Let's keep him in the paddock closest to the barn," says Ruth. "He needs to stay isolated from the other horses for two-weeks. Only feed him the bare minimum. I don't want to waste too much on him if he ends up being useless."

"Yip, ma'am," says the young man, taking my lead rope from Ruth and leading me away.

"Oh, and Wyatt," says Ruth. "Make sure you load the cabins with firewood before supper tonight. We've got twenty tourists arriving here tomorrow for the weekend."

"Yip, ma'am," says the young man, Wyatt.

Chapter 23

Wyatt and I walk by a pasture with a bunch of horses in it. I admit, a few of them have some dang impressive singing voices and moves while others, not so much. Normally, I'd be performing up a storm for these guys, showing them what real talent looks like. But I'm not in the mood. Besides, maybe I'm not as great as I thought I was. Ruth keeps calling me useless, maybe she's right.

There's a stirring among the horses. My eyes shift only enough to see what's going on. Some of the others run, kick and buck. All trying to show off for me. I listen to a few amateur singing voices as I walk, but there's one that perks my ears and gets my heart beating faster. It's the call of Tex.

My head lifts and I call back. Although Wyatt is still leading me, I pick up my pace while looking all over the place for Tex. I call out again, then he calls back. I attempt to run a circle around Wyatt, but he doesn't allow it.

"Easy, boy," says Wyatt, gripping tightly to my lead rope and pulling me closer to him. "I know you're excited, but I need you to go easy now."

It isn't until Wyatt and I get closer to a two-story barn made of horizontal tree logs that I spot my friend. I nicker and whinny as loud as I can, trying to be easy with Wyatt. It's just so dang hard to contain my excitement, though. I never thought I'd see Tex again, and here he is!

"That's right," says Wyatt, smiling at me and rubbing the side of my neck. "I forgot you and Tex met while you were staying with Lorraine."

I'm super excited to see my horse friend, but feeling Wyatt rub the side of my neck the way Lorraine did makes me crave more. I settle down and lower my head close, so he has an easier time of rubbing in the right spot.

"You like neck rubs, buddy?" he says with a chuckle. "Yip, me, too. I'll remember that when I'm training you over the next couple of months."

I'm led into a paddock, tall with grass on one end, and a shelter with a water trough on the other. It's nice and all, but the best part is that it's right next to the paddock Tex is in.

"Lucky for you, Ranger," says Wyatt. "You and Tex can be roommates again for the next couple of weeks, since you both need space from the rest of the herd."

Wyatt closes the gate to my paddock once we're both inside then reaches up to unfasten my halter before slipping it off from my head. Once the thing is off, I move a few steps away from Wyatt and kick things up a notch. When I turn my head to the side, I notice some of the other horses are still watching me, so I decide to give them a little show.

At first, I display my finest trot, completing a full circle around my paddock. Then, I canter for another lap as fast as my small space will allow, flipping my glorious hair as I do. To really show the others what I'm made of, I continue with my fine moves and belt out a loud song. Hopefully, I've done enough to impress, especially some of the ladies I've been smelling out since arriving.

"Looking good, Ranger," says Wyatt from perched atop the fence separating mine and Tex's paddocks. "Even though you're still limping a little, you can trot and canter just fine, as far as I can see."

Breathless, I trot over to Wyatt and lean my head on the fence next to where he sits. From this position, I have a closer look at Wyatt's face. His eyes are a brilliant blue, and his nose has clusters of small freckles that remind me of a starry sky.

Wyatt rubs my neck for a minute before Tex approaches and stands on the opposite side. We smell each other for a few seconds and Tex nickers, letting me know he recognizes me. I nicker back, glad to be with him again.

"See, you've already made one friend," says Wyatt. "Yip, I think you could do fine here if you keep up to Auntie Ruth's expectations. Mind you, she's got some weird expectations."

Wyatt moves his hand to scratch behind my ears. My body instantly relaxes, and my eyes droop with contentment. When Wyatt stops scratching, I lean in closer and nudge him with my nose, just to assure him that he doesn't need to stop with the scratching.

Wyatt chuckles, then moves to scratch behind my ears again. "Auntie Ruth can be a grumpy old cougar at times," he says. "And she comes from a long line of old school ranchers. Because this is a working dude and outfitting ranch, all animals must work and earn their keep, just like the humans. So, I'll work with you in the evenings, Ranger. Yip, you could do fine if you try. Just focus on that, little buddy. Try hard, work hard and then you'll be useful and can stay. Something tells me you're a rarity."

I nicker as Wyatt's scratches, and words, settle in.

Chapter 24

Useless. The word repeats in my head like a bad song for several days. Each time Ruth goes out with the horses she passes by me without a second thought. Then, the word becomes louder. Useless… useless… useless.

Ruth wasn't kidding when she told Wyatt to only feed me the bare minimum. There is a flake or two of hay placed in the corner of my paddock each night, and I've had to learn to make them last until the next serving. The first night, I gobbled down the hay so fast, accustomed to the large spreads of food served by Lorraine each day, only to find there was no more for a long time after. I ate through the tall grass within in my paddock in a hurry, too. Left now with a few sprigs reaching from the ground in some places.

I've never been this hungry in my life, and it's ruining to my once voluptuous figure. There's much admiration among horses for those who look like they're fed well. After all, it means they're lucky and loved enough to be eating regularly.

Not much has happened over the last several nights. I haven't even seen Wyatt aside from getting my feed. But today, as the morning sun stretches its arms through the surrounding tree branches, I'm pleased to see some new activity.

Songs sung by the local birds is interrupted by the loud noise of an engine. I walk over to the edge of my paddock and reach my neck over the fence as far as I can manage. The noise grows louder, and dust billows from the road leading into the ranch.

Then, a black vehicle moves into view before stopping in front of the barn and ranch office.

I learned the word, tourists, last weekend when this place was filled by people coming to stay in the small cabins. A few of them stopped by to say hello to me, but none stayed long nor have they returned after their stay. I can tell the vehicle that's arrived has tourists by the way Ruth walks out from the office to meet them; wearing her wide smile reserved for such people.

Two adults and three smaller humans leap out from within their vehicle and move to meet Ruth. They all talk and smile, and I nicker a little, wishing I could join them and their group huddle. The smallest human, blonde with pigtails and short legs, leaves the pack and wanders in my direction.

She takes a few steps, then bends over to pick a plump dandelion. She repeats this pattern until her small hand holds a large bouquet of the vibrant yellow flowers. The little one is only a short distance from my paddock, so I nicker to say hello. Thankfully, she hears me, then smiles and giggles a little.

"Hi, horse," she says, her words altered by missing teeth.

Hello, darlin. I nicker again, then move my head through the small opening between the middle and top fence rungs. Now my face is more aligned with hers. The little girl takes a few more steps before she's standing directly in front of me. I nicker, she giggles and smiles. Her hand free of flowers lifts from her side and reaches close to my nose. Although I'd rather she gives me a long neck rub, I'll take any form of human connection at this point, so I tolerate her little hands where they are.

My nostrils flare the second I pick up the scent of freshly picked dandelions on her fingers. Then, my stomach growls and a little drool pools at the side of my mouth. My tongue slips out from within my mouth and gently tickles the little girl's hand and she giggles. The empty feeling from within my stomach swells as I taste the yellow flowers on my tongue from licking the girl's hand.

Wanting more, I lean my head further out through the rungs of the fence and inch my way closer to the cluster of flowers within the little girl's hand. I sniff once, twice, then an uncontrollable instinct takes over. My lips twitch and quiver before opening and wrapping around the bouquet of delectable dandelions.

Once my mouth is full, I pull back and chew. But before I can swallow my meager treat, a hideous sound comes from the little girl. She squeals like a baby coyote, but louder than a pack of them. It scares me, but I'm concerned for the little one, so I push my head back through the fence rungs to try and get a closer look.

Tears rush from the little girl's eyes. I notice the other humans, including Ruth, rushing toward she and I and something scares me more than the little girl's cry. Fear floods the eyes of the largest humans, and I can feel it coming off their bodies, too.

Why are they so afraid? Is there a wild beast nearby? Should I be afraid, too? But what about the little girl? I want to run away from whatever is causing the humans fear, but I should stay close to her until they get here if she needs my help.

"Sara!" shouts a tall female human. "Sara, are you hurt?"

"Ranger!" shouts Ruth. "Ranger, get back!"

"Sara!" shouts the tall female human again.

"Mommy," shouts the girl with pigtails. "Mommy! The horse bite."

Mommy quickly scoops the little girl up into her arms once she's close. Now that the little girl is safe, I pull my head back out from between the fence rungs and trot quickly around my paddock. With so much fear in the air and holding strong for the little girl, I'm full of anxiety, and I need to try and eliminate some of it.

"Is this horse wild or something?" asks Mommy.

I whip my head and buck my back legs a little until some of the fear subsides, and I feel like I can stand still again. Once I'm still, Ruth quickly climbs over the fence and rushes toward me. I'm so excited to have her visit me as I desperately want her to love me and think I'm useful. The parts of me that crave love have me walk closer to Ruth, hoping she'll soothe some of my fear and rub my neck.

Instead, she lifts her hand and strikes me in the nose, harder than I've ever been struck before. I wince and cower.

"Bad horse, Ranger!" shouts Ruth. "Don't you dare ever bite anyone; do you understand me."

She strikes me again, then elbows me hard in the ribs. There's a throbbing pain in my side and nose, but the worst pain is radiating from my heart. Ruth rushes away from me, full of anger and loathing.

"Useless horse," she mutters under her breath.

My head sinks as low to the ground as I can get it as I move off in the opposite direction to the humans.

Chapter 25

Surely, I'm doomed. Most likely, Ruth has already made her mind up to ship me off to the next auction. Even though I understand the woman hates me, I still don't want to leave. Tex is here, and a bunch of other horses I haven't even met yet. Heck, I haven't had the chance to show them all my best moves in the field, or my greatest singing hits. What a shame it would be for them all to miss out on such talents.

The pain in my nose and side have subsided, but not from my heart. Why did I let my hunger get the better of me and steal that little girl's dang flowers? If I could have just controlled myself and left them alone, then maybe Ruth could have seen me close to that little girl and think I could be useful. Instead, she believes I'm even more useless than before. And only because I ate the flowers from the little girl's hand.

I take a deep breath and release it slowly through my nose. Then, a flicker from the sky grabs my attention and I look up. It's amazing how stars always find a way to shine brightly. Even if there's a nasty storm surrounding us on the ground, you know they're up there still spreading light, just in case one of us might need it.

The sparkle reminds me of Lorraine. I sigh heavily and my hurting heart sinks. I miss her. An image of Shadow pushes into my mind, I miss my old friend something awful. I wish he were with me now, in this paddock, standing close and watching over me.

I focus, with all my energy, on the sparkling star, hoping its light will reach me and fill me up a little. Then, for reasons I don't understand, I begin to think about my life as it is and as I'd like for it to be.

Although Ruth obviously doesn't love me, maybe if I try and love her and the others harder, they'll see how wonderful my love is. If they understand that, and if I show others how to love, then someday, I'll find someone who'll love me back. I don't know what something like that might be called, but I feel that's the right thing to do.

Perhaps my eyes are playing tricks on me, but the more I consider giving love, the more the star seems to shine brighter in the sky. This encourages me to keep going.

If I promise to be good and kind, all I ask in return is for someone to treat me in the same way. If you can find a way to always show love, will love eventually find a way to you?

Chapter 26

After several days of alone time, finally, the cycle is broken. With the evening sun settling behind the trees, Wyatt approaches my paddock from the direction of the barn. At first, I'm not sure he's coming toward me, or if he's moving to see the other horses. So, I move to the space of my paddock that's closest to him and watch.

He's carrying something in his arms. My heart flutters with excitement at the thought of it being more food. It isn't. Instead, he's carrying something that looks like a massive bug. I don't care much for bugs.

If it is a bug, it's about the scariest dang thing I've ever seen. Heck, even the largest horse wouldn't have a chance squashing it with its hoof. As Wyatt gets closer, my eyes widen. The bug he's carrying has a large, hard shell, and is black as the darkest night sky. There's a couple of long, dangling legs hanging down, and some other long things that might be stingers. The bugs with stingers are the worst.

Why on earth would Wyatt be carrying that thing? Furthermore, why in the heck is he bringing it toward me? I walk backward the moment Wyatt is next to my fence. Then, I rush back farther when he places the hideous looking bug onto the top rung of my paddock fence. Perhaps instead of taking me to the auction, Wyatt is here to let the giant bug eat me.

I call out, loudly, trying to warn the other horses that danger is nearby. Then, I kick up some dust, so they really get the message. As Wyatt climbs over the fence, the giant bug stays still, like it's stalking me and waiting to pounce. I'm not letting that ugly thing get anywhere near the likes of me.

"Easy, Ranger," says Wyatt, walking slowly toward me. "Easy, now. You're okay."

My nostrils flare and each breath leaves them forcefully. Maybe I can scare the nasty bug away with my fierceness. I stay in the corner farthest from it and allow Wyatt to come closer. I don't take my eyes off the bug for one second as Wyatt moves to stand next to me. Worried he might hit me like Ruth did, I flinch and blink my eyes as his hand lifts.

Worried the bug may have moved in the time I blinked my eyes; I widen them further and look to the last spot I last saw it in. It's still there, thankfully. Perhaps my fierceness is working after all. Then, I feel something that I haven't for too many days and nights. Wyatt is rubbing my neck and whispering close to my ear.

"Easy now, boy," he says in a soft voice.

My muscles soften slightly, but I don't take my eyes off the scary bug. Wyatt's hands stroke from the base of my ear to the top of my withers. And it feels mighty nice.

"Here's the situation, Ranger," says Wyatt. "Ruth is ready to send you off to auction. But myself, well, I believe you to be a rarity somehow. Can't explain why, I just do."

My heart sinks and knots form in my stomach. I don't want to be sent off to another unknown place where my future is uncertain. What the heck is a rarity?

"Yip, I convinced Auntie Ruth to allow me to work with you exclusively," says Wyatt. "I know I'm only thirteen, but I have more experience than some adults. My approach is much different to hers, and I'm really going to need you to cooperate with me. Otherwise, I won't be able to save you from the truck that'll take you out of here."

Wyatt walks toward the large bug, but the thing doesn't move. Then, from next to the creature, he grabs my halter and a lead rope before walking back to me. Wyatt strokes my neck again a few times, lifts my halter and places it onto my head. It itches at my nose, but I decide not to fuss. After all, Wyatt and I are having such a nice time, I'd hate to spoil it.

"The only way to stay on this ranch is if you're working," says Wyatt, leading me to the middle of my paddock. "In order for you to be working, you need to be saddled."

Wyatt holds my lead rope with one hand before removing his denim jacket with the other. Then, he does something super ridiculous. He lifts his jacket and places the thing onto my back. I hope he knows that thing will never fit a body like mine.

Just when I didn't expect Wyatt to get any loopier, he uses one hand to rub his silly jacket all over my back. I don't fully appreciate the way the material scratches at me, and I can't help but fidget a bit as he rubs. What in the heck is this ding-dong thinking right now?

"Easy, boy," says Wyatt, still rubbing his jacket on my back and then over to my sides. "I'm just using my jacket to get you used to having something foreign on your back. Don't worry, I'm not going to hurt you."

I nicker and speak up a little as I fidget a few minutes longer. After I've finished letting the jacket annoy me, I settle and stand next to Wyatt as he finishes whatever it is he's doing.

"Good, boy," says Wyatt. "Yip, that's the way. See, that was easy and painless. Let's try the next step."

I protest with exaggerated fidgeting as Wyatt gently slaps his dang jacket all over my back and sides. Holy heck, I don't care much for this step. I mean, it doesn't hurt or anything, but it's quick and a little scary. What on earth is he doing?

This ridiculous game goes on for quite a long time until I'm just too annoyed to react. And although I'm no longer reacting, Wyatt keeps going with the jacket shenanigans. Funny thing about it is, it doesn't hurt nor is it scary anymore.

"Good boy, Ranger," says Wyatt, rubbing my neck and pulling his jacket away from my body. "We should try the saddle pad."

Wyatt leads me over to the piece of fence with the giant bug resting on it. It hasn't moved an inch, and although I can't see the thing's eyes, I'm sure it's watching me. Close to the bug is a small blanket, which Wyatt grabs and allows me to smell. There's the scent of another horse on it, but nothing else that makes me afraid. Then, he slowly places it onto my back and allows it to rest there. I don't mind it, and truthfully, it's kind of cozy.

"That's the way, Ranger," says Wyatt. "Now comes the most important step."

Wyatt places his hand on the giant bug he keeps calling a saddle. I can't help wondering if it'll bite Wyatt, but it remains still and doesn't. I consider what Wyatt has said about being useful. It's crazy to me that the only way I can be useful in this place is by wearing a big bug on my back. I mean, I can help mow the grass, keep it clean and tidy. Heck, I'll work at that all day and night if they want me to. If there's any dummies around here, I can play with them and work with the rope like Spencer taught me. Do Wyatt and Ruth know how many babies I saw born when I lived with Lorraine? I'm basically an expert at that. They could put me in charge of delivering all the newborns around here – even though they do tend to drive me nuts. Couldn't I be useful by doing any of those things other than wearing a giant saddle bug on my back?

Wyatt keeps hold of my lead and inches closer to the saddle. He moves slowly and watches me carefully. My eyes stay fixed on the bug. I take in several deep breaths through my nose as Wyatt moves the bug off from the fence and closer to me. Each second the dang thing approaches, I tense up and my eyes squint. And although I'd love to run, buck, and kick up a fuss, the word useful repeats in my mind and I understand I must do all that I can to be that word. So, I allow Wyatt to put the bug on my back.

I remain tense and wait for the thing to bite me. I wait, and I wait longer, but all I feel is Wyatt rubbing my neck. My eyes open and I arch my neck around to look at the bug resting on my back. It still doesn't move, not even its long legs or stingers hanging from its shell. Maybe this bug isn't going to hurt me after all.

"Good boy, Ranger," says Wyatt, still rubbing my neck. "Yip, I knew you could do it. All right now, let's tighten the cinches so you really get a feel for the saddle."

Moving slowly, Wyatt walks to one side of my body, reaches below my belly, and pulls one of the bug's legs up to touch my side.

"I'm going to tighten the cinch now," says Wyatt.

He pulls up on the bug leg, which he calls a cinch, so it's against my belly. Then, he pulls on the thing so dang hard my eyes bulge from my head and a loud fart releases from my behind.

"Whoops," says Wyatt. "Maybe that cinch is a little too tight."

Chapter 27

Tex has moved on from the paddock close to me and rejoined the other horses in the field. I'm quite jealous of him as I'm still stuck in my small space. Not only does Tex get to hang with the others, but the field they're all in is also plump with tall grass and wildflowers. I would love to get in there and eat away at some of that.

Although I'm still confined to my tiny space, Wyatt comes to see me with the saddle every day. He places the thing on my back, then climbs up and sits in it before we walk around my paddock in circles until I feel dizzy. Wyatt also uses something called a bridle. It's an awkward contraption that sits in my mouth like a stick, but I'm used to that now, too.

We've been walking around in circles for long enough that my neck is forming sweat. Not only that, but I'm also getting tired of this game.

"All right, boy," says Wyatt, reaching his hand down to rub my neck. "I think you're ready for something more."

Wyatt squeezes my belly and I move forward. We walk over to the gate for my paddock, and Wyatt climbs down. Then, much to my delight, he opens the gate and climbs back on.

"Let's get a better look of the place," says Wyatt.

I inch toward the field with the other horses, but Wyatt has another direction in mind. He pulls at my bridle and leads me toward the large log house where Ruth lives. We move beyond the house toward a worn dirt path resting among a cluster of trees.

Wyatt sits still and relaxed on my back, so I relax, too, and keep walking.

It's nice to have a change of scenery. Birds sing and fly from tree to tree, against a backdrop of soft blue and pink sky. The air is warm, and the ground is soft beneath my feet. We casually walk through the trees until they break away into a small clearing.

My eyes grow wide when I notice the clearing is empty of other horses, but full of food. Wyatt walks me into the middle of the space and with each step, my head dives down toward the grass at my feet. I would give anything to eat this stuff all up. But Wyatt won't allow my head to lower further than it's upright position by holding strong to the reins.

"Not yet, Ranger," says Wyatt. "You can't just dive down and eat whenever you feel like it. If we get you out riding on the trails, you must wait until one of us gives you permission to eat."

I kind of understand what he's saying, but I still can't help myself. My head just wants to dive down into the grass and eat. But the harder I try, the more Wyatt resists until finally, I just give up. Funny enough, once I stop pulling, he relaxes his grip on my reins and says something.

"Good boy, Ranger. Go ahead and eat now."

My head dives down and the second my mouth connects with something green; I eat it quickly. This is some of the finest dang grass and foliage I've ever tasted in my life. Wyatt kindly sits in the saddle and allows me to eat for quite a time. He doesn't say much, just looks around and relaxes. We stay until the blue and pink sky shift to grey and the air cools. He must know night is coming, so he pulls my head up from the grass and directs me back toward home.

I feel better than I have since arriving here. Not only did I get to leave my paddock and stretch my legs, but my belly also hasn't felt this full since leaving Lorraine. Maybe my life is finally moving on the right track. When Wyatt and I reach the end of the path and approach Ruth's house, we find her sitting in a wooden chair on the wrap-around deck.

"Would you look at that," says Ruth, standing up and walking over to Wyatt and me. "You actually broke the useless thing."

Wyatt takes a breath before answering. "Yip, ma'am. It didn't take much work to be honest. Ranger here is a special horse – smart, gentle and kind. He's got a lot of positives going for him. Honestly, I think this horse is a rarity."

"Smart is one thing," says Ruth. "But gentle? He bit that little girl. I can't have that behavior around here."

"It shocks me to hear that Ranger would try and bite someone," says Wyatt. "You'd think with all the stuff I threw at him – my jacket, the saddle and bridle, that he would have bit me if he were really that kind of horse. But he didn't."

"Well," says Ruth. "I still haven't made my mind up about him yet. What about his injury – is he limping or tripping at all?"

"Honestly, his walk is a little different, but not to the point where I think it's bad or anything."

"Let's see if he can be useful this weekend when we have tourists here. You ride him out with the other horses and see how he does. Then, I'll decide."

"Fine with me. I suppose we'd better let him get to know the others before we do that."

"Yip, I suppose it's time we introduce Ranger to the rest of the herd. Go on, let him go in the pasture tonight."

"Yes, ma'am."

Wyatt and I walk away from Ruth, and I stay on my best behavior for the woman. Although I can tell she still doesn't care for me, I want to let her know I can be useful and a dang good friend if she lets me. I manage to remain calm and relaxed for quite a distance until Wyatt stops me in front of the field of other horses. Then, I kind of lose my cool.

Chapter 28

The moment Wyatt leads me through the gate, I run. Yip, I've never been so dang excited to be in a pasture in my whole life. The herd picks up energy as the other horses realize a newbie has entered their space. Although I've only been a short distance from them for the last few weeks, some of them approach to get a better look at me.

The first to get close is a smaller horse, white with grey spots all over it. I allow it to smell me, and I help myself to a smell of its belly, too. I can tell right away that the horse is a dude, like me. We both squeal ceremoniously as we smell and get to know each other. I'm so excited to be close to another horse, and all I want to do is show him some brotherly love, but the bastard bites me on the butt – hard.

I call out to relay the message that I'm hurt before getting the heck out of there, running in the opposite direction of the mean flea-bitten grey horse. Thankfully, he doesn't follow me, but a dark-haired horse, a little taller than me, approaches with its head held low. Because this horse seems unthreatening, I lower my head and approach.

After quickly smelling this raven-haired Canadian horse, I can tell it's a lady. I've heard that Canadian girls have a lot of spunk, but I wouldn't mind that. My eyes widen at the possibility of getting close to a girl, even though I was made into a gelding long ago and can't make babies, I still wouldn't mind a girlfriend. We could take long walks together, roll around in the tall grass, look up at the stars late into the night or snuggle in close when the weather gets cold. I'll need to impress the darlin first.

I lift my head and puff out my chest before trotting around her in a few circles. Then, I flip my glorious golden hair around, so she can see just how handsome I am. She approaches again, forcing my heartbeat to quicken and each breath to become short. Her head is low, and her eyes don't leave me. She's really getting a good look at me, which means she's obviously smitten already. She might end up being one of those girlfriends who shares her extra feed with me. I am feeling dang proud of myself right now.

Then, the raven-haired darlin quickly lunges in my direction before gouging her teeth into my backside, not far from where the first horse bit me. I consider she may just be a rough gal, and that she's showing me how handsome she thinks I am with this bite. But then, the old bag lunges and bites me again, this time on the neck.

My feet take off in the opposite direction to her. Whether that was a love bite or not, I'm not interested in a girl with a mouth like that. I run a short distance before finding Tex. He's not as interested in me as the other horses, likely because he already knows me. Instead of stopping to check out any of the others, I decide to just go and stick close to him. Hopefully, he won't bite me too.

When I'm near Tex, another horse rushes in front of me and intercepts my pathway. The male stink is strong on this fella, I don't even need to get close to his belly to figure that one out. He has muscles rippling up his legs to hindquarters. I need to lift my head to look up at him; a tall draft horse likely a hundred hands tall.

I swallow a lump down my throat and try not to appear like a dang ding-dong in front of this brute. I swear the earth shakes a little as he takes a step closer to smell me. His bay coloring is brilliant and slightly knotted in places to give him a strong and rugged appearance. I bet this guy works out, a lot, and he must get all the ladies.

Once the guy is close, I feel his hot breath against my neck as he smells me. My knees shake a little, but I hold still, something inside of me says this horse is the boss of the herd and I'd better just allow him to smell whatever he likes. After an agonizing amount of time, he lifts his head away and stops smelling. I'm so relieved. My muscles relax and I turn myself to try and get close to the massive draft horse. He'd be a great bodyguard and protector from the other horses.

But the big guy doesn't care for me getting close, and he lets me know it. Not only does he bite my neck hard, but my hair is also ripped out from its roots, and he turns his backside toward me and kicks. I've never felt pain like that before in my life. Swallowing my pride, I rush away from the big horse and all the other horses so I can get a break from their torment.

This seems to satisfy the rest of the herd once I've found my own space; they huddle together and keep their distance. My heart sinks and I feel defeated as I stand alone, again. The bite marks and kick site throb. I was so excited to be with other horses again, but it would seem they are less than enthused about having me here. Will there ever be a time in my life where I feel loved and accepted again?

Maybe if I can think of something nice to do for them, they might welcome me into the herd. I'll keep finding ways to show them love, so hopefully they'll see I'm a loveable guy and mean them no harm.

Chapter 29

It's taken some time, but I feel as though the herd has finally accepted me. Or perhaps they're tolerating me, but that's still better than being bullied. I'm still holding out hope that one day, one of the mares might pick me to be their beau. For now, I'm happy to be part of a family again.

The tourists only come when the weather is warm. We ride out together on the same paths each time a new crowd arrives. I'm still only ridden by Wyatt when he works for his aunt in the summer months, and Ruth still says she's making her mind up about me. She's been saying that for the last four full summers and I keep wondering when she'll finally make up her dang mind. Nevertheless, it is the longest I've ever lived in one place.

Life on the ranch stays consistent each day, the only thing that changes are the faces of the tourists. I keep wishing on the stars that one day I'll be surrounded by a consistent love and companionship. If only Wyatt could be here permanently instead of only in summer, then, I believe, my wish would come true.

After all these years, I've come to learn where the best patches of grass grow within the pasture. The spaces nearest the small creek meandering near the back fence is epic for eating. Another spot that smells disgusting and which Wyatt refers to as the septic field has the tallest, greenest grass around. Since I've eaten my way through those spaces, I've decided I ought to wander around through the trees at the back end of the pasture and see if I can round up any grub there.

I'm thrilled when I find dandelions and tall grass, so I bend down and bite as much as my mouth will hold. It's flavorful and sweet; the air is warm, a light breeze tickles my face, and the birds are singing with gusto. Everything is perfectly placid and serene, until there's a loud bang and the roaring of an engine.

My heart races and leaps into my throat. The birds scatter from the trees and rush up high into the blue sky. The engine sound gets louder and closer, then, there's another bang. My body moves fast as I examine each direction and find that I'm alone. With high anxiety, I run at full speed through the trees and back toward my herd. As I run, there's another loud bang; accompanied by the roar of men's laughter.

Once I'm back within the clearing of the pasture, I spot my herd; all huddled together and running, scared as hell. My lungs burn as I push myself to run faster than I knew I was capable of to catch up with the other horses. Ruth and Wyatt rush out from within the tourist office. A second later, they're met by a large white truck.

"Whoop, whoop," shouts a man's voice through the open window of the truck.

Wyatt's face is long and pale, like he's scared out of his wits. Ruth stands close to him and they both watch as all doors for the truck open and four men climb out. They leave the music playing loudly and adjust their shirts by tucking them into their jeans. The other horses and I run around a little longer before easing and walking close together and nearer to the house.

"Were you guys shooting a gun or something?" asks Wyatt.

"I was shooting my gun," says a man with a round belly and puffy face. "I'm determined to shoot a buck while I'm here."

"We aren't that kind of outfitting company," says Wyatt. "And you can't exactly shoot a buck from a moving vehicle."

"Oh hush, Wyatt," says Ruth. She leaves his side and walks closer to the group of men. She's behaving strangely; goofy smile, a slow walk, and her hands on her hips. "These are our only guests this weekend, and as the owner of this ranch, I'll allow a little hunting."

"Maybe I'll just focus on hunting you down, woman," says the round man with the gun. His remark induces laughter from the other men. "What's your name, anyway?"

"Ruth," she says, pursing her lips and pushing one hip out to the side. "What's your name?"

"My name is Duke," says the round man. Then, he points at another round man who looks like a younger version of him. "And this is my brother, Hank. He's the one getting married next weekend."

"I see," says Ruth, her voice softening. "And what about you, Duke? You married?"

"Not yet," says Duke. "But Derrek and Josh are, so it just so happens that I am looking for a wife." The other men erupt into laughter again and mumble under their breath while shaking their heads.

"Let me show you guys where your cabins are," says Wyatt, stepping forward and interrupting the obnoxious men. "This way."

Wyatt leads them away from the truck and toward the small cabins. He's annoyed by these men, angry even. There must be something wrong with these tourists if Wyatt is angry because I've never seen him act as such before. Admittedly, I'm not too fond of these guys either; especially not that loud gun they brought. Thankfully, tourists typically only stay for a day or two, then leave. It shouldn't be long before these men are gone and out of our lives.

Chapter 31

The noisy men and Ruth stayed up until long after the sun went down for the night. They played loud music, laughed a lot and shot their gun into the air a few more rounds. By the time they all went to sleep, I wasn't too afraid of the loud noises.

Wyatt was up at first light, as per usual, and had us horses all fed and ready to ride. He paced next to the fence and glanced at his watch every few minutes, mumbling and cursing under his breath. I could feel sweat forming under my saddle as we stood under the sun, growing hotter and higher in the blue sky with each passing minute. After Wyatt watered us horses a few times, Ruth finally made an appearance.

"It's past eleven," says Wyatt, approaching his auntie.

Ruth rubs her forehead with two fingers and moans before responding. "Our guests were up late last night."

"Yip, I know," says Wyatt. "I heard you all talking, shooting and drinking 'till all hours of the early morning. But I've had the horses ready for hours, just like you asked me to, and they're getting hot and tired."

"Don't get all high-and-mighty with me," says Ruth, giving Wyatt a pained look. "Just because you're almost eighteen, don't mean you know everything, boy. They're just horses, and they're fine if I say they're fine."

Wyatt's jaw clenches as he steps away from Ruth. He's changed so much this past year; his hair kempt short and neat, stubble growing on his chin and a tall body filled in with muscles.

Wyatt moves toward me and pushes his face close to my neck. His breath is hot against my already hot body, and I can tell he's mad and upset. Although I'm weary from standing in the hot sun, I bend my neck and tuck my face in closer, just to let him know I'm here if he needs me.

"Good morning," says Duke, walking up behind Ruth. Then, he swings his hand back before slapping it into Ruth's backside. She giggles and gives him a look.

I didn't know humans liked rears just as much as horses do. Do they bite one another on the butt, too? If one wants to eat what another is eating, will they bite to move them off? Or if one is watering for too long, will a human bite their butt or neck to have them get out of the way? Interesting.

"Are you guys ready to move out?" asks Wyatt, leaving my side and approaching Duke. "The horses have been saddled and ready for hours, they need to move out."

"It's just me and my brother today," says Duke as Hank drags his feet to walk up to the others.

"Yeah," says Hank. "The other two wussies can't handle their alcohol and are too hung over to come out today."

"Fine," says Wyatt. "I'll let two of the horses go, and then we need to get moving."

"I want to ride that palomino," says Duke, pointing in my direction. "They're my favorite color of horse, and I want that one."

"Ranger?" asks Wyatt. "Sorry, he's my horse and isn't used to anyone else riding him."

"He's my horse," says Ruth. "And if a guest wants to ride him, I say he can ride him."

Wyatt's face flushes red with anger and he stays silent.

Duke's breath smells funny. Even when he was still a fair distance away from me, I can smell it. His feet shuffle up dust as he approaches my side and I bend my neck to say hello. He doesn't even glance in my direction, only shifts his pants under his full belly before grabbing hold of the horn on the saddle. Duke places one foot within the saddle's stirrup, then all his weight as he stands on one side of the saddle. This brief act forces me off balance and I shift my feet to try and regain it.

"Is he acting up?" shouts Ruth from atop her horse. "Give him a smack if he's not being respectful."

"I know how to handle a horse, woman," says Duke, grunting before swinging one leg over and into the other stirrup. Then, he sits down into the saddle and relaxes all his weight.

My eyes bulge a little from their sockets and all the air in my lungs pushes out with a quick blow. Duke's weight aches on my back and I can feel my spine sagging into my stomach with each passing second. I feel a little weak in the knees, so I try and dance around to shake it off and find my balance.

"You settle down now, Ranger," says Duke in a loud, deep voice.

I want to settle down, but I fear if I stop moving, I'll shift too much and drop Duke onto the ground. Knowing how bad that would be, I ignore him and dance around a little more, just to find my footing. Then, I feel his hard fist jam into the side of my neck.

I wince and take in deep breaths to ease the pain of it. After a few short seconds, Duke rams his heels into my gut and says, "Walk on, Ranger."

This guy needs to make up his mind. Does he want me to stand still, or move? I'm not sure I'll ever understand the mind of a human. Nevertheless, I move my feet forward as instructed. Each time I place a foot onto the ground, it digs into the earth and pinches at my knees. I trip as I step, too, the old injury on my leg aches even more with Duke on my back. But he doesn't know nor understand that.

"Keep your feet steady, stupid horse," says Duke.

I understand what he's referring to, and I want to stay steady, and although I will myself to keep a smooth walk for the most part, every few steps, I can't help but trip.

"This horse trips a lot," says Duke. "Is he dumb or defective?"

"He has an old injury," says Wyatt, coming to my defense. "He trips from time to time, but you'll get used to it. I have."

Usually when I'm out for a ride with Wyatt, I take in the scenery. But today, with Duke on my back, all I can focus on is moving forward in the heat with the aching weight of the man on my swaying back.

Thankfully, Duke is just a tourist. I only need to endure him on my back and the odd smack a little longer. Then, I'll be back with Wyatt and all will be right again.

Chapter 32

Duke hasn't left. It's been many days and nights, the summer is almost at an end, and he's still here. He's not considered a tourist anymore. Each night when the humans go into their dwellings, Duke and Ruth always retire together in the main house. Sometimes, the strangest dang sounds come from within that house after the lights go out. Almost like they're being attacked by a pack of squirrels or something. It's quite disturbing, so I move as far away from it as possible until morning.

I've adapted to Duke's weight within my saddle, even though my back always aches and feels funny. He still hits me, which I'll never get used to, but not as much as he did in the beginning. The oddest thing about Duke being here is that because he thinks I'm useful, Ruth suddenly thinks I'm useful, too. The worst thing about Duke being here is that he insists on always riding me, which means I rarely get any time with Wyatt.

When I do see Wyatt, I notice a huge change in him. He rarely smiles and once his work is done for the day, he hides in his cabin instead of walking around or going for a ride. I miss him and wish he were still the only one to ride me.

Wyatt pauses in front of me after giving all of us horses our morning feed bowl. He sighs heavily, and I can tell he's missing me, too. Although I have a large bowl of food at my feet, I lean in close, and allow him to rub my neck. I get the sense that rubbing my neck feels as good for him as it does for me. We haven't had this much time to simply be together in ages. When the stars come out tonight, I'll make a wish to have Wyatt's love surrounding me in the future.

Our peaceful moment is interrupted by a loud holler from Ruth near the main house. Wyatt and I both jump and pause as loud footsteps rush toward the barn.

"Wyatt!" shouts Ruth from beyond the door of the barn. "Wyatt, where are you?"

Wyatt rushes from me and toward the barn door. "I'm here, auntie."

Ruth appears within the door, and Duke is just behind her. They're both smiling, wider than I've ever seen them, and Ruth is holding out one of her hands.

"Duke and I are getting married," says Ruth in a giddy tone.

"What?" asks Wyatt, flat and expressionless.

"I asked your aunt to marry me," says Duke, his chest puffed out. "And she has said yes."

"What?" repeats Wyatt.

"Are you deaf or something, boy?" says Ruth while laughing. "Duke and I are getting married, and as soon as possible."

"You've only known each other for a couple of months," says Wyatt.

"When you know, you know, son," says Duke, slapping Ruth on her butt.

Ruth giggles and leans into Duke. "I'm not a youngster who doesn't know what she wants, Wyatt," she says. "I am in love with this man, and I can't wait to marry him and grow old with him on this ranch."

Duke walks away from Ruth and stops to stand in front of me. Worried that he'll take me from my food, I eat as quickly as I can. Then, he shocks me by rubbing my neck as I eat.

"I'm giving Duke that useless horse as an engagement present," says Ruth, walking over to Duke and me. "I can't understand why, but he sure does love this silly guy."

"I told you, palominos are my favorite," says Duke.

"You're giving Ranger to him?" asks Wyatt. "But he's basically been my horse for the last four years. I've been the only one to ride him or care for him until Duke came along. How could you not even ask me about it?"

"Because he isn't your horse," says Ruth. "I'm the one who pays for him to be fed and all of his upkeep. You're a great hired hand, Wyatt, but just because you're family, doesn't mean you have any say in the way this ranch is run. You'll need to accept that if Duke is my husband, he and I will be the ones to make decisions around this place."

Wyatt crosses his arms firmly across his chest. His jaw is clenched, and his eyes are stuck on Ruth. It takes a bit of time, but eventually, he responds to Ruth's last comment.

"I'm not sticking around here to watch you and this idiot make a mess of this ranch," says Wyatt in a calm and even tone.

"What did you just say?" asks Duke.

"I'm done here," says Wyatt.

"Wyatt," says Ruth. "You're acting like such a baby."

Wyatt walks over to me and looks at me. He rubs a hand between my eyes for a few seconds before stepping back and walking away. I feel a pain in my heart as he leaves, and something inside of me knows that another person who loves me is gone from my life.

Chapter 33

Maybe the stars I've been wishing on are broken. Is it possible that a star is only allocated a certain number of wishes before it just fizzles out and loses magic? Or maybe the problem isn't with the stars at all. Is it possible that my wish of finding the unconditional love of a human not coming true because I'm the problem? Should I be doing more, loving more?

The sky is littered with stars against a veil of darkness. The stars I typically gaze at sparkle, but a different one in the opposite direction appears brighter to me somehow. I walk toward it, keeping my eyes locked on it as I do.

Wyatt's image immediately floods my mind. He's such an amazing human with so much love to give horses. Why did he leave? A better question may be, why did Ruth and Duke push him away? I wish I could have Wyatt's love back in my life.

But he's gone, so perhaps I should think about the kind of person I'd like to be my forever companion. Maybe I should instead imagine what their love could feel like – imagine what their soul would be like. Maybe if I wish hard enough, Duke will end up being this for me. After all, and although I don't like it, he is now officially my person.

Spring seems to have sprung overnight. The past winter wasn't as harsh as normal, which must be why the season changed as easily as it did. Typically, I'd be giddy with the arrival of Spring; eager to dine on fresh food growing vastly within our pasture.

Usually, I'd be anticipating the arrival of tourist season, especially with the knowing that Wyatt would arrive for his summer job shortly. But this year, without Wyatt coming, Spring feels lackluster.

Duke walks into the pasture with a halter and lead rope in his hands. My back stiffens with thoughts of another day with his weight on my back. After our rides, I always feel stiff, like an old man. But I shouldn't because I'm still quite young.

"Ranger," shouts Duke from a short distance away. "Come on now, Ranger. Time to come in with me."

I sigh heavily and my head hangs low as I slowly walk toward Duke. My body aches only thinking about him saddling me and climbing up onto my back. After he halters me, we walk slowly together through the pasture and to the barn. Instead of a saddle there waiting for me, there's a human instead. I recognize him to be the farrier, Darren.

"This is the one?" asks Darren, looking at me with examining eyes.

"You bet, Darren," says Duke.

"I remember this one. You know that old injury has completely thrown off his gait," says Darren. "He's got crooked feet – pigeon toed. Does he still trip a lot when he's walking?"

"He's always tripping and it's embarrassing as hell."

Darren runs his hands from the top of my rump, then all the way down the length of my leg and to my foot then says, "Why on earth would you want to use this guy? I mean, he's not exactly a looker or anything. And if he's tripping all the time; what's the point in even keeping him at all?"

Excuse me? Who the heck does this guy think he is? He must be partially blind if he thinks I'm not a looker. And even though I do trip, I'm always able to regain my stance and balance. Why are humans so dang critical of the appearances of others? If Darren would take a little time to get to know me, he'd see I'm one heck of a charming guy.

"Can we just get on with this, Darren?" asks Duke, releasing an anxious sigh through is nose.

"Yeah, yeah," says Darren, kneeling closer to my side. "Foot, Ranger."

I dutifully lift my back, right foot, and Darren holds it firmly within his grasp. Although I can't see what he's doing back there, I feel him pull and poke around at my foot, but nothing serious. Then, Darren rubs the bottom of my hoof with smooth, even strokes. When the farrier cared for me while I was with Lorraine, she'd say I was getting a pedicure. I like them well enough.

"How are things going for you, since you moved in?" asks Darren.

"Its fine, just fine," says Duke, scratching his head with two fingers. "This place does well enough, but I'm interested in making some serious money, you know?"

"This place has been stuck in a time warp for decades," says Darren. "I've been fixing horses feet out here for thirty years, and nothing has changed. Seems to me, though, that the family appreciates the steadiness of all they've built."

"Well," says Duke, shrugging his shoulders. "Now that I'm married to Ruth, I own half of this place. And we have so much land that isn't being used to its full potential. The future of ranching demands that we diversify – and I know just how to do it."

Chapter 34

We can hear it before seeing it. I can tell by the way the engine sounds that the vehicle approaching the ranch isn't a car full of tourists. The horses in my herd seem to notice, too, as some pace the fence closest to the driveway. There's a distinctive energy coming from the area of the road, too, which doesn't feel human – more animal in nature. My energy escalates and I join the others in pacing the fence, kicking up my back legs periodically and whipping my head.

Ruth and Duke emerge from their house and walk out to the base of the driveway. As the engine noises reach their loudest, a massive vehicle appears. I've seen one similar at the auction when I was sold to Spencer. A large, silver truck with a bunch of wheels and the largest horse trailer imaginable. The truck kicks up dust as it moves along the road toward the common areas of the ranch before stopping.

Are there another hundred horses in that trailer? Maybe there's a few new darlin's in there that I can show around the place. A loud ruckus of stomping and sounds not typically made by horses echoes from around the trailer. My heart sinks when I consider that maybe I've heard these noises made before, when I spent time with Lorraine at her vet clinic.

The large truck backs up to an open gate leading out to a large pasture. Then, a few humans climb out to meet Ruth and Duke. The other horses and I run around and make a fuss as they all talk and shake hands. After several minutes of conversing, one of the humans opens the back door of the trailer. I pause and watch.

The scene grows chaotic once the door is open. A rush of black animals, making obnoxious noises, flood the pasture on the opposite side of the road. My eyes grow wide and I flare my nostrils. Once I've gotten a good smell and look of them, it dawns on me. It's a bunch of dang dummies.

Does this mean I must become a roping horse again? Holy heck, is Duke planning on becoming a roping cowboy in the rodeo circuit? It's tricky enough for me to carry him on my back while walking on trails, how will I run like a roping horse with that dang man on my back?

Perhaps Duke has other plans for our new neighbors. Although I'm not sure what other use these dummies have aside from being in the rodeo. How could they possibly be useful on our ranch? Will tourists begin riding them instead of us? That doesn't seem logical. Knowing Duke, the way I do now, I'd say nothing he does ever seems logical anyhow.

The worst thing about having the new dummies living on our ranch is the lack of fresh pasture space for us horses. In the past, we'd be turned out to fresh and tall grasses each week, but that's no longer the case.

Thankfully, Duke hasn't decided to become a roping cowboy which means I'm not expected to run with him on my back. I'm mighty relieved of that. I still don't understand how the dummies are useful, and I can't say I've thought of any good reason for keeping them.

But the dummies aren't the only new thing around here. In the months since Duke has lived on the ranch, he's brought all kinds of new things here. First was a new truck; we can hear the dang thing coming up the road from miles away. It's red with black decals on the side and has giant wheels.

He's always wearing new hats that smell artificial. Boots, too; I'm sure he must have a hundred pair. Not only that, but it also seems he's wearing new clothes daily. Crisp new pairs of jeans and brightly colored shirts with designs that make me dizzy.

Although tourists have come and gone regularly, Duke and I don't ride out with them as much. Does Ruth mind us not going out with tourists anymore; always pushing how all who live on the ranch must remain useful. But she only smiles and giggles wherever Duke is concerned.

As I bite down on a sparse patch of grass, Duke's truck rolls up the driveway. It's loud as ever, but sounds different, deeper, and as if it's struggling. Still chewing the stale grass in my mouth, I lift my head to look for Duke and his truck. Maybe he'll come out and see me today. If that's the case, I'd better walk toward the gate closest to the house.

With each step I take, Duke's truck gets louder and closer. Once I'm at the gate, I turn my head to look at the driveway. Duke's truck climbs the high spot of the road, but I'm surprised to find he's hauling a flashy trailer behind it. I really hope he isn't bringing home any more dang dummies. I'm already surrounded by them out here.

Ruth rushes out of the house and walks down off the front verandah, using her hands to smooth her floral shirt and hair as she does. Then, as Duke's truck pulls up closer to the house, she stops in her tracks, puts her hands onto her hips and stares.

"What do you think of this beauty, huh?" asks Duke, climbing out of the driver's side of his truck and walking around the trailer.

"What in the hell have you bought now?" asks Ruth, her

voice raised.

The energy and tone of her voice grabs my attention and perks my ears. They aren't calling for me, but something about the way they're talking to one another makes me want to listen and pay attention.

"Just hear me out, baby-cakes," says Duke to Ruth, moving to the side of the trailer closest to me.

"Did you buy this thing?" asks Ruth. "Or is it a loaner?"

"Think of it as an investment," says Duke. "Think of all the places we can travel together with our horses in this unit."

"How much did it cost?" asks Ruth.

"It has all the finest components," says Duke. "We can haul four horses, and our bed is a king size. There's a full kitchen, fireplace and two televisions."

"How much?"

"Not much. I haven't told you why I bought it yet – that's the best part."

Ruth stands firm in her stance, her hands still on her hips and a tightness in her jaw.

"We've been invited to ride in the parade at the fall fair in town to represent our ranch," says Duke. "Do you know what an honor that is?"

"Our little ranch was invited. Why?"

"Well, technically I applied for a spot and may have elaborated a little on what our entry will look like, but nonetheless, they accepted our application and we're in!"

"What in the heck do we need to be in a parade for? Have you lost your damn mind?"

"I've got plans, Ruth. You must trust me, baby-cakes."

Duke walks over to Ruth and warps his arms around her waist. Then, he leans in close and smooshes his lips into hers.

Whenever he does this, it always calms Ruth and instantly shifts her mood where Duke is concerned.

"So, being accepted to ride in a local parade means we needed a new horse trailer that costs more than we make around here in a year?"

"We need to make an impression while we're there, Ruth. Show everyone we're a high-class operation. It'll be a great opportunity to promote our dude ranch, but also tell everyone about our new cattle venture, too."

Although Ruth and Duke are still arguing, they walk away from the new trailer and into the house. Now that I can't listen to what they're saying, and it's clear Duke isn't coming to see me, I bend my head down and eat some more grass. Besides, I have no idea what a parade even is, and I'm sure there's no reason for me to know anyway.

Chapter 35

I look like a ninny; completely ridiculous and utterly embarrassing. Knowing Duke's own style and fashion sense, I should have expected as much when he said I'd be wearing a costume for the parade. Although, at the time, I had no idea what a costume even was, and I still have no dang idea what a parade is either.

Despite all that, the parade is apparently where we are now headed. Duke loads me into the fancy new horse trailer dressed up in my parade costume: a green blanket with the picture of one of our free-range dummies, some words I don't know, something called a brand, and long strings of beads and neon feathers attached to my halter. It's hot, awkward, and itchy as heck, but I don't have much choice in wearing the outfit. Duke looks just as embarrassing as I do, wearing a long-sleeved shirt identical to my blanket, only with long tassels hanging from the sleeves with his round belly hanging over his tight, black jeans. His boots and hat match, both black with green, shiny dots all over them. They also have silver things that make noises each time he walks, similar to the new shoes the farrier put onto my feet.

Once me and two other horses are loaded into the trailer, the door closes behind us and we begin to move. The long ride to this parade thing we're headed to is quiet and uneventful. My favorite part about riding in the trailer is to look out the windows, but my halter is so heavy with crap, it hurts to lift my head up and look.

When Duke's loud truck stops, it's noisy beyond the walls

of the horse trailer. Voices of many humans, laughter and footsteps are all I can hear. Then, the backdoor to the trailer opens, and those noises intensify along with the sounds of other horses. My ears perk up and I nicker, excited about the possibility of meeting new friends.

"We don't have much time before the parade begins," says Duke, rushing around to unload us horses. "You gave me the wrong start time, woman."

"I can't keep up with all your stuff, Duke," says Ruth, her voice angrier than usual.

I sigh loudly and wait for the pair of them to finish another fight. It seems like that's all they ever do these days. As they continue with their banter, I check out my surroundings. The day is hot with nothing but blue sky and a vibrant sun. There are humans everywhere, walking tightly together in lines. Beyond that are massive machines harnessing humans that spin, lift, and drop. I can't say I've ever seen farm equipment like those before.

"We need to water them, Duke," says Ruth.

Water, the word is music to my ears as the sweat pools on my back below my thick costume.

"No time for that now," says Duke. "They'll have to wait. They still need to be saddled."

"It's hot out, they need watering before we walk them all that way."

"You can stay here, but Ranger and I are heading to the parade line. I'm not gonna let you ruin this for me."

Duke saddles me quickly, then leads me away from the horse trailer and toward a bunch of other horses. Some of them sing out, so I lift my head and proudly serenade them with some of my best tunes. It gets some attention as a few other horses respond. I shift my backend and sing louder, pulling a little on the lead rope in Duke's hands.

"Settle down, Ranger," says Duke, smacking me in the nose with one hand. "You'd better not embarrass me and make me regret bringing you here."

The other horses continue to sing, but I hang my head low and don't respond, worried I'll get another hit to the face. I walk with Duke until we reach a patch of cement packed with horses all dressed like me. I'm grateful I'm not the only one here who looks like a dang ding-dong.

My mouth is dry and desperate for water as the heat leaches sweat from my body. There's a large trough full of water at the edge of the space, but Duke mustn't see it. Instead, he hoists himself onto my back and sits within the saddle. His weight on my back just makes me hotter.

Loud music crashes from ahead of the pack of horses before we all begin to move in a long line. After taking a few steps, Ruth and her horse move up and align next to Duke and me. My eyes grow weary, and I'm certain my body is dripping sweat onto the pavement. I stand still in my position before Duke rams the shiny things on the heels of his boots into my gut. Sharp pain makes me wince and clench my belly before moving my feet forward to follow the other horses.

After taking a few steps, I trip.

"Stay straight, Ranger," says Duke in a stern voice. "Do not embarrass me with your gimpy leg."

Even though I'm hot, sweaty and tired, I want to make Duke proud. So, I muster up every ounce of energy I have within me to keep myself balanced and straight footed. And I manage to do so for a while, moving us from the concrete holding space and onto a long road lined with the thousands of people.

The humans are smiling and clapping as we walk past. I can tell Duke is proud by the way he's sitting. I desperately want to feel pride, too, but each step I take makes me hotter and more exhausted. The noises around me begin to sound distant, even though they're all right next to me. Then, I trip again.

"Damnit, Ranger," says Duke before ramming me in the sides with his sharp heels again. "Stop tripping."

I repeat Dukes words in my mind as I walk, stop tripping, stop tripping, hoping it'll keep me on my feet. But it doesn't. Instead, I feel myself tripping even more. And with each trip, Duke becomes angrier. I breathe deeply and focus on walking, but then we approach a round metal thing in the middle of the road. I've never seen anything like it before, and that scares me. My butt shifts around, and I trip again as I sidestep to try and avoid it.

"Smarten up," says Duke, slapping the side of my neck with his reins.

But I disobey his wishes. The round metal thing in the road gets larger the closer I get to it. I call out loudly and shift my butt around again, faster this time than the last. Then, the weight on my back disappears and the humans lining the streets gasp and point at me.

I shift myself around a few more times before I'm away from the round metal thing. Then, Duke rushes up behind me on foot and yanks forcefully on my reins.

"Stupid horse," says Duke. "That's it, I'm done with you."

Even though there's so much happening around me, I can only focus on Duke's energy. He's angry with me, and I feel as though he loves me less. I lean into him and walk straight, trying to show him I can do what he needs me to if he gives me another chance. But he doesn't climb onto my back again. He and I walk the rest of the way until we're back at the horse trailer. Duke ties me up and walks away.

Chapter 36

Ruth and Duke seem to have forgotten us. The sun has risen and sunk twice since we last saw them. Anything edible within our enclosure has been bitten so far to the ground that hardly anything other than dirt remains. We need food, and we need it soon.

The other horses and I pace the fence closest to the house, and bite at each other out of anger from being hungry. Occasionally, we start calling out loudly, hoping Ruth and Duke will hear us and remember to come out and feed. Heck, even the dummies are becoming loud and rowdy, I'd suspect for the same reasons my fellow herd and I do. But our humans haven't even left the house since we came home from the parade. The only reason we know they're in there is by the loud yelling coming from inside their dwelling.

As the sun nears the end of another shift, the front door to the house opens with a crash. The noise grabs my attention and I pause to look. Duke rushes out with his hands full of large bags. Only a second behind him is Ruth; her hands are empty and instead are tightly bound into fists and resting on her hips. Immediately, I can tell she's angrier than a swarm of angry wasps.

"Don't you dare walk out on me," says Ruth. "We aren't finished talking yet."

"Woman," says Duke, rushing over to his truck with the horse trailer still hitched from the parade. "You can talk until you're blue in the face, except I won't be here to listen for another second."

"When will you be back then?"

"I'm leaving you, Ruth, for good. I can't stand to be around you."

"You can't leave me, Duke. We're married – what about that, huh? Doesn't that mean anything to you?"

"It doesn't mean a damn thing to me! You're suffocating and controlling, and I must feel like I'm free to live my life as I see fit."

"So, you're just going to leave forever?"

"Yes, woman! I'm done with you!"

Duke loads his large bags into the back of his truck before rushing over to the barn. Ruth follows him close and keeps talking. I move toward the fence line closest to the barn and watch. Hopefully, they're fixing to feed us.

"What do you think you're doing?" asks Ruth, moving at a quicker pace to try and get in front of Duke.

Duke storms toward the fence where the other horses and I are standing and pacing. There's such a rush of horses, all moving quickly and in front of me, making it difficult to get a good view of the ensuing altercation.

"I said, what are you doing?" says Ruth again, her voice louder than before.

"I'm taking my horse," says Duke, walking through the gate and pushing his way through the crowd of horses.

"What?" says Ruth. "What are you talking about, your horse?"

I stand back and watch. Duke continues to move through the other horses and toward me. Once he's close enough, I notice he's holding my halter and lead rope.

"Ranger, come on," says Duke.

I nicker and walk toward him. Maybe I'll be the first one to eat. Once I'm at Duke's side, I lower my head and allow him to halter me.

"You can't take Ranger," says Ruth, moving to stand in front of me. "He's my horse."

"You gave him to me," says Duke, moving with me around Ruth.

Instead of leading me toward the barn, Duke rushes quickly toward another gate along the fence closest to the main house.

"Stop, Duke," says Ruth. "You can't leave me, and you can't take that horse with you. Where will you go?"

"I'm getting as far away from you as I can – Arizona," says Duke. "You'll never see me again."

"You can't take Ranger to Arizona without a bill of sale and special permits. Just leave him here."

Duke and I reach the gate and walk through. We walk across the gravel driveway until reaching the back of the new horse trailer. The other horses call out again, still hungry, and angry. I call out to them, too. I'm not sure what an Arizona is, exactly, but it sounds like Duke is taking me there to find out.

"Stop, Duke," says Ruth.

The tone of her voice has changed. I shift my focus from the other horses and look at her. She's crying, which is something I've never seen her do before. There's a deep sadness radiating from her, and although she's never thought of me as a useful horse or even one worthy of love or food, I feel badly for her. Ruth moves to stand near Duke and look onto his eyes. I lower my head and nuzzle in close to her, hoping to show her enough love to help her feel better.

"Good-bye, Ruth," says Duke. "You'll be hearing from my lawyer soon."

Duke opens the back door to the horse trailer and steps inside. I notice the feed bags are still full of hay, so I eagerly walk in and begin to eat. Once I'm secured in my stall, Duke rushes to close the back door then climbs into his truck. As he starts the engine, Ruth is still speaking, her words broken between sobs.

As the truck rolls forward, I pull a large amount of hay into my mouth and chew. Then, I move my head and look out the window. My fellow herd, my family, are still pacing and unsettled. Duke and I leave, and I'm not sure when exactly I'll be back from Arizona.

Chapter 37

Hay has a different taste depending on where you are eating it. When I was living with Justin and Mara, it tasted sweet and floral. The hay at Spencer's house was tricky to chew and had little flavor. When I was with Lorraine, the hay tasted close enough to fresh grass, and often had dried leaves of clover in it. Ruth's ranch was surrounded by pine trees, so I found the hay tasted a little like the green needles that would fall from the tree branches. The hay I'm eating now tastes of dust and like it's been here for longer than I've been alive.

Yip, I'm still eating the stuff, though. I have been in this new place for more than a week, and I've quickly learned there's nothing else for us to eat anyway. So, to fill the rumblings within my belly, I eat the stuff without complaint.

When Duke and I arrived in the place I assumed was Arizona, it was late and dark. Sadly, I didn't get an opportunity to check out the scenery and new environment. I was led directly to a small pen with tall, wooden walls which had cracks not large enough to see through. Thankfully, I'm outside and can pass the time watching clouds and birds fly overhead.

Duke hasn't made an appearance again since we arrived here either. I'm not sure what to make of it. There are other horses here, several in fact. They've been arriving few by few since I got here. And there's a bunch of people bustling about and doing odd jobs.

"Number these quarter horses in the pens along this line,"

shouts a man from beyond my gate.

My ears perk and eyes widen. I hope to hear Duke's voice because at this point, I don't care much for Arizona, it's boring. I'd like to go home to my herd.

A young woman arrives at the gate of my pen with her hands full. She manages to open it and step inside while juggling all that she carries. Desperate for a little human affection, I rush up to her and nuzzle in close.

"Palomino... palomino... palomino, ah here you are," she says, looking at a sheet of paper affixed to a wooden clipboard. "Are you, Ranger?"

I nicker and nuzzle in close. She smiles and gives me a quick scratch on the neck before saying, "Your number is 338."

She grips onto a small piece of plastic attached to another sheet of paper. The small tag is yellow with black numbers on it. Then, she removes something from the back of the thing before placing it onto my rump close to my tail. Another tag is placed onto the other side of my rump before she moves back toward the gate and leaves.

Now it all makes sense to me. Now I understand why I thought I'd been to Arizona before. I've been in a situation just like this one in the past. It was the time I was sold to Spencer, at the auction. Duke has brought me to an auction. Is that why I haven't seen him in a few days?

I lower my head and move away from the gate. Finding the corner, I push my head into it and stand still. I'm not in Arizona, I'm being sold at auction. Which means some random person who knows nothing about me is about to take me to another new home. My stomach tightens and I sigh heavily. What am I in for next?

Once night falls, I look up at the stars in the sky. I make a wish. This one was simple – please let my new home have someone to love me, and a herd I can call my family. I wish to find a forever home and never be abandoned again.

Morning arrives quicker than I anticipated, and the place is filling with people. They walk slowly past my pen, looking and pointing as they go. A few humans stop to check me out, it excites me, a little, until they begin commenting about me.

"He seems incredibly kind and gentle," says one man. "But look at that lump above his front leg. Never buy a horse with an old injury like that. It'll cause nothing but trouble."

A woman with a little girl in tow pauses to look at me, too. They stroke my neck, which felt nice, and the little girl even scratched between my ears. I wish I could have a girl like her to care for me. But once the mother takes a closer look at my body, they move on.

Feeling defeated by the comments about my appearance, I turn myself away from the humans and tuck my head into a corner. With only my butt and my number facing the onlookers, I hide the pieces of me humans always seem to find fault with.

A few more try to prompt me from my place to look at me, but I ignore everyone and stay put. But then I hear a melodic voice so sweet within my presence, it reminds me of my mama.

"Hey, sweet boy," says the female voice from behind me. "Look at you, beautiful palomino boy."

The way she speaks evokes an emotion within me. One that swirls bubbles within my belly and tickles at my ribs. A feeling so strong, all I can do to express it is sing. I lift my head high into the air and deliver the best song I've ever sung in my life. Then, I turn around.

A woman with short, silver hair holds out her hand and looks right at me. The sun beyond creates an orb around her, making her appear angelic – or maybe she just is. Her smile is kind and wide, and her blue eyes beam love and kindness. My heart pounds within my chest, begging to be close to her.

I move to the woman as quickly as I can. The moment I'm close enough, she uses one hand to rub my neck and the other is still outstretched to me. Something I've never seen before lays within the palm of her hand and smells dang delicious. So, I reach over and delicately take the object into my mouth. My insides do a jig as intense flavor hugs my taste buds. As though she can read my mind, she reaches into her pocket and gives me another one.

"You like my treats, sweet boy?" she asks. "Let me take a good look at you."

My stomach sinks low as she steps away from the gate and looks at my front leg. She'll probably see me the same as the others do – defective and useless. After spending a few seconds looking at my body, she prompts me closer to her again by holding out another treat. I move in and take it. Then, she holds my head in her hands and stares into my eyes.

She and I remain this way for quite a time, and all the while, I feel pure love move from her hands and into me.

"Your eyes tell me more than anything else your body ever could," says the woman. "I can tell you are kind and gentle, and I bet you have a lot of love to give."

Yes, I sure as heck do. It's like this woman can read my mind. Is she magic, or just an exceptional soul?

"Vickie," shouts a woman from a few enclosures over. "Come and take a look at this one."

"I'll be right there," says the woman named Vickie.

Our eyes remain locked for a little longer before she steps away from my pen and moves on.

Chapter 38

A loud voice sounding like a howling coyote explodes all around me. I remember this sound from the last time I was sold at auction. A young man comes to fetch me from my square pen and leads me away from it for the first time in days. It feels good to be walking in a more open space, even if it does mean I'm about to enter the place where the loud coyote man is calling from.

The young man and I walk past more horses than I can count, and a bunch of dummies, too. I never knew there were even this many animals in the entire world let alone in one place. There's an energy around here, a sadness. It leaches onto me with each horse I pass, making my head hang low and feet drag.

I'm led to a huge building with a massive door open to the outside. We inch into the building where I'm astonished to find more animals, plus a bunch of machines I'm used to seeing in the places I've lived. More humans crowd the inside, too, lining the outer walls or sitting on seats stacked up from floor to ceiling.

The loud coyote-voiced man announces it's time for the horse sale, before offering brief instructions to the crowd. Then, he begins speaking faster and faster, first rambling on about a three-year-old bay quarter horse, broke and ready, easy to ride – then a bunch of numbers before shouting, "Sold!"

I inch closer to the round pen where the horses are being shown off for the spectators, listening to the way each one is described. Hearing words like, sound, gentle, broke, good footing, and so on. Until it's finally my turn.

"Here we have a palomino quarter horse gelding," says the loud coyote man. "We don't know it's exact age, but we'd expect him to be around ten."

The young man leads me into the round pen and we walk around in front of the spectators.

"This palomino horse has an old injury," shouts the loud coyote man. "We don't have a history on this one, but he has a growth above his leg that we aren't sure about either. Looks like he walks incorrectly – his gait is off and he's pigeon toed. A lot of uncertainty about this guy."

The young man leading me quickens his pace from a walk to a run, forcing me to trot and keep up.

"His gait is off and looks like he's tripping a bunch," says the loud coyote man. "Not sure he can keep up to anything too rigorous."

What the heck is the loud man talking about? Can't he see me now? Keeping up to the human as he runs. Heck, I can ride a trail for hours without stopping. They'd know that if they just got to know me a little. Why aren't they saying anything nice about me?

"He seems gentle enough," says the loud coyote man. "He's saddle broke, but again, not sure how he'd keep up. Looks like this guy could benefit from an easier life. Let's start the bidding at two thousand dollars."

The young man leading me stops in front of the crowd, and all eyes are on me. Loud coyote man keeps repeating the words, two thousand dollars, two thousand dollars. There isn't a response from the crowd. This means nobody wants me.

"All righty, then let's go down a tad to eighteen hundred dollars," he barks out loudly. "Do I have anyone willing to buy this gelding for eighteen hundred dollars. There, yes, I see you lovely lady with a bid of eighteen hundred dollars. Do I have anyone else? Going once… going twice… sold to the lady in the third row!"

I lift my head and look at the crowd. Sitting not too far off is the silver-haired woman with the blue eyes named Vickie. She's looking at me and smiling. I sigh and move out of the round pen to go and meet my new person.

Chapter 39

She smells like other horses; too many for me to count. The other profound scent I pick up is the treats from the pocket of her jacket. Remembering how good they tasted, I peck my nose around the area, hoping I can access some.

"You like my crunchies, sweet boy," says Vickie, reaching into her pocket and placing one below my mouth for me to eat.

I devour the small, tasty treat in seconds before pushing my nose toward her pocket again. This time, instead of offering me another morsel, she uses her free hand to rub my neck. Vickie's touch relaxes my body and I lean into her a little, wanting to absorb as much of it as possible. Her hand radiates a loving energy I've never felt from a human before. The kind of touch that makes me feel safe, and a sense of belonging. Even though I've only just met Vickie, I desperately want more than anything else in the world to only be with her for the rest of my life. Perhaps the last star I wished on was the lucky one.

"Let's get you loaded into the trailer and home to meet your brothers," says Vickie, leading me to a long horse trailer with beautiful pictures of horses and mountains, and black lettering on its side.

Another woman, younger than Vickie, walks around the side of the trailer and opens the back door. I take a good look at her, she, too, has kind eyes and gives off the signals of being a person with a warm, loving heart. What are the odds I'd be taken to a home with two loving humans?

"Shall we get this sweet boy to Eagle Feather?" asks the young woman.

"Yes, Catherine," says Vickie. "This guy has spent enough time in this auction lot."

What's an eagle feather? Vickie leads me to the back end of the horse trailer and climbs inside first. There's room for six horses back here, but I get the place to myself. As far as I can tell, they've got enough hay out for six horses, too. But if I'm the only one riding back here, that means I get to eat it all myself. Maybe my new home will finally allow me to get the kind of body I've always longed for – a glossy coat of hair and a plump, round belly.

"Look how easily he just climbs right into the trailer," says Catherine, walking in behind Vickie and me. She extends her hand out and touches my back before giving it a scratch, and I sigh heavily with contentment.

The women maneuver me into a safe position. Before walking away, they both use two hands to rub my neck and back, prompting another loud sigh and groan. So far, this is one of the best dang days of my entire life.

"We have a bit of a drive to your new home," says Vickie, moving to stand next to my head. "And when we get there, you'll meet your new brothers – there's forty-seven of them. And because you are my new baby, I'm going to rename you. From now on, we will call you, Karma."

The drive to my new home is taking some time, but I don't mind. There is more than enough hay to keep me occupied on the journey. I've eaten through half a feed bag, and much to my surprise, I find some of Vickie's special treats buried at the bottom. Using my nose, I dig my face all the way down and eat them up as fast as I can.

Bright light from the afternoon sun beams in through the small windows of the horse trailer, warming my back for the entire drive. I reached my neck up to look through the window. Other vehicles whip past the horse trailer going in the opposite direction, but beyond that, I notice something familiar.

Massive mountains stretch along the horizon; their white peaks illuminated by the spotlight in the sky. I remember having a view of those when I lived with Spencer and Shadow. How is my old friend, Shadow, doing? Where did he and Spencer end up? Is my new home close to the old one I shared with them?

The truck and horse trailer slow down on the highway before making a turn onto a small, gravel road. I reach my neck further, hoping to get a better understanding of where we are, and that's when I spot them. A lot of horses. My heart rattles within my ribcage as I consider that I've only ever seen this many horses in one place at an auction lot. Is Vickie taking me to another auction? I thought she was taking me to my new home. Did my wish not come true after all?

Once the vehicle has stopped, Vickie and Catherine exit the truck; both women speaking with joy and exuberance. Then, the backdoor of the horse trailer opens, and sunlight floods the space. Vickie enters the trailer and releases the barrier keeping me in my spot. Then, she attaches a lead rope to my halter and gives me another treat from her pocket. I don't think I'll ever get sick of eating these things. She leads me toward the backdoor of the trailer and prompts me to step out. Before I do, I take a little look around.

My nostrils flare as I draw in a deep sniff of this new place. With the end of summer looming, the air is perfumed with a mixture of both sweet and drying foliage. The mountains I saw while travelling is visible beyond a small ridge of the property. There are a bunch of white buildings with green roofs, some that look like human dwellings, and others for horses. A few trees border a small space at one end of the property, but otherwise, it's open fields. Within the open fields are a lot of dang horses.

One calls out singing from nearby, pacing the fence. The song is nice enough, but I can do better. I lift my head high and sing out as loudly as I can, throwing in an extra high-pitched note at the end.

"You have a beautiful voice, Karma," says Vickie. "Come on out now, sweet boy. You're home."

Slowly and steadily, I step out from within the trailer and onto gravel. With Vickie close by my side, I walk toward the open fields where the other horses are. But before I'm introduced to my new herd, we stop in an area covered by a large roof but otherwise open to the elements. Yip, I'm thrilled to find this space is full of hay with another covered area next to it also filled to the roof with bales. With Vickie, there seems to be a heck of a lot of food everywhere.

Vickie walks me into a small paddock beneath the covered area, which is away from the other horses, but close to the human dwellings. Once the gate for the paddock is closed behind us, she removes my halter and gives me a handful of treats. I eat them up in seconds then turn my head and find a massive pile of hay in the corner of the fenced off space. Although I'd love to stay and cuddle some more with Vickie, the hay is calling for me to come and eat it.

"He'll stay in this paddock for two weeks, to quarantine after being with all of those other horses at the auction lot," says Vickie.

With a mouth full of hay, I lift my head to see if she's

speaking to me; not that I mind much where she keeps me, so long as she keeps bringing me an abundance of hay to eat. To my surprise, my stall is already surrounded by a crowd of humans. They're all different ages, shapes, and sizes, but all are admiring me. I'm glad for all the attention, so I nicker a few times, to let them all know they're welcome to hang out with me anytime.

A few of the onlookers stretch out their hands through the fence rungs of my paddock. It's possible they all want to give me handfuls of treats, so I move away from my hay and approach them. Hands from all over pet various parts of my body and I sigh heavily with the feeling of love surrounding me.

As the human love continues, I'm taken from the moment when I scan the faces in the crowd and land on a specific one. My heart hammers within my chest and I feel as though my tummy is full of butterflies. A girl, young but not a little kid, stands a few feet back from the crowd. Her green eyes, vibrant as spring grass, are on me and her lips are parted in a half smile. Her long, straight hair is the same color as mine, and her face is spotted with freckles that remind me of stars in the sky. And although I'm surrounded by other humans, and although this girl is standing back from me, something about her forces me to fixate only on her. I can't explain it, but for some reason, I feel like I've met that girl before. But have I met her before? And if I have, who in the heck is the little darlin?

Chapter 40

All I've done since arriving in my new home is eat – and I'm not complaining one dang bit. Heck, at this rate, I'll have the full figure of a well-fed gelding that all horses admire in no time. Not only is my belly full, but my heart is also full. Several humans stop by my paddock to see me each day, all eager to groom and pet me, and feed me handfuls of crunchie treats, too. Finally, it feels like my wish has come true, a home full of love.

"Good morning, sweet Karma," says Vickie, her voice melodic and soothing.

I sing her a song and trot over to the area of my paddock closest to her. I'm mighty eager to see her this morning, even more so when I notice the giant bowl of food she's brought for my breakfast.

"Eat up, sweet boy," says Vickie, placing my bowl on the ground before me and giving me a good rub all over. "You've been cooped up in this paddock for two weeks, and today is the day you will finally get to meet your brothers."

Although living in this paddock, being fat and lazy, suits me fine, the prospect of being released into the herd really has me excited. I've been watching the others closely, and there's a select few I'm quite keen to meet. The others, though, seem like a bunch of ding-dongs. Nevertheless, it'll be nice to feel like I have a family again.

"Are you excited to meet your brothers?" asks Vickie, looking at my empty bowl laying on the ground. "You ate your bowl quickly. All right then, let's go."

Vickie grabs a halter she's hung on the fence of my paddock then brings it closer to me. She's not a tall woman, so I lower my head to give her easy access to my head. Once my halter is in place, Vickie grabs the lead rope, and we walk out of my paddock and closer to the sprawling fields housing the other horses.

"Is he going out with the others today, Vickie?" asks a man to our right.

"He sure is," says Vickie with a smile.

I glance in the direction of the man's voice and see a small group of humans has congregated beneath a sheltered space lined with several mangers full of hay. They all smile at me, so I nicker, to be polite. Before I look away from the group, my eyes lock on an image. It's the girl I saw on the first day I arrived here, the one with hair the same color as mine. She's staring at me and smiling sweetly. I don't know what comes over me, but I feel like I must sing her a song. Her smile widens when I do, which tells me she must like my singing voice.

After walking a few more steps with Vickie, the group of humans leaves my sight and is replaced by horses instead. A wide metal gate with chipped, green paint creaks when Vickie pushes it forward to open. My heart quickens and each breath I take feels short; my nerves are getting the better of me.

Once Vickie and I are through the gate and within the proximity of the herd, we stop. My sense of smell is in overdrive now that I'm this much closer to the other horses. I turn my head in every direction to look at them all. A large black and white paint horse with kind eyes is the first to get close. I can tell he's the boss man because all the other horses either remain behind him or at his side. It's difficult for me to keep it together as he approaches, wondering what he might want to do to a new guy like me. Then, I really lose my nerve because Vickie reaches up and with one swift motion, she takes my halter off and steps back.

Where in the heck is she going? And why does she feel the need to step away from us? Did she just release me into a herd full of trouble?

The boss man paint horse stops walking once his head is next to mine, only an inch of air separates us.

"Be nice to him, Legend," Vickie says, speaking to the boss man horse.

I nicker, both from nerves and as an offering of peace. Legend doesn't reciprocate the peace offering, instead, he pushes his nose into my neck and smells me. His breath on my neck kind of tickles.

"Good boy, Legend," says Vickie. "Be nice to our sweet Karma and show him around the place."

Feeling a bit braver, I lean my nose into Legend and breath in his scent, hoping this will show that I'm interested in him, but not a threat to his herd. The dude scares the dang crap out of me as he squeals like a crazed lunatic. What's this guy's problem, anyway?

Not keen to find out, my legs quiver before moving back. Legend steps closer to me again, and some of the others follow, like a gang. I spot an opening to my left, so I take off running toward it, feeling overwhelmingly nervous in my new surroundings.

Thundering hooves from running horses sound out behind me, pushing me to run faster. I whip my head and sing out as loud as I can. I'm still ahead of the horses running behind me, and I feel good with my current position. With my long hair whipping in the wind, my speed, and a new full-figured body, yip, I'm guessing I look like one heck of a magnificent stallion in this moment.

It feels good to run again, but it's been a while, so my lungs heave with the effort. And although I'd love to show off a little more, my body is protesting the exertion and begging for a rest. My feet slow to a trot, allowing the horses following a chance to catch up. We trot in unison for a distance and sensing no danger, I slow down to a walk before standing in place.

With all that running, I've ended up far away from where the humans are, and into a large, open field. Specks of green grass mix in with the dry, and the sky is a vibrant blue. Several hawks float overhead, looking for their next meal, and the odd bug darts about. As much as I'd like to take more time to view the scenery, my attention shifts fully to the horses swarming around me.

My ears perk, stretching tall, and both of my eyes are wide open. As I take in the air, my nostrils flare and become huge. A flea-bitten grey Arabian moves in next to me and pushes his nose into my body. I squeal loudly, unsure if he'll bite me, but too petrified to move either. Thankfully, he just smells and moves on, making way for a buckskin quarter horse with dark socks and a mane colored to match.

Because things went so well with the Arabian, I relax, just a little, and allow this dude to smell me. He squeals, scaring me enough to tense up again, and then I squeal. Something tells me to shift myself away from this guy, so I shimmy backward only to run into another horse. But instead of smelling me like the others, this one immediately sinks his teeth into my butt, pulling out some of my hair in the process. I buck my back legs and turn around to find a huge Draft, black with grey flecks down his rump and legs. What a dang jerk, biting me like that. We all do that sort of thing to each other, but I wasn't being pushy or trying to hurt anyone, so he should just lay off already.

Before the pain fizzles from the Draft's bite, another bite pushes into my neck. I buck and quickly turn to find a bay-colored horse with a black mane close by. His ears are pinned down and it looks as though he might come at me again. Yip, I'm getting the heck out of here.

I'm tired, but I run away from this pack of horses and closer to the humans again. Maybe they'll take pity on me and put me back into my paddock. I could use a break. I run straight and fast, all the way to the fence where Vickie is watching. Once I'm close to her, I stop, sweat trickling down my neck and stinging my fresh bite wounds. I keep my eyes fixed on her, hoping she'll get the message that I don't want to be with these bullies anymore.

"Beginnings are always the hardest," says Vickie, rubbing a spot on my head between my eyes. "You'll need to earn their respect, but don't be afraid to defend yourself. It'll take time, but not too much, and then you'll be one of them. You'll see."

I turn my head and see more horses approaching to check me out. I really hope Vickie is right.

Chapter 41

Some of my bite marks are fresh, while the others are beginning to heal. Yip, Vickie was right, beginnings can be the most difficult, and meeting my new herd certainly has been for me. But, thankfully, she was also right in saying it'd only last a short time.

After a couple of days, my new herd is used to me being around. None of them are keen to be my friend yet, though, but hopefully that'll change in short order, too. At least none of them is biting me anymore, except for the moments when someone else wants the pile of hay I'm eating. Or if I'm at the water trough and one of the longstanding herd members wants to drink, they'll push me off and make me wait. When I first arrived in my new home, I thought my wish for a loving forever home had finally come true. Although I feel that coming from the humans around here, I'm still not feeling it as such with the herd.

Cool air flips my mane around and bites at my sparse-haired neck. With the grass growing dryer by the day, and the nights getting longer, I can tell a change of season is not far off. I nibble at what green grass I can find when there's a magnificent song carried by the wind.

"Karma," sings an unfamiliar voice.

I nibble at the grass again, feeling the voice delivering the song absorb into my ears before seeming to travel to my heart. It's the kind of song I could listen to every day. One that flutters my soul and makes me feel warm.

"Karma, come here," sings the voice again.

It makes me feel giddy, so much so that I can't help but lift my head and look for the source of the most beautiful singing voice I've ever heard in my life.

"Karma, over here," sings the female.

My heart pounds within my chest and I've overcome with joy. I don't know why, but something about the voice is making me feel this way. That's when, I spot the darlin. Her eyes are only on me, even in this field of nearly fifty horses.

I stare back, waiting to see what the darlin with hair like mine and specks like the stars on her face will do next. I wish her singing were for me.

"Karma," she sings again, then walks closer toward me, not taking her eyes away from mine for a second.

Wait a minute. That's right. She is singing my name. I almost forgot; Karma is my new name.

"Karma," she sings, her voice louder as she gets closer.

I lift my head and sing loudly, so she'll be sure to know I've heard her. Soon the young girl is standing next to me with a halter in her hands.

"Hello, sweet Karma," she says, leaning in close and rubbing my neck.

My body instantly melts, and I lean in closer to her, too. I can't describe why, but the way this girl strokes my neck feels like no other I've felt before. It's strange, but when her hand connects with my body, a surge of electric heat pushes from her and onto to me. It's incredible.

"Hello, Karma," she says again, her voice is soft and soothing. My eyes relax, as she continues. "My name is Kiyomi. I get to bring you in and feed you today."

Kiyomi – it's neither a word nor name I've ever heard

before, but it makes me giddy.

"Should we put your crown on?" asks Kiyomi. She's smiling widely and giggles a little after saying it. "I know it's called a halter, but it's decorated with so many beautiful and sparkly beads that it reminds me of something special."

Her small hands hold my blue with white beaded crown and lift it close to my head. Knowing I'm much taller than her, I bend down at the neck, so she has an easier time of placing my crown.

"Good boy, Karma," she whispers in my ear, tying the ropes so my crown stays in place.

Just when I can't imagine this moment getting any sweeter, Kiyomi reaches into her coat pocket and pulls something from inside. She stretches her thin arms toward my mouth and holds her tiny hand open just below it. Resting within her palm are two crunchie treats, the same ones that Vickie always gives me. Carefully, I part my lips and take both treats into my mouth and chew them gratefully. Then, Kiyomi curls her small hand into itself, leaving only her pointer finger out. She slowly moves her finger toward my face and gently touches my nose with its tip.

"Boop," she says, then giggles and smiles.

I don't know what she's just done or what the word 'boop' means, but it makes me feel special somehow. Kiyomi moves in close to my side before leading me toward the covered feeding space. Her short legs move slowly, so I mimic her pace. I don't want to get too far from this sweet, little darlin.

"I'm going to take you for a ride today, sweet Karma," says Vickie, rubbing my neck and holding a treat in her hand for me.

I eat the treat, but I'm distracted. Kiyomi handed my lead rope to Vickie after bringing me into the feed space, but I haven't seen her again since. Although I love Vickie, and she's always kind to me, there's just something about that young girl that tugs at my heart strings.

"We're doing a lesson today with some of the other horses and a few kids, so I thought you and I could go along," says Vickie.

My back aches a little as the words 'take you for a ride' settles into my brain. Although I've really enjoyed my time of eating and laziness, I suppose it would be wise to get a little bit of exercise. And it's not the exercise itself that's making my back ache, it's the prospect of a heavy saddle that I'm never thrilled about.

"Let's circle up before we move out for our ride, everyone," says Vickie, calling out to the crowd of people sharing the same space as us.

The humans aren't the only ones here. Several of the horses from my new herd are lined up in rows; tied up neatly to wooden posts and prepping for the ride. I scan the faces of the horses and I recognize them all – some have bitten me recently while others haven't. The humans, big and small, leave their horses and form a small circle around Vickie and me.

"I'm excited to be taking Karma out for his first Eagle Feather ride today," says Vickie, she has a big smile, and her hand strokes my neck as she speaks. "If each of you can be aware of Karma's spacing from the other horses today, that would be helpful. Also, I wanted to say something about Karma and his name. His name represents a motto which essentially means you get what you give out of life. I believe the same philosophy is true with horses. The more love and respect you show them, the more love and respect they will show you in return. I suppose you could call it horse karma. Does that make sense?"

All humans forming the circle nod their heads and some say

yes. An energy radiates from them, a beautiful feeling of kindness. It makes me yawn and sigh deeply, like a release of anxiousness leaving my body.

"Let's water our horses, and head out for a beautiful ride," says Vickie.

Vickie releases the knot for my lead rope keeping me in my spot. Then, she lets me drink from the water trough before leading me out to a large penned off area with weird wooden structures placed all over it.

"Ready for our ride, sweet boy," says Vickie, whispering in my ear and offering me a treat at the same time.

I glance around the pen at the other horses. To my surprise, none of the horses are wearing saddles on their backs, nor do any have bridles in their mouths. Then, Vickie swings the lead rope over my neck before walking around to the other side of me. Her hands are busy below my neck, and I wish I could see what she's up to.

Yip, she must be getting ready to throw a saddle onto my back as she leads me over to one of the wooden structures that looks like a small set of stairs.

"Whoa," says Vickie, stopping me alongside the wooden stairs. "Easy, Karma. Easy, boy, stay where you are. That's a good boy."

I remain in place, as instructed, and watch the forgetful woman walk up the stairs before slowly and gently swinging one leg over my back and sitting down. Does the ding-dong realize she forget to put my saddle on? I'm practically naked, and she's just climbed onto my back like it's no big deal. What if the others see us traipsing around together like this? I glance around at the other horses to see if anyone has caught us in our state. However, all the other horses are without saddles and have riders on their backs, too. What the heck kind of outfit is this anyway?

Vickie squeezes my belly gently with her legs, and it tickles when her pants move against my body this way. I flinch a little, and squirm, but Vickie doesn't react, which calms me. I walk forward and allow Vickie to guide me through another gate which leads down a grass corridor and into a large pasture at the back of the property.

As I walk, I'm shocked by how free and light I feel with Vickie on my back. Without the weight and straps of a saddle, my back doesn't ache at all. Taking confident strides and feeling light footed, Vickie and I continue to ride. It's liberating to move without feeling constrained. I turn my head to the left and see fluffy white clouds rolling in; they're beautiful and make funny shapes. The air is warm and smells sweet, and I feel like I'm going out riding for the very first time. It's so exciting.

While taking in my surroundings, I lose a little focus on my walking, and trip. My body immediately tenses, and I wait for my rider to smack me for making this mistake, just like Duke would. Vickie's hand reaches forward, and I prepare myself for the pain of a blow. Instead, she rubs my neck.

"It's okay, sweet Karma," she says. "Don't be afraid to trip, I don't mind. You are free to be exactly who you are – we will love you no matter what."

What a dang minute. Did she just say she doesn't mind if I trip? Is she rubbing my neck after my blunder instead of smacking me? Doesn't she want to tell me I'm disabled or that I'll be useless if I don't walk straight and refrain from tripping? Is she really okay with the way that I am?

I lift my head high and pick up my feet with pride. I'm going to really like riding naked with this lady.

Chapter 42

Vickie and I have had some wonderful rides together over the last couple of weeks. Yip, riding without a saddle is great. It's as though I can read her thoughts better when we ride this way. Although it does limit us a little to be without a saddle, it's fine by me. We still walk, trot and canter when we ride around the ranch. And now that I'm basically an expert at carrying riders bareback, Vickie says I'm ready for something new.

"All right, Karma," says Vickie, placing a bowl full of food down at my feet. "I'm taking you out on one of our beginner lessons today, sweet boy."

I devour my food as she brushes me from forelock to dock, and although I can't see my reflection, I can tell I'm going to have a dang good hair day. Vickie picks manure and rocks from my feet and primps my mane a little before stepping back.

"Hi, Vickie," says a young voice.

My ears perk at the new sound and I turn my head to look. Standing next to Vickie is a small boy with brown hair and matching eyes. His hands are folded together and clenched, like he's holding something precious within them.

"Hello, Samuel," says Vickie. "How are you today?"

"Fine," says Samuel. "Who's this?"

Vickie lays her hand on my side and encourages Samuel to do the same. A tiny hand gently touches my belly, so I reach my head around to get my nose closer. The young boy must have eaten something sweet before arriving. I'd like to lick his hand

and have a taste, but I'd hate to scare him and have him think I want to bite him.

Samuel smiles, each time a breath from my nose hits his small hand. Then, there's a tickle within my nostril and a split second later, I sneeze loudly and forcefully while simultaneously releasing a thunderous fart. Once it's over, I glance at Samuel as he stands next to me expressionless. He has green goo from my nose and mouth on the front of his jacket and a bit on his hand. Worried I may have done something wrong, I move slightly away from the boy, then look at Vickie's face, then back to the boy for a reaction.

"Gross," says Samuel, wiping his hand on his jeans.

"Are you okay?" asks Vickie.

Samuel smiles and giggles before touching my belly again. "Yeah. Did you hear him sneeze and fart at the same time?"

"I sure did," says Vickie.

"That was awesome," says Samuel. "Can I ride him?"

"Absolutely," says Vickie.

I release a loud sigh, then yawn. I'm so glad and relieved I didn't get into trouble for sneezing on the young guy. The last time I was this close to a small child, she accused me of biting, and I was given a harsh punishment. Thankfully, Samuel doesn't seem to mind that things got a little weird for a moment.

After taking a few more bites of hay, Vickie leads me into a squared off pen to join a bunch of other horses. I've come to learn that this is the place where people get onto horses before going for a ride. Vickie leads me to a mounting block and stands in place at my head. Then, I feel the slightest weight on my back.

Thinking a bug has landed back there, I arch my head around to the right, and then the left. Sitting there is little Samuel with a huge smile on his face.

“This is going to be fun,” says Samuel, running his tiny fingers through my withers.

Vickie hands me a treat and says, “Good boy, Karma. You are such a sweet boy.”

I lift my head high and my chest puffs out a little. Feeling useful and knowing I’m doing something good in my new home is the best.

Vickie and I continue riding and taking young ones in beginner lessons for several weeks. My herd has finally accepted me and stopped taking bites out of my butt too often. Things are finally beginning to feel settled in my new home.

“Karma,” sings out a familiar voice.

I lift my head and look, recognizing fully now that this is my new name in this place. And although a human is calling out my name, it isn’t coming from Vickie.

“Karma, come here,” sings out the voice again.

Finally, I find her. It’s Kiyomi calling for me. She’s an awesome human, so I walk toward the sound of her voice. Although it’s fine that she’s the one singing my name, I’m a little disappointed that it’s not Vickie. She and I have been spending so much time together, and I’ve come to really love her. Perhaps Kiyomi is just catching me, and Vickie will be waiting for us in the tie-up area.

“Good morning, Karma,” says Kiyomi, holding out her hand and offering me a treat once I’m close enough. “How are you today?”

I nicker and take the treat before lowering my head and allowing her to place my crown onto my head.

“I have the best news ever,” says Kiyomi with a huge smile and love beaming from her heart. “Vickie has asked me to take care of you now that she's gone. Isn't that great?"

Wait, did she say Vickie is gone? Gone where? Has she gone to the feed store to buy me more food? Is she getting her feet trimmed? Could she be sick and need a check-up by the Vet? What does Kiyomi mean, gone?

Nudging my nose into Kiyomi's pocket where the treats are stashed, I nicker. She smiles and gives me another. Kiyomi, full of excitement, leads me to the tie-up area. Once we're there, I still see no sign of Vickie. And it's the same thing the next day, and the next. Many days pass which makes me think that Vickie is no longer here.

Where did she go? Will she come back or abandon me like all the others?

Chapter 43

Thy sky is a sheet of white as small snowflakes spiral to the ground. My back is covered with the fluffy white stuff, too. I'm trying to get into the shelter with the group of other horses already congregated there, but they won't let me in. Each of them is a horse high up in the herd, and not keen to share their covered space.

To make matters worse, there's still no sign of Vickie around here. Sure, I'm still being fed, ridden, and loved on, but it's not the same. I genuinely believed Vickie was my forever person. Now, I'm beginning to feel like just another handsome face in a crowd of others.

Perhaps Vickie changed her mind about me. I did my best to behave and be good, so she'd see I can be useful to her. And although I still trip when being ridden, and although Vickie did say it was okay for me to do so, maybe she changed her mind about that. After all, I've heard enough times in my life that no one wants a disabled horse.

I hear my name called from way over by the tie-up area.

I lift my head to look. Funny how that name instantly grabs my attention now. It feels like such a long time ago when I was called Ranger. And when I'd hear the names Golden Flash or Saturn seems like a lifetime ago. Of all the names I've had in my life, Karma is my favorite. It's melodic and beautiful how it rolls from the mouth of whomever is calling it.

"Karma, come here," shouts the voice again.

I turn my body to walk toward the voice. I recognize that Kiyomi is the one calling me. She's been here every day to feed me since Vickie left. My feet move slowly through the snow as I inch my way closer toward her. Don't get me wrong, Kiyomi is a wonderful human. It's just that I was beginning to bond with Vickie.

"Karma, come on," says Kiyomi. "I have a big bowl of food ready for you."

Hearing this, my feet pick up pace. Nothing, not even my low mood, will keep me from eating a meal.

"Good boy, Karma," says Kiyomi, rubbing my neck once I'm standing next to her. She pulls a treat from her pocket and offers it to me from her tiny hand, covered by heavy gloves. Gently, I picked it up using my lips and chew it while she places my crown onto my head.

We walk together into the tie-up area and stop in front of a large black bowl overflowing with food. I dive into it the second we're close. As Kiyomi ties me to a nearby wooden post, I dig around my food a little with the end of my nose. Deeper within my soaked hay cubes and beet pulp I find chunks of apple and pieces of carrot. Although I'm making a mess by pushing my food around, I continue to do so and eat all the pieces of fruit and vegetable before anything else. It was nice of Kiyomi to add these extras to my meal. She's not such a bad replacement to Vickie after all.

"Do you need help over here?" asks a woman with a kind voice.

A woman has moved in to stand next to Kiyomi. She's older than the young girl but looks similarly to her in the face. Then, the woman reaches her hand toward me, allowing me to take in her scent. Funny, she smells a little like Kiyomi, too.

"Hello, sweet Karma," says the woman, stepping in closer to me and looking into my eyes. "There's definitely something special about you, isn't there?"

"Isn't he awesome, Mom," says Kiyomi to the woman.

"He's beautiful and has such kind eyes and a gentle disposition," says Mom. "Do you need my help with him at all?"

"Nope," says Kiyomi, smiling proudly. "I've got it all under control."

"You sure do, sweetie," says Mom, rubbing me again before walking away.

Mom isn't so bad either, I guess.

"I hope the other horses are being nice to you, Karma," says Kiyomi. "It's hard being the new guy."

While chewing a mouthful of food, Kiyomi leans in close, so I lift my head, before resting it onto her small shoulder. Food dribbles from my mouth as we cuddle, some falling into her long, silky hair.

"Karma," Kiyomi says through a laugh, shaking the pieces of food free from her hair. "Thank you for trying to share your food with me, but I don't want any, thanks."

I'm not trying to share my food with you, darlin. You're nice and all, but I don't share my dang food with anyone.

Kiyomi sits next to me on the ground and gazes up. She removes a glove from one hand and balls it up into a fist. Then, she extends her pointer finger and gently moves it toward my nose before touching it. "Boop," she says with a wide smile and giggling. She seems to really love this game, so I lean my nose into her face and touch hers with it. She laughs and there's a gleam in her eyes.

"Did you just 'boop' me, Karma?" she asks. "That can be one of our special games, then."

When I move my face away from Kiyomi's to eat, she pulls something from her pocket. Figuring she's trying to give me another treat, I lower my mouth closer to her hand and get myself ready.

"It's not a treat, silly boy," she says, with sparkling eyes. "It's my phone. I was doing a survey on this fun app while we were driving here, and I didn't get a chance to finish it."

I take another bite of food, then glance back over at the girl. Her fingers are busy with the phone. Bright lights flicker from the thing and from time to time, noises come from it too. It's distracting and a little odd, but not threatening, thankfully.

"Let's do a survey together, Karma," says Kiyomi, her fingers flipping and clicking on the phone. "Here, let's do this one."

She holds the phone toward me, showing me a picture like I'm meant to understand what the heck she's up to.

"Are you and your new friend bestie material," reads Kiyomi. "Let's see how you and I do on this one, shall we?"

I sigh heavily and continue to eat. Although this kid keeps talking and asking me questions, interrupting my feeding time a bit, I like listening to her talk.

"First question," she says. "Does your new friend make you smile? That's a yes for me, Karma. You make me smile. I'm going to answer yes for you, too, because in time I'm going to teach you how to smile for treats."

Did she say treats? I lower my head closer to her hand. She smiles and pulls a treat out of her pocket before offering it to me.

"Next question," she says. "Do you and your new friend enjoy similar activities? I'll answer yes for both of us on that one, too. We both like riding, eating and being around horses."

I nicker then lower my head so I can see Kiyomi's face. She's so happy and kind; it warms my heart just to be near her.

"Do you think your new friend would do anything for you? Keep secrets and always support you?"

She glances up from her phone and fixes her eyes on mine. I pause from eating and stare at her, too. I reckon I would do anything for this little darlin, and I suppose she'd do the same for me.

"I'm going to answer yes to that, too," she says, reaching her hand up and gently stroking the space between my eyes.

Kiyomi continues to talk and smile. We stay this way for as long as it takes me to eat a nice-sized pile of hay after finishing my bowl of food. Then, she stands up and gets close to my head.

"Looks like you and I are destined to be besties, Karma," says Kiyomi. "According to my survey app, that is. I'm glad because I already like you – a lot."

Kiyomi grabs a brush from a small bucket nearby. As she uses it to stroke my hair, I tuck in my back leg to relax and enjoy her gently grooming me. I suppose I like this young girl a lot, too.

Chapter 44

After all that talk of besties with Kiyomi, I have a good understanding of what that means. According to her survey, it seems like a bestie should be someone you have a lot in common with. Perhaps all the time I've spent in the past looking for a human to be my ultimate companion has been the wrong strategy. Don't get me wrong, I still need the love of a human in my life, but maybe I should begin focusing more on someone that's more alike me than a human could ever be. It might be time to look at my herd for a bestie of the horse variety.

Strolling leisurely from the water trough and through the herd, I casually look at each horse I pass by. Some of these guys have already formed their own groups or small herds within the herd, so they aren't likely to be the best candidates for my new bestie. So, I believe I should focus on considering the lone horses, the ones who may be just as keen for friendship as I am.

A buckskin quarter horse named Bud is the closest lone horse I can see. I saunter toward him, keeping my head low and made to look like I'm searching for food. My plan is to take the casual approach with these guys, not come across as too desperate.

Bud lifts his head once I'm only a few feet away. He pins his ears back and keeps his gaze locked onto me. I'm not too worried about his stance in the moment as we all do the same thing when any horse is nearing us. Keeping my head low, showing him that I mean no harm, I keep my eyes on him, too. We stay in this position for quite a time, both of us waiting for the other to do something, anything. So, I take in a deep breath and another step closer to Bud, hoping he'll let me stand with him awhile. Instead, Bud lunges toward me and attempts to bite my butt. This certainly means he isn't at all interested in being my bestie and quite frankly would rather I move on from him. Message received, Bud.

After walking quickly away from Bud, I sigh heavily and lift my head. I scan the herd and look for another lone horse to approach. Maybe things would go better if I found a small pile of hay and offered to share it with someone. That would make one of these guys keen to be my bestie for sure. After all, the way to a horse's heart is through its stomach.

I walk around and look for a hay pile, but before I find one, I spot a chestnut-colored Arabian named Titan standing solo near the fence line. This guy has the nicest dang hair I've ever seen on a horse. Does he use something special on it for growth and shine? Perhaps if we become besties, he'll share his beauty secrets with me.

Titan is using one of the wooden posts to scratch his butt, and this immediately grips my attention. Scratching my butt on a fence post is one of my favorite things to do. And it isn't an activity Kiyomi or any of the other humans would partake in with me. Which is a pity because they really don't know what the heck they're missing.

Seeing Titan scratching his behind on the fencepost feels like a sign. So, I walk on over to him and stare as he scratches. He catches me looking and although he looks away and seems like he'd prefer I do the same, I don't. I continue to watch as he scratches himself, just to let him know how much I admire what he's doing.

Just as I take a few steps closer to Titan and prepare to join him, a flea-bitten grey Arabian rushes toward us from the right. This guy is Willy; his ears are pinned, and he looks angry. Not only that, but the dude is also coming straight for me with his teeth ready to bite. Yip, I forgot, Titan already has a bestie, and that is, Willy.

I rush away from Titan and Willy, and thankfully, they don't chase me too far. Walking along the fence line, I move until I'm at the very back end of the pasture and find another palomino horse named Poco. He's standing alone and his eyes are closed. Maybe he's sleeping? I enjoy sleeping, and Poco and I look almost identical. Perhaps because we look the same, we'd make good besties.

As quietly as possible, I sneak up to where Poco is sleeping. If I'm already standing next to him when he wakes up, maybe he'll think I'm a good guard for while he sleeps and want to be besties. I stand next to him, and close my eyes, too. The sun is shining brightly in the sky, warming my back and body through. I feel so cozy, and sleepy.

I'm not sure how long I was asleep for, but sadly, when I awake, Poco has gone and I'm standing alone once again. I'm sure I look like a ding-dong right now. I guess Poco didn't wake up and see me as a possible guard or bestie after all. But if not him, then who?

The herd all seems to be grouped or paired off with someone. I sigh and lower my head, hoping for a nibble of something on the ground. At least while I'm still a lone horse, I don't need to share any of the food I find on the ground. Although, I sure wouldn't mind if it meant having a bestie.

Chapter 45

Kiyomi is back. This time, when she sings my name aloud, asking for me to come and meet her, I don't hesitate. In fact, I sing back so she knows I've heard her and am on the way.

She and I have been doing this same song and dance every day for several weeks now. And although I still miss Vickie and wonder each day where she may have gone, I'm beginning to love the darlin a little more each time we meet.

I walk through the snow blanketing the ground until I'm next to Kiyomi. She's bundled up in a blue snowsuit with a hat covering her head. The only parts of her visible are long strands of hair and her beautiful and kind eyes. There's a glove on her hand when she reaches toward me, and within that glove is a cookie for me to eat. I could eat these dang cookies all day long.

"Are you ready for a different kind of day, Karma?" asks Kiyomi, placing my crown onto my head.

She and I walk together toward the tie-up area, and I notice there are several humans out catching horses just now.

"Today you need to be the sweet, gentle guy I know you are, Karma," says Kiyomi. "They need us to take a rider out today with the lesson group. You and me. It's a big deal for them to be trusting me to take a little boy out with the group, so we need to do our best."

I nicker and lift my head to take a thorough look of the tie-up area. There are already around ten other horses there eating hay, and several more coming in behind us. When Kiyomi and I arrive to a spot for me, I'm thrilled to find a huge pile of hay and a hearty portion of food. One thing is for sure, Kiyomi is mighty good at keeping me fed.

"Remember, Karma," says Kiyomi, leaning in close to my head as I eat. "Be the gentle and sweet guy I know you to be."

Once I'm finished eating my bowl, Kiyomi approaches me from behind, but she's not alone. I lift my head while chewing hay and turn to look. Walking alongside her is a small human and another one more grown up than Kiyomi.

"This is Karma," says Kiyomi.

"Isn't he beautiful," says the grown-up human, placing her hand onto my back and stroking.

"Yes, he is beautiful," says Kiyomi, smiling at me. My heart swells with pride. "And he's kind and gentle. Would you like to brush him, Jackson?"

The small human nods his little head before moving to stand next to Kiyomi. She hands him a small brush and shows him how to groom me properly.

"What's wrong with his leg?" asks the grown-up human.

"We're not sure," says Kiyomi. "I was told that he was injured at one of his old homes and that's mostly just scar tissue."

"Is it safe for my son to ride an injured horse?" asks the grown-up human.

I sigh heavily and keep eating my hay. I understand what is being said about me. I've heard these words so many times before. It hurts that people often only see my flaws before understanding me fully.

"He's been ridden a lot since coming here," says Kiyomi. "And each time the riders have been perfectly safe."

"How old are you?" asks the grown-up human. "Do you have enough experience for this kind of thing?"

"I'm twelve," says Kiyomi. "Almost thirteen, and I've been working with horses since I was five."

"I'm going to walk with you guys, just in case Jackson needs me," says the grown-up human, folding her arms and watching me speculatively.

After eating, we move out into the space for riders to climb onto our backs. There are at least twenty horses here, some with riders already poised and ready to ride.

Kiyomi has my lead rope tight within her grasp, holding it close to the base of my crown. On my other side is the grown-up human and the little boy, Jackson. All of them are anxious, and I'm trying my best to remain calm. Since the other horses here all seem calm enough, it eases me.

"Let's line up here, Karma," says Kiyomi, standing in front of me and leading me next to one of the small wooden staircase contraptions. "This is our mounting block. Jackson, you can climb up these stairs and slowly get onto Karma's back."

"Okay," says Jackson.

His mother hovers close behind him and holds his hand as he climbs up the stairs. My heart is thundering in my chest as I sense Kiyomi and Jackson's are, too. I hope I don't mess this up. Then, I feel the slightest weight on my back and little hands rubbing the hair around my neck.

"Good job, Jackson," says Kiyomi. "Do you feel comfortable in your seat up there?"

"Yes," says Jackson, gripping his hands into my withers and holding tight.

"Good boy, Karma," says Kiyomi, offering me a cookie from the palm of her hand.

The other horses begin to move out with riders, and other humans walking along the ground next to them. Kiyomi remains close to my one side and Jackson's mother on my other.

The humans with me are all quiet for quite a stretch of the ride. With each step we take, each of us eases up a little and relaxes. My stride is slow and steady, I only trip the slightest a couple of times. Then, the silence is broken by a soft sound.

"Like a rhinestone cowboy," sings Jackson, quietly and softly from his perch on my back. "La, la, la, la, la… at the rodeo. I'm a rhinestone cowboy."

"He's been playing that song over and over and begging me to ride a horse for months now," says Jackson's mom. "This is a big moment for him."

"I love your singing, Jackson," says Kiyomi.

I nicker and sing out a little. Kiyomi smiles and giggles once I do.

"Like a rhinestone cowboy," sings Jackson again. "La, la, la, la, la… at the rodeo. I'm a rhinestone cowboy."

"Karma seems to like your singing, too," says Kiyomi.

And I truly do. Not only that but as Jackson sings from my back, I'm walking within the middle of the herd and no one seems bothered by me at all. I lift my head a little higher, proud to be part of this place.

Chapter 46

She's barely said anything since arriving here today. When she called my name, I walked over to her immediately, so she never said it again. And she's said nothing else since.

There's a sadness seeping from her, and I can feel its heaviness. While I'm eating, she brushes me and cleans each of my feet. I nicker a few times, attempting to lighten the mood, but still, she says nothing.

Once my food bowl is empty, she leads me over to a small covered space with a giant bale inside of it. There are scraps of hay strewn all around it, blanketing the ground. Kiyomi places my lead rope over my back then sits within a soft pile of hay next to the bale.

I stand still and look at her then over at the bale. It's so green and full, and I desperately want to eat it. But am I allowed? If I take a bite, will I get into trouble? But why would she lead me to it if she didn't want me to eat off it? Is this a test? Am I meant to hold my ground even when amid temptation? Awe heck, I can't resist all this food when it's this dang close.

I lunge my head toward the bale and take a quick bite before stepping back. While chewing, I wait for Kiyomi to have a reaction. She does nothing. Just sits next to the bale while twirling a long strand of it between her fingers. Boldly, I lean in and take another bite. Still, she doesn't react. So, I do it again, and again. This is awesome.

Kiyomi sniffles and wipes her nose with the back of her

hand. Her head is hung low, so I lower mine to get a better look at her face. A small tear leaks from her eye and rolls down her cheek. I nicker and rub my nose against her cheek, hoping to wipe the tear away. Then, I gently touch my nose to hers, wishing I could say the word 'boop'. Thankfully, she smiles and looks up at me.

"Sorry, Karma," she says. "I'm having a rough day."

I nicker again and hold my gaze on hers. Even though I'm standing in front of a huge bale, and I'd like nothing more than to consume the entire thing, I pause. She needs me. Her eyes stay locked with mine before more tears flow from them and she looks away. I remain frozen in my place.

"Sometimes I really hate school," says Kiyomi.

I nicker and move closer. She leans her head and rests it on mine, tears soaking into my hair from her eyes.

"There's this girl at my school," she says. "Her name is Twyla, and she's so mean. Yesterday, she pushed me on the playground and told everyone I must never shower because I get zits on my forehead."

Kiyomi cries harder now, and I sense her pain. I wish I could take her pain away somehow. I don't know what zits are, but I do know that Kiyomi is perfect in every way. She's always defending me when humans ask about my leg injury. Yip, I would like to defend her from the people who hurt her feelings, too.

"But I do shower," says Kiyomi. "And because Twyla is so mean to everyone, and because everyone is so scared of her, all the other kids in my class laughed at me. I never want to go back there."

I must leave here and find this ding-dong, Twyla. How dare she make Kiyomi cry this way. This little darlin is the kindest and sweetest human I've ever met. Perhaps if I find a fault in the fence somewhere, I could push into it and get out of here. Then, I'll find Kiyomi's school and when I figure out who Twyla is, I'll bite her nice and hard in the dang butt. That should chase her off from Kiyomi and teach her to leave my girl alone.

"I wish I could just stay here with you forever, Karma," says Kiyomi. "You always make me feel better."

I wish she could be with me forever, too. For now, I'll just stand next to her and soak up as much of her pain as I can, hopefully easing a bit of her burden.

Chapter 47

The stars' brightness is shrouded by the intense light of a full moon. I was hoping to make a new wish on a star tonight, but I'm struggling to keep one in focus. Just when I think I've found one that could be wish worthy, something highly irregular happens.

"Karma," Kiyomi sings. "Karma, come here."

I sing back, looking all around, desperately trying to locate her. But it's nighttime, dark, and I'm not used to her coming out here so late, it's disorienting.

"Karma, come here," sings Kiyomi again.

I sing back and turn toward the sound of her voice. Because I can't see her, I'll need to trust my instincts and try to find her. I walk several steps before she sings my name again. This time, it sounds closer, so I must be on the right track for finding her.

"Karma," Kiyomi sings again.

Her voice is so close now, I'm sure I must be nearer to her.

"Karma," she says. "I'm right here, silly. You walked right past me."

From behind me is Kiyomi's voice, so I turn around and finally see her. She's standing in the dark with only a beam of moonlight to illuminate her. Next to her is another human, but I'm not sure who. I walk to Kiyomi and take the cookie she has for me in the palm of her hand. As she places my crown onto my head, the other human places her arms around my neck and hugs me. Now I recognize it's the one Kiyomi calls Mom.

"Hello, Karma," says Mom, kissing me below my eye.

"Boop," says Kiyomi, gently tapping my nose with her pointer finger. She and her mom lead me toward the tie-up area, and I'm surprised to find we aren't the only ones here this late at night.

"We're going on a moon-lit ride, Karma," says Kiyomi. "I've never been on one before, and I'm so excited that I get to take you with me. Especially since this will be the first time I ride you."

Although I've already eaten today, Kiyomi has made me another heaping bowl of food. I dive into it and eat fast, even though I'm not particularly hungry.

"How is he doing?" asks Kiyomi's mom. "Have things been going well since you began working with him?"

"He's the best horse ever," says Kiyomi. "I love him so much."

Wait, did Kiyomi just say that she loves me? I mean, I knew she really liked me a lot, but love. That's all I've ever wanted from a human.

"I'm so excited that I finally get to ride him," says Kiyomi, leaning into my neck and wrapping her arms around me.

"I'm glad," says Mom. "I'm excited that I get to come along with you two tonight."

After eating my food, Kiyomi and I walk out to the pen where the riders climb onto our backs. Although Kiyomi has tied my lead rope into reins, her mother clips another one onto my crown and stands close. Before Kiyomi climbs onto my back, her mom hugs me again, then kisses me in the same spot as before.

"You're such a beautiful boy, Karma," says Mom.

"I'm getting on now, Mom," says Kiyomi.

I can tell Kiyomi is nervous. Even though it's dark, I assess our surroundings to see if there's anything we should be concerned about. Another animal lurking beyond the bushes perhaps? Is there a horse getting in too close and wanting to bite me? Could that Twyla girl from school be here and making Kiyomi nervous? As far as I can see, there's nothing to be afraid of.

"Are you nervous, Karma?" whispers Kiyomi, leaning down onto my neck and getting close to my ear. "I am, a little."

A gentle vibration moves through her neck as she remains close to me. Sound, soft and gentle, moves from her mouth and captivates me. Each muscle within my body relaxes, one by one, as the melody she's creating infiltrates my ears.

"I always hum when I'm nervous, and it always helps me to feel better," she says.

I sigh loudly and release the tension in my body. The humming is helping me relax, too.

"Here we go," says Mom, walking forward with my lead rope in her hand.

We follow closely behind ten other horses and riders. The night air is cold, and the snow crunches beneath my feet. The coolest thing, so far, is that the light of the moon is reflecting on the snow's surface, making it sparkle like stars on the ground.

After walking a few minutes, Kiyomi relaxes on my back, so I relax a little more, too. With her mom leading the way, I'm not as concerned with watching my surroundings as closely as if she weren't. As we walk, there's an odd sensation coming from Kiyomi and onto my back. It's a magnificent heat, not like the feeling of the sun, but a heat that tickles. She has one hand on the reins and the other hasn't stopped stroking my neck since she climbed on. It's a wonderful feeling.

"How does it feel to be riding him, honey?" Mom asks Kiyomi.

"I've never experienced a better feeling in my entire life," says Kiyomi.

We stop for a break and Mom wraps her arms around my neck and kisses me – again. She sure is a hugger, and she's smothering me a bit, but I can't complain about being loved too much. Especially when there were times when I felt no love at all.

Once we are walking again, I look up. Although the moon is still bright, I finally find the sparkling glow of a star. Before I lose sight of it, I focus on a new wish I want to make.

"Do you see that star, Karma?" whispers Kiyomi from my back.

Is she talking about the same star I'm looking at now?

"I'm going to make a wish on it," she says.

Wait, I was about to make a wish on it. Can we both make a wish on the same star? Which wish will come true if we use the same one?

"I wish that you could be my horse," says Kiyomi. "Forever and ever."

Maybe we can both make a wish on the same star. Especially since we are wishing for the exact same thing.

Chapter 48

Kiyomi has fed me at least ten cookies already, and we haven't even gone on our ride yet. We've only been together for a few minutes, and her pocket seems to be an endless treasure trove of treats. Like the other days she and I have spent together, this is shaping up to be another amazing one.

"Are you ready to ride now, Karma?" asks Kiyomi, rubbing my neck in the spot I love most. "Today is a big day. I'll be riding you solo, without a co-pilot or any other assistance. Just you and me."

Kiyomi softly hums while stroking my head. Loving that sound, I nicker and nuzzle my head in close, letting her know I like the idea of it being just her and me. Then, my attention is gripped by a dramatic shift of energy among the herd. There are around fifteen horses in the same tie-up space as me, and we all seem to feel it. Whatever it is. With my head lifted high and my ears perched straight, I search for what is causing such a surge in our once peaceful space. Then, I understand what's happening.

"Hello, everyone," says Vickie, walking toward us horses with a huge smile on her face.

Some of us nicker and others sing aloud. I do a combination of both. Vickie pauses to hug and greet a bunch of humans, but also stops and says hello to the other horses, too. The energy among the herd isn't the only shift I feel. Kiyomi seems disappointed, and the smile she usually wears is gone from her face.

"How's my horse, Kiyomi?" asks Vickie, stopping at my neck and rubbing the spot I love most.

"He's amazing," says Kiyomi. "I really have loved being with him while you were gone."

Vickie looks different. Her skin is darker, and she smells of salt and sand.

"You did a great job taking care of Karma while I was in Maui," says Vickie. "Thank you so much, sweetie. I really appreciate it."

"You're welcome," says Kiyomi with a crooked smile. "Do you want to ride him now with the group?"

"No, you go ahead and ride him today," says Vickie. "Since you've already gotten him ready."

Vickie offers me a cookie and rubs my neck, then my back. I lean in a little, loving the attention.

"Thank you," says Kiyomi. "I'd love to ride him today."

Vickie walks on to greet another human, leaving Kiyomi and I alone. Tears have formed in Kiyomi's eyes, she's breathing heavily and rubbing me like it's the last time. Then, she hugs me tightly, like it's good-bye.

What's going on? Is this the last time I'll get to be with Kiyomi? Now that Vickie is back, will I be her horse after all?

I feel agitated and anxious. It's a feeling I've felt before, just before I was handed off from one human and onto another. I don't like this feeling, but I don't know how to fight it in this moment. I love Vickie, but I love Kiyomi with a deep profoundness that I've never experienced before. What should I do?

Kiyomi leads me to the mounting blocks and climbs onto my back. She's so light and the same warmth and tickling energy passes from her and onto me that I felt on the moonlit ride. Although in addition to that, I feel a deep sadness coming from her. I don't like it when she feels this way. I need to do something, but what?

"Let's head out, everybody," says Vickie from atop her horse, Titan. She looks at me and smiles.

Kiyomi and I follow the other horses and ride out into the back pasture. Typically, she would have told me a bunch of stuff by now. Like, what her day was like at school – thankfully, that Twyla has stopped teasing her. Sometimes she'll fill me in on something gross her older brother did. Or something she saw or experienced that she couldn't wait to tell me about. But so far, she's said nothing.

We walk up next to Vickie and her horse, and she looks at Kiyomi and me. "My boy is looking so good, Kiyomi."

"Yeah," says Kiyomi. I feel a surge of sadness from her heart.

It's too overwhelming for me to handle all the sadness she's carrying with her. So much so, that I need to do something to help get rid of this feeling. So, I trot forward, hoping it'll ease my anxious energy.

"Whoa, Karma," says Kiyomi. "We're just walking today."

But the trotting is helping me expend this anxious energy and has me feeling a little better. Now that I'm doing it, I don't know if I can stop. Even for her. I slow down for a moment and walk a few steps, but this only has me feeling Kiyomi's sadness again. It's too painful for me to bare. My feet pick up again, but instead of trotting, I lope. Kiyomi sits back in her seat and pulls on my reins.

"Whoa, Karma," she says with fear in her voice. "I need you to slow down and walk. Please."

But I can't. If I do, I'll only feel the pain coming from her, and the pain I'm feeling inside, too. So, I slow down to a trot, but nothing more.

"Whoa, Karma," says Kiyomi. "Please, walk."

"Do you need help, Kiyomi?" shouts Vickie from behind us. "Get off if he's not walking for you, honey."

Then, I feel Kiyomi's hands hug my neck before she slides her body off from my back. She's gone. Was that the last time I'll feel her love while out riding? I'm overwhelmed by emotions. I'm so glad Vickie has brought me into her home and wants to love me. And I love her, too. But something happened between Kiyomi and me while she was gone, and I never want to let that go. What do I do?

A new rush of energy and sadness pushes through me. So much so, that all I can think of doing is to run. And I do. I run as fast as I can toward home, leaving Kiyomi and the others behind.

Once I've run as far as I can go, I wait. Breathless and tired from the exertion. After a time, Kiyomi walks up with the other horses and riders following. I step toward her and lower my head, feeling badly about what I'd just done. As Kiyomi gets closer, she's crying. I expect her to stop and hug me tightly, but instead, she walks past and leaves me where I stand.

Chapter 49

Her hands are soft and full of love. When she looks into my eyes, I feel safe and wanted. I've been wishing for a love like this my entire life. And I've finally been blessed with it. There's nothing more I've ever wanted other than to be loved the way I am now, and to have a home exactly as I do. So, am I being selfish? Is it wrong for me to want something different still? Rather, for wanting to be with someone different.

I'm still very keen to have Vickie in my life forever. After all, she's the one who found me and granted my wish. My life will be amazing with her as my human. But I can't shake the feeling of needing another human in my life, too. My thoughts are consumed by all that I've shared with Kiyomi.

Will she come back? I freaked out the other day when we were riding, and I didn't mean to upset her. But the fact of the matter is, I did upset her. I made her cry; scared her and watched her leave. It's been several days and nights since then, and the little darlin hasn't come back to see me. I could live the rest of my life perfectly happy with Vickie. But why does my heart ache for the young girl whose freckles remind me of my wishing stars?

"Karma," sings out a voice. "Karma, come in and see me, sweet boy."

I lift my head and sing loudly. As I walk toward the tie-up area, I search for the one who has called me – for Vickie. It's funny how each human can say my name, but the way they say it always sounds different. The same is true with horses. We all sing and nicker, but our voices are all different. I'm excited to hear Vickie say my voice, but it doesn't push the same spark of energy into my heart the way Kiyomi says it.

"Good boy, Karma," says Vickie, rubbing my neck and offering me a cookie.

Then, she places my crown onto my head and leads me into the tie-up area. We walk slowly, I don't feel a particular pep in my step today. Once we arrive under the covered space, Vickie lays a bowl of food at my feet, and I eat – one small bite at a time.

"Hey, Vickie," says Catherine, walking toward us. I haven't seen much of Catherine since she and Vickie brought me home from the auction. Whenever she sees me, though, her kind hands rub my neck.

"Hello," says Vickie in return, as she uses a brush to groom my back.

"How is Karma today?" asks Catherine.

"Well," says Vickie. "He's beautiful as ever, but he seems a little sad today."

"Awe," says Catherine. "I wonder what we can do to cheer him up?"

"I'm not sure," says Vickie. "But I'll ride him in the lesson today, spend some time with him, and see if I can figure it out."

"Now that you're riding him," says Catherine. "Who should Kiyomi ride in the lesson tonight?"

I abruptly lift my head with wide eyes at the sound of her name. Did Catherine just say what I've been longing to hear most? An enthusiastic nicker leaves me, just at the sound of Kiyomi's name.

"Wow," says Vickie. "Karma's energy has certainly shifted dramatically. Interesting."

I keep looking at the humans within the area, scanning each

face, hoping to see Kiyomi. Then, just in case she's near and can't find me, I lift my head higher and sing loudly.

This pushes the other horses to sing out, too. Each of us trying to outshine the others. Those dang ding-dongs, I can't hear anything other than all the racket they're making. I sing out again and look in each direction, then shift my body from side to side a bit, hoping to see more human faces and ultimately hers.

"Easy, boys," says Vickie. "Easy now, Karma."

"Was it something I said?" asks Catherine, chuckling with a smile.

"I think, possibly, it may just have been," says Vickie.

Chapter 50

The sun has climbed and fell several times since I last saw Kiyomi.

The days are getting longer and warmer, and the promise of green grass is nearing. Thoughts of the imminent arrival of spring typically makes me giddy. Today, however, it's still not enough to make me feel better about losing Kiyomi. Will she ever come back? I didn't mean to hurt her. I didn't know how to handle my feelings in the moment I ran and she fell off my back.

"Karma," sings out the most amazing voice in the world. "Karma, come here."

Am I dreaming? Or is it her?

"Karma," she sings out again. "Karma, come here."

I lift my head and sing as loudly as I can. Then, I look everywhere in search of the source of the angelic voice singing my name. That's when I find her. My heart races and I sing out again, louder than I've ever sang before. It's my girl – my Kiyomi.

Instead of walking toward her, like I'd usually do, I run as fast as I can, singing along with each step. I'm so excited that I whip my head, tossing my hair into the air, and even buck a time or two with pure joy. When I'm only a few steps away from her, I slow down to a trot before stopping right in front of her.

She's smiling and staring into my eyes. I stare into her eyes, too. There's a sparkle and a light within them that I love so much. I lower my head and nuzzle in close. She rubs my head then moves onto my neck. I can't believe she's back. I'm so happy that she's back. Not only that, but she's here to see me.

Kiyomi isn't alone. Standing close behind her is my human, Vickie. She's smiling, which eases me; knowing she isn't upset that I've run toward Kiyomi rather than to her. As Vickie watches, Kiyomi wraps her arms around my neck and squeezes. Her breathing is rapid and deep, like she's pained from the inside.

"I love you so much, Karma," says Kiyomi. "Even though you are Vickie's horse, I'll do whatever I can to see you as much as possible."

I nicker and sigh heavily, feeling and hoping to release some of the pain transferred from Kiyomi to me. Also, some pain of my own that I've been harboring, too.

"Would you like to ride Karma in the lesson tonight, Kiyomi?" asks Vickie, walking over to join us. She rubs my neck and hands my crown over to Kiyomi. Vickie then places her hand gently onto Kiyomi's shoulder. There seems to be a transfer of kindness from one to the other.

"I really, really want to ride him today," says Kiyomi, pulling my crown over my head. "But what if he does what he did last time? What if he spooks or runs off on me again?"

I won't, Kiyomi. I promise to be cool, calm, and collected. I nicker, hoping this will convey the message I desperately wish I could say with human words.

"We won't know until we try," says Vickie. "You'll be calm for Kiyomi tonight, won't you, Karma?"

I nicker and lower my head, nuzzling it into Kiyomi's chest. She giggles and rubs between my ears. Her pointer finger extends and gently taps my nose as she says, "boop." I tap my nose onto hers, and it makes her laugh.

"Did you teach him to do that?" asks Vickie.

"I did," says Kiyomi. "It's just a silly game."

"It doesn't look silly to me," says Vickie. "I'm impressed at how much he responds to you. Well, what do you say? Will you ride him?"

"All right, Karma," says Kiyomi. "Let's go for a ride."

I lift my head and sing aloud. She leads me toward the tie-up area, remaining close by my side and humming softly. As we walk, the best feeling comes from the girl to me. And I don't feel quite as afraid of losing her as I did before.

Chapter 51

Kiyomi and I ride every day. Sometimes, we stay in the outdoor arena at the front of the property. Just her and me meandering around and chatting. Other times, we go out with more of the horses and I behave like the perfect gentlemen.

What's interesting is the more Kiyomi and I ride together, the more in sync we become. I might sound like one heck of a dang ding-dong, but I swear Kiyomi and I can read each other's minds. Like when she wants me to move my body to the right, I begin doing it before she even moves her hands on the reins. If she wants me to backup, I seem to know exactly when to do that. And she must be reading my mind, too. Whenever I want to stop and eat some grass, I just lower my head and we do. If I'm craving a cookie, she hands me one within a second, even if she's riding on my back. Although, granted, I'm usually thinking about eating cookies almost every second of every day.

Whenever we ride with the others, Vickie is always nearby. She still rides me sometimes, but never when Kiyomi is around. From time to time, she watches Kiyomi and me. I still feel very loyal to Vickie, and I do still love her very much. But there's just something so unique about the love I feel for Kiyomi. I hope Vickie doesn't mind that too much.

Kiyomi and I have ridden our way right into summer. The grass is sweet and vibrant, and the birds are back filling our space with music. My only issue with this time of year, however, are the dang mosquitoes who bite me in regions I can't reach with my tail to swat them away. I hate the little buggers.

Luckily, I've found a primo piece of green grass near the end of the back pasture. So far, since I'm still without a horse bestie, I have it all to myself. No one has followed me here, so I don't need to share. Yip, it's pretty dang sweet.

With the sun warm on my back, I leisurely eat grass from my special patch. I'm relaxed and content until I'm startled by a presence.

My heart flutters within my chest as the grass rustles close to me. This is the biggest downfall of not having a horse bestie, no one else around if a predator should approach. I move my feet, pacing back and forth, then spot the intruder.

A fuzzy grey and black dog, with curly hair and big dopey eyes, moves in close. My nostrils flare so I can smell it and try to sense its intentions. I've been around plenty of dogs before, so I'm not too scared of them. Unless they try and bite at my heels, which has happened, and which I hate. So, the question remains, what in the heck is this beast's intentions.

"Journey," shouts Vickie from a short distance away. "Journey, come back here."

The dog looks back at Vickie, responding to her voice and its name. But he doesn't do as he's told. I bet he's in trouble now. Since he interrupted my meal, I'll smugly watch him get a lecture about listening.

"Journey," says Vickie as she moves in next to him. "Silly dog, you need to leave the horses alone and come when you're called."

Journey doesn't get into trouble – Vickie is all love. I sigh with disappointment, knowing I won't be getting an entertaining show at the dog's expense today.

"Good afternoon, Karma," says Vickie, the bright sun

evoking a glow onto her skin. "I need you to come with me, sweet boy."

She holds a cookie in her hand, so I walk toward her and take it. Then, she places my blue rope crown onto my head and begins leading me back to the tie-up area.

"Today is a big day for you, my friend," she says as we walk slowly. "Although I think you are an amazing boy, I've come to realize that you and I are not destined to be partners."

What? Did she just say we're not destined to be partners? What is she getting at? Have I done something wrong? Is she sending me to an auction? Will I be going to live in another new home?

"I hope you'll be okay with it," she says. "I've decided you'll be much happier in the care of another."

I nicker again and again. Wishing desperately that I could speak human and beg for Vickie to reconsider. What does she mean I'll be much happier in the care of another? Why can't I make human sounds with my mouth? I must tell her that I don't want another new home.

Journey runs up behind us and barks. I'm so frustrated right now, and his barking and carrying on is the last thing I need. I lower my head as Journey moves in close to me. Just close enough for me to lunge my head and snap my teeth at his butt. I taste fur and feel satisfied for pushing that dang dog away. How can Vickie honestly believe I'll be better off in the care of another?

My heart is racing once we reach the tie-up area. I look all around, hoping to create a lasting impression of this place. Wanting to engrave all that it is into my mind to hang onto forever. Why is this happening? Why can't I just be loved and left to live in one place?

Vickie ties my lead rope to a wooden post before attaching something red and shiny to my crown. I don't know what it is, but I don't care either.

"Looks like your new family has just arrived, Karma," says Vickie, rubbing my neck and taking a deep breath.

Oddly, a group of humans, regulars in this place, all surround me. It's like they're hiding me from something, but what? Then, Vickie speaks from a short distance away. With the humans surrounding me and all mumbling, I can't hear what she's saying.

Then, I sense something. It's a presence so familiar, I'd know it anywhere and under any circumstance. My heart feels as though it's being pulled out of me. What is going on? Finally, the crowd of humans moves away, exposing me to another small group of humans standing ahead with Vickie.

"Karma," says Kiyomi, moving to stand next to me.

I sing so loud, my throat aches. My girl is here! Maybe she can talk Vickie into letting me stay here.

"Kiyomi," says Vickie, moving to stand next to me with tears in her eyes. "I know you and Karma have been spending a lot of time together since he's arrived. And I can tell that you and he love each other very much. I've made a decision about his future, and it will affect you."

Kiyomi's face drops. Her mother moves in close and wraps her arms around my girl. There are tears in Mom's eyes, too, which makes Kiyomi tear up. What is going on? Where are they sending me? Why is everyone crying?

"What's happening?" asks Kiyomi.

"Karma is a very special boy, and I love him very much," says Vickie. "But I've come to realize that he just isn't meant to be my horse."

"Oh?" asks Kiyomi, the tears in her eyes intensifying. "What will happen to him?"

"He deserves the kind of love that only one human can offer him," says Vickie. "The kind of love that comes from a special bond written in the stars. A love destined from the beginning of time itself."

"You don't think he can have that kind of love here?" asks Kiyomi.

"I know I can love him forever," says Vickie. "But there's someone else who can give him a magnificent and powerful love. And that person is you, Kiyomi."

"What?" says Kiyomi, sobbing and walking to me, nuzzling her wet face into my neck. "What do you mean?"

"What I mean," says Vickie, moving in close to Kiyomi and me, "is that I think I brought Karma to Eagle Feather so that he could meet you. And you were destined to be his forever loving human."

"Mom? Dad?" says Kiyomi, looking to her Mom and a male human.

"Happy Birthday, Kiyomi," says Mom, wiping tears from her face.

"Seriously?" says Kiyomi, rushing over to hug her mom and dad.

"Seriously," says Dad.

"Karma," says Kiyomi, rushing back to me. "My wish came true."

I sigh heavily and nicker, tucking my back leg in and resting into Kiyomi's hug. My wish has finally come true, too.

Chapter 52

Being at the hay bale with Kiyomi is my favorite time. Not only because I can eat until my belly is full, and then keep eating some more. It's a time where she takes me away from the other horses and humans and tells me stuff which I'm sure only I get to hear.

Such as: her brother now has a girlfriend, and they hold hands and kiss. Someone in her class moved away and she's going to miss them. Her mom took her bra shopping, which was weird and a little exciting. Her mom ended up drinking too much red wine and behaved like a crazy person at a dinner party. Stuff like that.

Then again, when the grass has flourished, and dandelions have graced the ground with their sun-yellow beauty; the front pasture might be my favorite place to be with Kiyomi. She always feeds me my bowl of food first, then leads me away from the other horses and humans and allows me to graze all on my own on the grass and dandelions. Sometimes, she'll sit on my back as I eat, or lay all the way back so her head rests on my butt and watch the clouds roll by. Humming my favorite tune, of course.

When we go riding with the others in the back fields is also my favorite place to be with Kiyomi. We walk proudly together, feeling like one unit, exploring the small piece of world we can ride in. Kiyomi's always feeding me endless cookies as we ride, rubbing my neck and praising me for walking. I mean, if she's impressed by me just walking, she'd be dang impressed if we ran off into the sunset together. Maybe someday.

Yip, the weeks since Vickie gifted me to Kiyomi have been the best of my entire life, and I'd like to think the same is true for Kiyomi.

"Are you ready for an exciting adventure today?" asks Kiyomi, placing my new crown onto my head; one that's green with white and black beads. Then, she pushes her pointer finger into my nose and says, "boop."

Of course, I'm always ready for an adventure with you, darlin. I'm a legit adventurer ready to seize the day. What'll it be today: the bale, the front pasture, or a ride out back?

Once I've been fed, Kiyomi leads me away from the other horses and humans then in the direction of the front pasture. I'm dang glad she chose this spot for us today; I've been dreaming about eating mouthfuls of dandelions since yesterday when we were last there.

Instead of turning to the right and toward the lush green and yellow field, we veer off to the left and toward a space I've never explored with her before. I stop walking and Kiyomi stops, too. Turning my head, I nod toward the front pasture, trying to let her know we're going the wrong way. But Kiyomi only smiles and cocks her head, looking at me as though I'm the one behaving like a dang ding-dong. I don't want to be rude, but she's the one who's obviously behaving as such.

"We aren't going that way today, Karma," she says confidently.

I beg to differ; we ought to be heading that way. My head pulls on the lead rope, forcing her hands to lift in the air and hold tighter.

"Karma," says Kiyomi. "Please be a good boy. We aren't going that way today. There's something else planned instead."

Kiyomi reaches into her pocket and pulls out a cookie. My head lowers and relaxes, and I move to stand next to her. She knows I'm a sucker for treats and will do anything she asks in exchange for one. Once the cookie is in my mouth and I'm distracted, Kiyomi walks us further away from the front pasture. After only a few steps, we stop. And we haven't arrived at food at all, rather, a horse trailer.

I don't like where this is going. The only time I've been placed into a horse trailer was to be moved to a new home, taken to auction or to a parade with Duke. Neither of those destinations sounds appealing to me at all. Where in the heck is she taking me?

I'm guided further toward the horse trailer, and Kiyomi steps inside, urging me to climb aboard, too. My feet remain planted firmly on the ground, and I refuse.

"Come on, Karma," she says. "You can do it."

She pulls a cookie out of her pocket, but I don't go for it. If eating that cookie puts me inside of that trailer, and if being inside of that trailer has me going to a new home, auction, or parade, I don't want to get into the dang trailer.

Kiyomi and I stare at each other; she still coaxing me to climb aboard and me remaining still. Then, I feel a hand gently poke into my butt. It doesn't hurt, but it startles me enough to think I need to move on out of my position. Sadly, the only place for me to move is inside the trailer with Kiyomi.

"There you go, Karma," says Kiyomi. She rubs my neck then leads me toward a feed bag hanging in front of a small window. Once I'm in the correct position, she closes the metal gate to keep me in my place.

Thankfully, other horses are loaded into the trailer with me, too. At least I won't be alone if we do end up at auction, or another home. Heck, maybe they're taking us all to a parade. But none of us has been dressed up in costumes. Maybe they'll dress us up once we arrive in the location of the parade. I guess, given the choices, that's the best scenario. I'll dress up like a ninny and do everything I can to keep my cool in the chaos of a parade if it means I can stay with Kiyomi.

Driving to our destination only takes a short time. Once the truck and trailer stop, I lean my nose toward the open window and smell deeply. It reminds me of my home with Ruth and Duke. The air smells of evergreen trees and cool water. I also smell dirt and rock minerals, but not much in the way of horses other than the ones from my herd.

Instead of hearing crowds of people and smelling odd foods they'd eat at a parade, I only hear birds singing, leaves rustling in the breeze, and the voices of the humans from Eagle Feather. Where the dang heck are we?

The backdoor of the horse trailer opens, allowing the sunshine to flood in. Since none of the other horses seem too bothered by the place we've just arrived, I keep my cool, too. But with my eyes wide and nostrils flared, I'm ready to protect myself and Kiyomi in this new place should the need arise. After four other horses disembark the trailer, it's finally my turn. Thankfully, Kiyomi enters the trailer and walks toward me. She's smiling, and I'm so glad she's still with me.

"Are you ready for an exciting day?" she asks, releasing the metal bars that once barricaded me.

Kiyomi steps off the trailer first. Wanting to remain close behind her, I follow, my feet landing onto black pavement. From this angle, the only thing visible is the horse trailer I arrived in, and another parked close, leaving just a small lane for us to pass through. Kiyomi leads me through the laneway until we move past the trailers and are in an open space.

Everything is green. Clusters of trees, all varying species, hug the side of a small rock mountain. Beneath the trees are long blades of grass with wildflowers fighting for space. There's so much to smell and see here, and my heart is racing. Not only because we've arrived someplace new, but also because I'm so relieved Kiyomi has brought me to a place I wasn't expecting.

"We're all going for a nice trail ride, Karma," says Kiyomi.

I've done that before, and I'm dang good at it. This will be just fine. Kiyomi leads me toward some trees where I recognize a few other horses from my herd. I take another look around and she fixes my lead rope to be reins, ready for riding. There's trees and mountain as far as I can see. From Eagle Feather, we've brought three trailers all full of horses and humans. It eases me to see so many familiar faces from my herd in this place.

Once my reins are set, Kiyomi leads me over to a large rock. She climbs onto it and takes a cookie out of her jeans pocket. Focusing on the cookie, I walk forward until I'm standing parallel to the large rock. I open my mouth, ready to receive the cookie, but instead, Kiyomi swings her leg over my back and climbs on. It startles me a little, so I shuffle my back end around some.

"Easy, boy," says Kiyomi. "It's all right, we're safe here."

Humming quietly, her small hand reaches down next to my neck and toward my mouth. I can smell the cookie, so I arch my neck toward her, and snatch it from her hand. It helps me to feel a little better.

"Everyone good to go?" shouts Vickie, from atop her horse, Legend.

"We're good to go," says Kiyomi from my back. I feel

excitement rush from within her and through to me.

"Let's head out, everyone," says Vickie with a smile, moving her horse to the front and leading us all away from the trailers.

Kiyomi and I stay near the back, having a horse named Willy and his rider, Holly, behind us. Willy had better keep his teeth to himself, I don't want anyone biting my butt from back there. Especially since I'm already on edge in this new place and want to stay calm for Kiyomi.

We follow the other horses from the parking lot and to a small dirt trail carved out in the ground. It's framed by trees and the sun pushes light through the branches. Once on the trail, I spot birds, squirrels, and lots of bugs. There must be a million dang mosquitos out here. Great.

"Good boy, Karma," says Kiyomi, rubbing my neck with her hand.

After we walk up the path a distance, we arrive in a small clearing full of tall grass. I can tell the other horses are just as excited as me to see it all. Vickie must understand that, too, because she stops and allows us to eat.

I rip as much of the green grass from the ground with my teeth as possible. It hangs from my lips as I chew, it's much longer than the grass around our home. There's a profound sweetness to this grass, and I'm loving every morsel of it. Once I've cleared a small space of it, I take a few steps forward to find more. Tucked in between the tall, green blades is a purple flower. I've never tried it before, so I take it into my mouth and chew. I search the ground for more of them because it's one of the best dang flowers I've ever tasted.

"Let's move on and ride further," says Vickie.

I could sit here all day, but the other horses begin to leave, so I follow. We move back onto the dirt trail and walk. The path leads upward, and I find myself breathing heavily with the exertion. My legs feel tired, and I trip, jolting Kiyomi on my back. Her hands grip into the hair of my withers, like I've scared her.

"Steady, Karma," she says.

Sweat begins to form on my neck as I continue to climb the trail. Then, I trip again. I hope I'm not scaring Kiyomi too much.

"It's okay, sweet boy," says Kiyomi. "We'll get used to being on these trails, together. If you trip, I'll hold on. It's okay."

My heart swells to hear her say that. Even though I never mean to trip, I've gotten into trouble in the past for doing it. Knowing Kiyomi isn't too bothered by the outcome of my old injury, the thing others call a disability, something that makes me different from the other horses, only makes me love her more.

We walk farther, until coming to a clearing again. My heart swells more and flutters within my chest when I take a good look at where we've arrived. I feel like I've walked up into the clouds. There are trees, mountains and sky farther than I could possibly see. Although I've been on trail rides before, I never knew the earth was so big. At the dude ranch, we only took tourists on the same trails each time we rode out. Who knew there was so much more to this world than I could have dreamed?

Perhaps , being on a trail ride with Kiyomi is my favorite place to be.

Chapter 53

Certainly, I must look like a dang ding-dong. Kiyomi is making me do new tricks. She's teaching me things that make her laugh, which must mean, to her, that I look ridiculous. But because it makes the little darlin happy, I endure the humiliation and do it anyway.

During the beginning of mine and Kiyomi's relationship, she'd hand over treats to me at will, not requiring me to do much in return for one. Now, she has me doing all kinds of crazy things in exchange. And because she knows I'm highly hooked to the stuff she insists I perform for her to get one.

Kiyomi stands next to me, leaning into one of the horizontal wooden posts that make the tie-up area. A soft, warm breeze tussles her long hair, pushing pieces randomly into her wide smile. She's giggling a lot, too, especially when I flash my teeth at her. I've seen the inside of my brother's mouths, and it isn't pretty, I'd giggle at them, too, if I could. Especially right now as my teeth are feeling extra-long and sharp.

Pinching a treat within her fingers, Kiyomi lifts her hand into the air above my head. With wide eyes, I lift my mouth in unison with her hand and open it, ready to receive my treat. Instead of offering it to me right away, she moves her fingers up and down in the air, and I move my lips in and out as she does. This is when she giggles, making me move my lips this way over and over before finally giving me my dang treat.

"You look hilarious, Karma," she says, rubbing my neck.

"But I sure do love to see you smile."

There's a glow of happiness in her eyes when we do this trick, and I love seeing her this way. That's why, even though I have wretched teeth and an awkward mouth, I smile for her each time she moves her hands like this. And, of course, for the prize of a treat.

"Now give me a hug, Karma," says Kiyomi.

She leans in close and holds a cookie out in front of her. For me to reach it, I must arch my neck sharply around, which hugs Kiyomi's body as I do, and open my mouth to grab it. She doesn't ask me to hug her as much as she asks for the smile. Probably because her mother is constantly smothering everyone with hugs, and she feels satisfied by that. Heck, Mom is often hugging me and the other horses, too. So, I can relate.

"Boop," says Kiyomi as she gently taps my nose with her pointer finger.

In response, I tap my nose against hers. Luckily, this little exchange always results a treat, too.

"Let's head out to the front today, sweet boy," she says, untying my lead rope and walking us away from the tie-up area.

I follow her willingly. I'm not in a rush to get back to the herd, still feeling friendless and alone whilst there. And besides, being with Kiyomi is always the highlight of my day.

Kiyomi and I meander through the front pasture, pausing every few steps so I can take a bite of grass and the odd dandelion. She's telling me about a boy at school named Kenny. Each time she says his name, my eyes widen, and I pin my ears. The way she keeps saying this boy's name sounds awfully like the tone in which she says mine. And I don't like it. It would seem to me that she might like this kid, Kenny, a little too much. And yip, it bothers me. I'm the only boy she needs in her life. I may need to find this Kenny, bite him in the butt and chase him off my girl.

We walk far enough for Kiyomi to say the name Kenny a bunch more times, and to reach the end of the front pasture. I like this area as it's shaded by a small cluster of large evergreen trees. Kiyomi removes the lead rope from my crown and lays it onto the ground. Technically, I could make a run for it, and go wherever the heck I please. Instead, I stay close to Kiyomi as there's no other place I'd rather be. And I'm so glad my girl trusts me enough to know this, too.

"Want to play a game, Karma?" asks Kiyomi.

The only game I'm fixing to play right now is how many dandelions can I fit into my belly in a short amount of time. I lower my head and pluck a few before chewing.

"Karma," sings Kiyomi.

I nicker and softly sing back for a second before pulling a few more dandelions into my mouth.

"Karma," she sings again.

I lift my head and look, but I don't see her. Where the heck did she go? I still smell her, feel her presence, but I don't see her.

"Karma," she sings.

I turn my head in all directions, then shift my body to the left and right, but I still don't see her. Then, she giggles and pops her head out from behind the trunk of a large tree. I nicker and sing, which makes her giggle again. But after a few seconds, she disappears.

With the tree Kiyomi was just behind in my sights, I trot directly over to it, not even pausing to eat more grass or dandelions, which means I'm quite serious. But when I come around to the other side of the tree, she's not there.

"Karma," sings Kiyomi from a short distance away.

What the heck kind of game is she playing? How does she make herself disappear like that? I must find her. Following the sound of her voice, I trot toward another tree and look around to its other side. Standing there, with her body pressed tightly into the bark and a huge smile on her face is Kiyomi.

"You found me, Karma," she says, rubbing my head and gifting me a treat. "See, hide and seek is fun. Let's keep playing."

She runs away from the tree, and I follow her as she giggles. Together, we move from tree to tree. Kiyomi's giggle shifts to a loud laugh, and I nicker with every other breath. I didn't know that dancing in the trees with my girl could be so much fun.

After quite a time, Kiyomi and I are both breathless. She stops within the middle of the trees and lays down in the grass, looking up at the sky. I stand close to her, but instead of laying down, I eat grass.

"That was fun," says Kiyomi. "Good job following me without a lead rope, sweet boy."

The truth is, I'd follow this girl anywhere and at anytime.

Chapter 54

The pampering in this place is next level. Last week, Trudi came out and did my feet. Sure, I've had my hooves trimmed before, but nothing quite like the experience of having her do them. She lifts my foot up and angles it in the most comfortable way. Then, she gently trims the longer bits of my hoof and frog. After that, she slowly files around the edges of my hoof. It's so dang relaxing. The best part is, she comes to do it every six weeks.

Today, Kiyomi says I get to see the Vet and have my teeth done. The first thing that comes to mind when she uses the word 'Vet' is that it'll be Lorraine. I always think of her when a human says the word Vet. She was one of the kindest humans to ever care for me. I'm super stoked to see what kind of pampering I'll be getting from the Vet today.

Within the tie-up area are a bunch of humans and horses. Following Kiyomi, I try to locate the Vet and hope to see Lorraine's face. Instead, there's some random guy with glasses looking into another horse's mouth. Darn, I did hope it was going to be Lorraine.

Kiyomi ties me up in front of a large pile of hay, and I dive right into it. While eating as much as my mouth can hold, the Vet walks up to me and Kiyomi, and asks her a bunch of questions. Then, I feel a small pinch at my butt that makes me flinch.

"Easy, boy," says Kiyomi, rubbing my neck and offering me a cookie. "You're okay, nothing to worry about."

Because I trust her so much, I sigh deeply and stand still beside her. After a few minutes, things become a little blurry and not quite right. I look at Kiyomi, my eyes heavy and blinking slowly. For some reason, she resembles a cloud-like version of herself rather than a solid human.

I lean over to nudge her for a cookie, but my balance is completely off, and my back legs don't want to stay straight. What the heck was in that last cookie I ate? Did they accidently feed me some funky dried morsel to make me feel like I'm flying in the sky?

Whoa, it's the middle of the day, and there are stars everywhere. I've never seen something like that before. What is going on with me today?

"Is Karma ready to have his teeth done?" asks the Vet, his voice sounding like a distant echo.

"Yeah," says Kiyomi with a laugh. "He's looking relaxed and super loopy right now. The sedation must be working."

Kiyomi releases my lead rope from the post and turns her body. I have enough mental clarity to understand that when she does this, she wants me to follow her. Does she seriously need me to walk right now? I can barely keep my legs straight, let alone walk in a straight line.

"Come on, Karma," she says sweetly. "You can do it. Follow me."

She holds a treat in her palm, and I turn my body to grab it. I lower my head toward her hand and open my lips, trying to pick the treat up. But I miss it. So, I lift my head and try again. I miss this time, too. Kiyomi laughs at me before pushing the treat into my mouth with her hand. I try to chew the thing, but it slips around on my tongue before eventually falling to the ground at my feet. I hope to try and pick it up again, but it's so far down to the ground that I don't think I can make it all the way there.

Dragging my feet, I stumble next to Kiyomi as she leads. I turn my head and see the horse from my herd named Thor. He's a freee – a freeezzin – wait, he's a friesssssss. Why can't I remember that word? The word that is his breed of horse. What is wrong with me? Thor is a Friesian. There, I did it. Finally. He's one of the biggest dudes in the herd and strong. But when I look at him now, he looks just as bad as I do.

Hey, man, did they feed you a funky cookie, too? What's in that stuff? Wait, did I just speak human, or am I imagining it? Thor doesn't respond, and none of the humans look impressed, so I'm guessing I wasn't just the first horse to speak their language. Too bad.

After taking more steps than I'm sure I've ever taken in my entire life, Kiyomi and I finally stop and stand in front of the Vet. He's holding the craziest looking crown I've ever seen and has tools laid out at his feet. Then, he comes toward me with the crown and places it onto my head. The thing scares the crap out of me, and I'd like to run away, but I can't seem to make my feet work. Dang it.

Once the crown is secure over my nose, the Vet picks up a long tool and pushes it into my mouth. Drool slips out from my bottom lip, and the tool rattles my brains. As if I weren't dizzy enough before, now, with the vibrating, I can't see a dang thing. What kind of torture device is this anyway?

After many, many minutes of the Vet vibrating my mouth, he pulls the tool out from within it, and steps back. "All done," says the Vet casually, like he hasn't just turned my world upside down.

"Good boy, Karma," says Kiyomi.

The vet takes the odd crown off from my head, and Kiyomi moves to lead me away. Thankfully, I can see a little straighter again and notice she's smiling at me. But she's the only one smiling right now, because I'm sure not happy with whatever pampering treatment that was supposed to be.

Chapter 55

"Karma," sings Kiyomi from the tie-up area.

Although I'm a far distance from her, I lift my head and sing aloud, so she knows where to find me.

"Karma, come here," she sings.

I sing back and quickly run in her direction. I don't want to miss a minute of being with her. As I run, the warm sun heats my body and not a single cloud can be seen in the sky. Today is going to be a hot, glorious summer's day, I can tell.

"Good boy, Karma," says Kiyomi with a smile as I slow to a walk before stopping next to her.

Even though she isn't holding a cookie in her hand yet, I get close and arch my neck around to give her a hug. She giggles and hugs me back before placing my crown onto my head.

"We get to go on a trail ride today, Karma," says Kiyomi with excitement in her voice.

Hearing her say the words, trail ride, instantly has me excited, too. I love going out to the mountain trails, seeing new things and especially, tasting different foliage. They truly are the best adventures.

"Come on, let's get you ready and loaded into the trailer," she says, walking next to me.

We've come to a new trail. I stay close to my herd brothers and smell. Although we are in a new place, nothing seems too odd or different when compared to the others.

Kiyomi leads me away from the trailer and fixes my reins. Then, she climbs aboard and allows me to start eating. My mouth waters when I spot one of the purple flowers I love so much. I eat it quickly, so none of the other horses find it and try to eat it first. Then, I spot more and head straight for them.

"We can't go over there yet, Karma," says Kiyomi, moving my reins so I'll stop.

We stand still and wait for the other horses, but they're taking so dang long. Do any of them need a little encouragement? I'd happily do a little butt biting so we can get moving. Keeping one eye fixed on the other horses and one eye on the purple flowers, we wait for an excruciating amount of time.

"Let's head out, everyone," says Vickie from the far side of the line of horses.

The flowers I've had my eye on are only a few strides away, so when Kiyomi relaxes the reins and prompts me to move forward, I trot over and eat the flowers in one big bite.

"Are you excited to head out, Karma?" asks Kiyomi, giggling under her breath.

We walk away from the horse trailers and onto a rock path. My feet hurt a little on this path as several of the rocks are large and craggy. Along the side is long grass and softer looking ground, so I move over there.

"Is this more comfortable on your feet, Karma?" asks Kiyomi, rubbing my neck.

As we ride through the tall grass and large trees, Kiyomi sporadically leans down onto my neck and holds tight so the branches don't hurt her. A few more steps ahead is a small shrub, almost as tall as my belly. With the weather so warm, I'm sweating, and I have an itch on my underside. Once I'm near the bush, I climb over it and pause. Sharp branches of the bush push into my belly and I sway my body back and forth a bunch. It's one of the best dang belly scratchers I've ever found in my entire life.

After scratching my belly thoroughly, I move on to stay in line with the other horses. The birds are singing in the trees, creating a harmonious orchestra. But suddenly, they stop. Instead of a joyful bustle in the air, there's an eeriness that ignites a fire within me. Something isn't right.

My ears pick up a sound and my nose a scent. Once I lift my head into the air and widen my eyes to look, the other horses do the same. This tells me something really isn't right. Then, a loud and frightening sound thunders all around us – a bang.

Kiyomi's little hands clutch to my mane and her heart is pounding, fast, just like mine. Then, the loud and scary bang rings out again. It's terrifying, but also, I've heard this sound before. It's familiar, but I still don't like it.

"Hello!" screams Vickie at the top of her lungs. "Hello! We have horses and riders here."

Kiyomi's hands hold tightly to my hair, and she lowers her body down to hug me and lay flat on my neck. My legs quiver and I desperately want to run – away from whatever is making that horrifying sound.

"Please don't run away on me, Karma," whispers Kiyomi in my ear.

I can tell she's crying and terrified. Even though I'm scared, I could never run off to save myself and abandon her.

The obnoxious sound pierces my ears again, this time, it seems closer, pushing me to jump and move my feet forward a little. A couple of the other horses from my herd run with their riders still on their backs. I don't know where they're going, but I'm sticking here with the group and my girl. Whatever is making that noise and posing a threat will have to go through me before it can get to her.

"Hello!" screams Vickie again. "Please stop shooting your gun! We have horses and riders here!"

A gun. I knew I'd heard that noise before. It's the same sound Duke made sometimes with his gun at my old home.

"Get as close to me as you can," says Vickie, waving her hand at the group of riders.

Kiyomi remains low to my body, but motions for me to move forward and huddle with the other horses. Broken sounds, her attempt at humming, come from her mouth. Usually this will clam us both, this time, it isn't dissipating the anxiety.

"Stop shooting your gun!" screams Vickie. "Stop shooting, we have horses and riders here."

Another shot rings out in the air, forcing more of us horses to jump and feel skittish.

"Get off your horses," says Vickie, doing the same. "Get as low to the ground as you can and let go of your horse if he decides to run."

Kiyomi slides off my back and crouches low to the ground. I move my head low and nuzzle in closely to her. Tears from her eyes drip down her face and some wet my hair. I'll lay down on her to keep her safe if I must.

"Stop shooting," screams Vickie.

The remaining horses stand still while the riders squat close to the ground. Everything is silent for a moment, and then it stays quiet for longer and longer. Until it seems the gun has stopped shooting.

"Is everyone all right?" asks Vickie, with tears, and fear in her eyes.

All the humans are crying and hugging. Vickie rushes over

to Kiyomi, the youngest rider in the group. She pulls her into her arms and holds tightly.

"It's okay," says Vickie. "It's over now. You're safe."

Kiyomi is sobbing and I feel how scared she is.

"Karma, good boy," says Vickie. "He stayed still for you, Kiyomi. He loves you and wanted to make sure you were safe."

Kiyomi moves away from Vickie and wraps her arms around my neck, gripping as tightly as she can. Vickie is right, I would do anything for my girl.

Chapter 56

After the trail ride with the gunshots yesterday, I've never been so happy to be at home. Somehow, after that harrowing experience, the grass around here seems much sweeter. Even some of the horses that irritate me don't seem as bad as they did yesterday.

"Karma," shouts a female voice from the tie-up area.

I lift my head and sing, but don't move. Someone is calling my name, but that someone isn't Kiyomi.

"Karma," shouts the voice again.

Then, the woman Kiyomi calls Mom walks in my direction with my crown in her hand. But I don't see any sign of my girl with her.

"Karma," shouts Mom again. "Come on, sweet boy. Come in and have something to eat."

I stay in place and watch Mom walk the entire length of the pasture until she finally reaches me. I nicker and she hands me a cookie. Once I'm chewing my treat, Mom wraps her arms around my neck and hugs me for quite a time. This lady must not get enough hugs at home, she's always smothering us horses with hugs.

"Come on, sweet boy," says Mom, moving out of our hug and pulling my crown onto my head. "I made you a nice full bowl of food and even put some carrots in there for you."

Mom walks toward the tie-up area with my lead rope in

hand. I follow, never one to pass up a meal, regardless of who has prepared it. Maybe Kiyomi is waiting for me up by my food bowl. Once Mom and I arrive, though, she's nowhere to be seen.

"Kiyomi couldn't make it today," says Mom, rubbing my neck.

For some reason, she has tears in her eyes. What's happened to Kiyomi? Is she okay? Why isn't she here? Did I do something wrong?

"She wants to be here," says Mom, "but she needs a little time to process what happened on the trail yesterday. She's still pretty shaken up by it all."

As Mom talks, I keep eating. I wish she could take me to Kiyomi so I could make her feel better. She uses both hands to rub my neck before hugging me again. Man, this lady really likes to hug.

"We love you so much, Karma," says Mom. "Thank you for taking care of my girl on the trail yesterday. I'm sure it was scary for you, too."

I grunt and sigh. Yes, I was scared. What does Mom mean by saying 'taking care of my girl'? She should know, Kiyomi is my girl, and nothing matters more to me.

Chapter 57

Mom ends up feeding me for a week. She's all right, but it's different from having Kiyomi here. I'm beginning to wonder if my girl is ever going to come back. And it's making me feel like I've done something wrong, or that she doesn't love me as much anymore.

"Karma," is sung into the air.

I lift my head and sing back – loudly. I turn my head to look in all directions. It's her, I just know it is.

"Karma, come here," sings Kiyomi.

Then, I spot her. My heart flips and my stomach twists as I sing using my best voice. And while I do that, I run. Using all the strength I have in my legs, I run to Kiyomi as fast as I can, whipping my mane and head around with sheer joy.

"Hey, sweet boy," she says as I move in next to her and stop. "Hey, Karma. I missed you so much."

I nicker and nuzzle in close as she rubs my neck and then hugs me. My chest heaves with deep breaths and I feel as though my heart might explode.

Kiyomi remains quiet while I eat my bowl of food. While there are other humans and horses around us, she doesn't make eye contact nor speak with any of them. Then, once I've finished and she cleans up after me, she leads me away from everyone else, and we walk.

We move together, side by side, until we reach a gate near

the edge of the mounting block space. The gate leads through to an open field at the back of the property. It's full of tall, green grass, and is a section used for rotating the herd to graze. For now, there aren't any other horses within the space. Kiyomi opens the gate and leads me through before closing it behind us.

"I thought you might like to eat some of these dandelions before your brothers are allowed in here and demolish them," says Kiyomi.

Yip does this girl know me well or what. All this grass and dandelions to myself – don't mind if I do. I rip up as much long grass as I can and eat. It tastes amazing, untouched by anything else other than the sweet sun and rain from the sky.

Kiyomi places my lead rope onto my back, allowing it to hang freely, and walks slightly ahead of me through the tall grass. For every few steps she takes, I take one, and eat the grass in between.

We walk together, she still not saying anything, and I still eating, until we've reached a small hill and the middle of the field. Then, she stops and sits. With her legs crossed and back straight, she looks out and stares at the mountains. I stop next to her and carefully eat within the space between us. These are the best dang dandelions I've ever eaten in my life.

"I've never been so scared in my life, Karma," says Kiyomi. "The only time I've ever heard gunshots is on television. I've never heard them in real life and so close."

She lifts a hand to her face and wipes tears from her cheeks. With a mouthful of grass and dandelions, I look over to her. Then, she wipes her tears away with her hand again. Her small chest heaves with breath and shudders a little. This prompts more tears.

"I was so scared that I was going to get shot," she says through the tears. "But worse, I was so scared that someone was going to shoot you, Karma."

Kiyomi looks at me, her eyes fiercely green against a background of red. Although I'm standing in a field of long grass and sweet dandelions, I resist them and stand still. Kiyomi reaches her hand over to my head and rubs between my ears. We stay this way long enough for the sun to move into a new location of the sky, far enough for me to take notice.

"I'm so glad you were okay," says Kiyomi, shifting her body and leaning close so our foreheads touch. "And I'm so glad you stood with me."

She cries a little more, and I concentrate on absorbing her pain, so she doesn't need to hold it all in her small body.

"Karma," Kiyomi says, her nose sniffling. "Did you know the same letters that spell hero's spells horse?"

I don't know what a 'hero' is.

"Well, okay, there's an apostrophe in the word hero's and not in horse," she says. "But whatever, they're spelled mostly the same. But the way you stayed with me when things got scary was so brave. You're always listening to my troubles and don't judge me. You are one of the kindest most loving beings I've ever met. Karma, you're one of my heroes."

I nicker and nuzzle in close. She leans her body against mine and cries a bit more, humming softly to me as she does. Time passes, as the pair of us sit in silence. Words aren't required in this moment any longer. Love is our language.

I've never seen a mane like that on a horse before. Heck, I've never seen anything else at all like the guy. What breed of horse looks like that? Is he a horse at all? Spending so much time living with a Vet, my Lorraine, exposed me to a few various kinds of animals. But this one is dang weird looking. I'd better get a good smell of him and find out what we'll be dealing with around here.

We horses all get a little nutty when there's new blood in our midst. What I mean is, anytime there's the scent of a new horse or other animal in our home, we act a little crazy. Initially, our instinct is to treat the new scent as a threat. So, naturally, we all huddle together and run around trying to avoid said threat. We make a bunch of noise, kick our legs, and stir things up. Acting like this should scare off the threat – or just make for a great show. Once the scent and presence has lingered for a while, and we figure our lives aren't in grave danger, we find the source of the scent and then make a big fuss all over again – again, to put on a great show.

Some horses in my herd are behaving as though the crazy haired newcomer is one of us, so this calms me a little. Others, though, are showing off for the guy. For now, I'm only interested in figuring out just what in the heck kind of animal this guy is.

His legs are short, which makes him smaller in stature to me, but he's solid muscle. The hooves on this guy are three times the size of mine. I wouldn't want to be on the receiving end of a kick from those. There's a small group of horses at the fence line separating us from him, which blocks my view a little. So, I move down the pasture a bit to get a better view.

The mane on this guy is shorter than any other horse, and it sticks straight up into the air, extending all the way down his solid and strong neck. Over his forehead is long, puffy hair which almost covers his eyes. He has kind eyes, thankfully. Oddly, his hair is the same color as mine, but otherwise, we don't look anything alike. But I can tell now that this thing is in fact a horse. Although, the most unique looking horse I've ever seen.

Horses are busy smelling the new guy, and he's smelling them, and they're all making a heinous shrieking noise. I remain standing at a slight distance, getting a good smell of the guy from over here, and watch. My ears perk and with wide eyes, I stare.

After watching the shenanigans of the others for quite a time, something odd happens. The solid new guy with spiked hair sees me standing away from the crowd. Once our eyes meet, a jolt pushes through my belly and pauses my heart for a beat.

The new guy nickers and grunts, almost sounding like a mix between a cow, llama, and horse – odd – and keeps his eyes locked on mine. I nicker once, then decide this occasion calls for a song instead. So, I lift my head high and sing a song, to welcome him to our home.

My singing always charms the heck out of everyone, and now is no exception. The new guy moves away from the cluster of other horses and walks toward me. Some try to follow, but I pin my ears back and show them my teeth. Thankfully, this tactic works, and they back off.

Now that the new dude is close, I get a better smell and look at him. We sniff one another's necks and squeal, then do the same thing again. Then, to my surprise, he licks my neck and starts grooming me. So strange – although this guy looks like the toughest, meanest horse around, he instead seems like a big softy. Not wanting to seem rude to the newcomer, I arch my neck around and groom him, too.

From the corner of my eye, someone approaches the new guy from behind. But the horse doesn't pay attention. Instead, he and I continue to groom one another and act like no one else is around.

"Are you making a new friend, Digger," says a sweet girl, around Kiyomi's age.

The new guy, Digger, stops grooming my neck, then grunts and nickers at the girl. Instead of walking away from me to be with her, he shifts his body close to the fence and closer to me. The young girl smiles and laughs. Mimicking Digger's movements, I do the same and lean in closer to him on the other side of the fence, too.

"Awe," says the young girl. "Look at the two of you. Seems to me you've already found your bestie, Digger."

My ears perk high, and another jolt moves through my body. Bestie – could Digger be the horse versioned one I've been looking for?

Chapter 58

After several long and excruciating days, today is finally the day they're releasing Digger into the herd. Because I've been searching for a bestie since arriving here, it's felt like the last few days with him on the other side of the fence have lasted forever.

Once Digger's halter is off and he's standing within the space to join the rest of the herd, there's commotion. I want to rush over to Digger and show him all the wonderful things that this side of the fence has to offer, but there are too many horses blocking my dang way. Most are high-herd guys, and it wouldn't be smart for a low-herd guy like me to try and move in where they are. They'd bite and kick the crap out of me.

Digger is doing well, though. Instead of trying to kick up a storm and boss the other members of our herd around, he stands still and allows them all to smell him. Some horses nip at him while a few push their dominance and bite hard. Digger squirms and squeals, but doesn't react, which is the right thing to do because after only a brief time and minor wounding, most of the other horses lose interest in him and walk away.

With merely a few low-herd horses near Digger, I make my move. I sing out loudly, so he knows I'm coming. Slowly and with my head low and in a non-threatening position, I walk toward him. He hears me; perks his ears and looks for me. Then, our eyes meet, and he moves away from the other horses and runs toward me.

It has crossed my mind that once Digger was introduced to

the rest of the herd, he might not want to be my bestie. With fifty horses, there's plenty of options around here for friendship. None of the other horses have been inclined to be my bestie, and so many humans have pushed me away. Am I good enough to be someone's choice?

My heart swells and I feel the need to sing out again. If I could cry in this moment, I would. Digger moves around all the other horses and runs straight to me before we're standing so close, not even air can move between us. He lifts his head and arches it around mine, hugging me in his own, unique way. Although this guy's neck and head are dang heavy, I stand still and absorb his closeness. I nicker and he nickers, too. For me, this seals the deal. Digger is officially my horse bestie.

I take my friends to all the best places. There's a fence post along the east side of the property with notches in the wood. It is by far the best post to get a good scratch out of. And I would know because I've scratched my backside on every dang post in this place. After careful contemplation, I decide this is the first place I should show Digger.

Excited to show Digger around his new home, but not sure if he'll follow me when I move, I decide to test our friendship and walk forward. To my surprise and delight, he remains next to me and we walk in unison.

As we walk, we pause every few steps to eat something off the ground. The weather is shifting from late summer to signs of early fall, so if we see anything green, we eat it. There'll be a short window on the green grass now, and we mustn't waste any of it. After our leisurely stroll, we arrive to the fence along the east side of the far pasture. I find my favorite scratching post, having used it at least a hundred times, and turn myself around.

Facing Digger, I back up into the wood until my butt connects with it. Then, I move side to side and scratch. I sigh heavily, feeling so much relief by scratching such a hard-to-reach area. Digger's eyes are wide as he watches me, which, to be honest, is a little awkward in this moment. Regardless, he watches me scratch and nickers and grunts.

To really test our friendship and see if Digger genuinely understands the kind of guy I am, I move away from the scratching post and pause. Digger looks from me, then to the scratching post, then to me again. I spot a small patch of green grass near my feet, so I bend down to snatch it between my teeth. Once I'm chewing the grass, I lift my head again to look at Digger. Within the few seconds it's taken me to grab the grass, he's backed himself into the fence post and is now scratching his butt, too. Yip, this guy does understand me.

Another of my favorite places is my secret patch of green grass near the back of the west side of our pasture. Although Digger and I have only briefly been besties, my instincts tell me I should share the patch with him. Once I've allowed Digger time to finish scratching his rear-end on my favorite post, I turn from him and walk in the opposite direction. Shortly after, he grunts and nickers behind me before running to align and walk with me.

Side by side, Digger and I walk past other small groupings of horses. Some try to interfere with our mission by lunging at us with open mouths, but the big dude and I manage to push them off. Alone we were easy targets, together we are one heck of a formidable duo.

The moment we arrive at my secret grass patch, I can tell Digger is impressed. He lowers his head and eats away heartily as I do the same. My eyes remain fixed on him as we graze. He can pack away a lot of food in a short amount of time. Which means I'll need to eat faster if I want the fresh greens. It's a sacrifice I'm willing to make for my bestie.

"Karma," sings Kiyomi from the tie-up area, far in the distance.

I lift my head and sing loudly so she knows I can hear her. Digger isn't responding and still eats. This is a dilemma. I have my new bestie next to me, but my girl who I love more than anything in the world calling me.

"Karma, come here," sings Kiyomi again.

I sing back, look at Digger, then decide I'll need to leave him and hope I can find him again when I'm finished being with my girl. My feet take off in the direction of Kiyomi's voice as she calls me again. Then, thunderous hooves move in behind me. Arching my neck as I run, I look back and find Digger is hot on my heels, following close.

Picking up my pace, I run full speed toward Kiyomi. To my surprise, Digger does the same. Once I'm with my girl, she places my crown on my head. My new bestie is so close, I feel like I'm sandwiched between the two of them.

"Hello, Digger," says Kiyomi, rubbing his neck and giving him a cookie.

Why in the heck is she giving him one of my dang cookies? I've already shared my secret grass patch with him, he can't have my cookies, too. There are limits to what a guy is willing to share with another, even if the other is his bestie.

"Sorry, I'm only bringing Karma in for today," says Kiyomi. "You can see him again after we're finished riding."

Kiyomi leads me away from Digger, but he remains close, like sap glued to tree bark. Once I'm led through the gate and Digger is still on the other side, he calls for me. I call back, letting him know I won't be gone forever. But he paces the fence and calls for me non-stop.

"Looks like the new guy doesn't like to be without you, hey Karma?" says Kiyomi as she ties me up to a wooden post.

I nicker then lift my head and call back while looking at Digger. His eyes are wide and his breathing quick, like he's panicking. Using one foot, he knocks the gate with the edge of his hoof, shaking the metal and producing an unpleasant sound. In fact, he's creating downright chaos at the gate. Humans nearby, including Kiyomi, approach Digger and attempt to calm his anxiety. But Digger is relentless and continues to call, grunt, and knock at the gate.

Although I understand his behavior is unacceptable, I can't help feeling smug. My chest swells with pride. It's nice to be such a wanted man.

Chapter 59

Digger thinks he's king of the poo pile. In just a few short weeks, the guy seems to have claimed the place as his domain. There's a lot of real estate options where we live, but for some reason, my bestie behaves like he's scored a castle or something. Does he know what he's standing on? It's a giant pile made from loads and loads of our herd's poo.

Sure, standing on top of the thing gives a certain viewing advantage. You can see longer distances from up there, and it is that much closer to the clouds. Also, it makes one feel a little like a giant horse, commanding and strong over the rest of the herd. But again, it's a massive pile of horse poo.

The truth is there are several horses within my herd that like to be on the poo pile. Maybe because so many others desire it makes it more appealing to a broader market. If it were up to me, I'd be staking my claim on the back corner of the large horse shelter. That's the spot that holds all the heat and doesn't get the wind. But that space is reserved for Legend, the master of our herd, so I wouldn't dare attempt claiming it.

Anyway, whenever Digger and I aren't eating or with our humans, he perches himself on top of the dang poo pile and acts like he's hit the jackpot. Because I don't know anything about his history, or the home he came from before here, perhaps the poo pile is the jackpot for him. From the stories I've heard the humans tell one another, I do believe that for most horses living here, this place is heaven on earth compared to where they left. Just like it is for me.

"Karma," sings Kiyomi from the tie-up area.

I lift my head and sing back. Then, Digger lifts his head and sings back, too. Well, singing is one way of describing it – the guy grunts and moans, producing a sound unlike anything I've heard coming from a horse before. Not that I'm judging him, though. When it comes to singing, I'm one heck of a tough act to compete with. Regardless, Digger is a dang ding-dong. His name wasn't called – mine was. Sure, we're besties; always together and sharing everything. But we can't exactly share a name.

"Karma, come here," says Kiyomi.

I sing back and move toward her. Digger rushes off the poo pile, bringing a scented essence from the place with him, and follows me.

"You can come, too, Digger," says Kiyomi's mom, appearing from near my girl.

I'm fine with Mom taking Digger and not Kiyomi, she's something I'm not willing to share with him. My bestie rushes to keep pace next to me, pushing his robust body in close. He's always keen to be as near to me as possible. Perhaps in his old home he lonely and longs for the connection he and I share. Or it could be that he's using me as a shield; I rarely see him defend himself against the other horses in our herd.

It'll be nice for Digger to have Kiyomi's mom spending time with him. That woman is constantly hugging the horses, and since Digger is constantly hugging me, they can smother each other and get their fill.

I'll allow my bestie to come in with my family as long as I still am fed the same number of treats.

Chapter 60

There's a wretched pain in my stomach. I'm not sure if I've eaten bad hay or something off the ground that's ripping through my insides. Now that it's Fall, I'll admit I've been eating things off the ground that I shouldn't because there's barely any green grass left. I just can't help myself, though. With the recent memories of summer, lazing with Kiyomi and eating grass to my heart's content, I'd love to find even a small morsel of that now. But something isn't right. My abdomen burns, aches, and has me weak and tired.

Digger must sense that I'm not well. He's pushed himself in close and keeps attempting to lick my stomach. But I can't even tolerate that. The moment anyone or anything tries to get close to my mid-section, I only want to kick and bite. I wish this pain would go away. I'm not sure how long I can take it.

"Karma," sings a voice, not Kiyomi's, though.

Slowly, I lift my head and look toward the tie-up area. Sighing heavily, I lift my feet, one at a time, and walk toward the sound of my name.

"Karma, sweet boy," sings the voice again. It's Kiyomi's mom. I can always tell because she sounds a little like my girl, but much, much older. Kiyomi always refers to her as my grandma. Which Mom always says she loves in a high-pitched voice and fake smile.

Each step I take hurts. As I walk, a giant fart passes from my backside. Usually, that relaxes me, but not today. Even the effort of doing that has exhausted me further and cramps my stomach. With heavy eyes and more calls by Mom, I finally reach her and stand by her side.

"Karma?" she says, looking at my face. "What's wrong? You look sick."

I nicker, but it hurts, so it's brief.

Mom places my crown onto my head then, from within the palm of her hand, offers me a cookie. I refuse it and sigh heavily instead.

"Oh no," says Mom, slowly walking with me toward the tie-up area. "What's happened, sweet boy? Are you hurt? Are you sick? I hope we don't need to call a Vet."

There's a large bowl of food waiting for me when we arrive in the covered tie-up space. I smell it, but don't eat.

"Vickie," says Mom, waving her hands frantically in the air. "Come here, I think Karma is sick."

From the other side of the tie-up area, Vickie moves away from her horse and walks toward Mom and me. She looks worried, and Mom does, too. Vickie smiles as she approaches, then stands close. Her hand has a small pile of cookies within it, and she offers them to me. Again, I refuse and lower my head.

"What's going on with you, sweet boy," says Vickie. She gently lays one hand on my neck and rubs softly. "Where's Kiyomi today?"

"She's having a terrible time, Vickie," says Mom. "There's a lot going on for her at school and with friends. I really hope Karma is okay because I don't think Kiyomi can take any more hardship right now."

"Interesting," says Vickie. With one hand on my head, she slowly glides her other hand down from my neck and toward my belly.

I tolerate it for a minute before my back leg stomps into the hard ground, my tail swishes rapidly in circles and I lunge at Vickie with barred teeth.

"What is that all about?" asks Mom. "Are you okay, Vickie? Did he bite you?"

Vickie backs away and smiles at me. She doesn't become angry nor react to my behavior. So far, it doesn't seem like she's preparing to punish me for lunging at her. I hope she understands that I didn't mean to bare my teeth at her. I didn't want to scare her, or anyone. My belly hurts so badly, and all I could think to do to express that was what I just did.

"No, he didn't bite me," says Vickie. "I think I know what's going on with him, but we'll need to monitor him for a few days to test my theory."

"Should I call a Vet?" asks Mom.

"Not yet," says Vickie. "If he begins laying on the ground for longer than normal, we'll call one then and check for colic. For now, there's a few things in the feed shed that'll help ease his stomach. Give him some of that in his food and try to get him to eat something and drink water."

They keep me in a paddock near the house for several days. Thankfully, they're allowing Digger to stay and hang out with me, too. I'm sure my bestie is loving it because they keep trying to feed me a bunch of food and when I refuse, they let him eat it instead. He'll have the roundest, most coveted belly among the herd soon if he keeps eating at this rate.

For as long as I've been in this paddock, Kiyomi hasn't come out to visit me. Her mom comes each day, spends time with me, but only says that my girl is going through a rough time right now. Whatever that is meant to mean, I'm not sure.

While Mom is here, I push myself to eat something, but little. Although my stomach is feeling a bit better with each passing day, it still isn't quite right.

"Hello, Karma," says Kiyomi, walking toward my paddock from the parking lot.

My eyes grow wide, and I lift my head. There she is, she's here, she's back. A loud song blasts from deep within me, stirring the aches from my belly and releasing them at the sight of her. I run from the far end of the paddock and over to the place closest to the parking lot, hoping to be as near to her as possible.

"I'm here, Karma," says Kiyomi. Her eyes are full of tears and the moment she's close enough, her arms wrap around my neck. "I'm sorry I've been away so long."

She hugs me for quite a time before climbing over the fence and joining me in the paddock. Mom takes Digger to another area so my girl and I can be alone. Kiyomi sits on the ground next to a pile of hay, so I lower my head to be close. Then, she cries harder.

"I didn't mean to be away for so long," she says, her words muffled through the tears. "Now that I'm in grade nine, I had to go to a new school – High School. It's been so hard."

For the first time in days, my stomach relaxes, and I feel hungry. There's a large pile of hay right next to Kiyomi, but instead of eating, I stay in place and listen to my girl.

"I hate moving to new places," she says. "The new school isn't anything like my old one, and it's scary. But I suppose you'd know all about experiencing new places, huh?"

I nicker and move my head close enough to gently tap my nose against hers. This makes her smile and laugh a little. Then, I rest my nose on her small shoulder and listen as she says more.

"There are so many new kids, the building is massive, and I

feel so lost all of the time," she says. "Not only that, but many of my old friends also changed over the summer. Even some of my best friends since pre-school have made new friends and I never see them anymore."

Kiyomi cries harder and pushes her face into my forehead. Tears soak my hair, but I don't mind. If I could, I'd take all her pain away.

"My stomach has been hurting so badly lately, too," says Kiyomi, wiping her eyes and nose with the back of her denim jacket. "Each day after school, I've been laying on the couch with the worst pains. I couldn't eat and I was so grumpy. I'm sorry I stayed away so long."

She rubs my face and neck, her tears slowing as she takes several deep breaths. She tries to hum, but it's broken by the crying.

"My stomach is feeling better now, though, and I'm making new friends and getting more used to my new school."

My belly roars, but not with pain, with hunger. I can tell Kiyomi is feeling better than when she first arrived, so I lower my mouth to the hay pile and take a large bite.

"You're eating, Karma," says Kiyomi with a smile. "I'm so happy to see you eating."

I'm so happy to see a smile from my girl. I'm happy to finally feel relief in my belly, too.

Chapter 61

The sky has a steely grey hue to it. A sharp cold within the air bites at my skin where my winter coat hasn't filled in yet. There's an ache in my bones, one that tells me winter is here. Our grass in the pastures is brown, dry and tastes poorly. Where colorful leaves once danced on the branches of trees is now bare.

Wet snow is the worst. As it lands on my back, it seeps down through my hair and pushes a deep cold throughout my body. It's dang irritating. The higher herd horses are all tucked in at the back of the shelter with dry backs, while the rest of us stand outside and watch. Thankfully, I have Digger with me now. This winter should be easier with him around. Because he's so big and hairy, my bestie generates a lot of heat. So, standing close to him warms me a little.

As the sky shades to the darkness of night, wet snow continues to fall. The temperature is dropping and now, I'm shivering with cold. Time ticks on slowly as the night carries on. Just before morning arrives, the clouds part and a few remaining stars shine above me.

Still shivering, I fix my gaze onto one. I haven't made a wish since Kiyomi became my girl, and Digger my bestie. Funny, after getting those two things, I haven't had a wish in mind since. Love was all I ever wanted, and now I have so much of it.

Before the star's brilliance is stifled by the sun, I thank it. I'm grateful for my new home, my new herd, and the life I have in this place. But also, I wish I could be warm and dry and stop shivering.

The second there's light in the sky, someone approaches me from behind. Snow blankets every inch of the ground, and the human is covered completely, aside from the eyes. In their hands is a large lump of pink and blue. Shivering and moving slowly, I move toward the human, and examine them with wide eyes.

Was I wrong in thinking this was a human after all? What if, instead, it's a snow monster? Perhaps it's a breed of wild beast I haven't seen before. Although, its movement is non-threatening. Unless it's the kind of predator that stalks its prey calmly before attacking. I am much larger than whatever it is, so I'm sure I could defend myself. But what am I looking at here?

"It's me, Karma," says Kiyomi, her voice muffled under a face covering.

I sing and move closer to her. She rubs my neck before handing me a hand-full of cookies.

"I'm so sorry, sweet boy," she says, pushing her hands into my armpit to check my temperature. "You're freezing, aren't you."

I nicker and nudge my nose against her pocket, attempting to prompt her for more food. Eating always helps me to warm up.

"I didn't realize the snowstorm was going to be so bad last night," she says again, lifting the pink and blue blob toward my face. "Here, what do you think of this?"

I smell the thing, but honestly, I don't think anything of it. Whatever it is.

"Good boy," says Kiyomi. "Let's get this on you and warm you up."

Digger moves in close and watches. Kiyomi's small arms lift the lump of blue and pink onto my back and lay it out flat there. It helps me to feel warmer within moments.

"This blanket should warm you up," says Kiyomi.

Once the blanket is in place, I arch my neck to look at the thing on my back. Yip, it's warming me up, but the thing is pink. It also reminds me of the dang costume Duke made me wear when we did the parade. I looked like a complete ninny then, and I'm sure I look like one now, too. How humiliating.

I'll be mighty glad when summer arrives again. Not only so I can stop wearing this ridiculous outfit, but also to feel warm again. The best part about summer, though, is the amount of time I get to spend with Kiyomi. She isn't in school so we spend time together every day. Not only that, but there's also summer camps, so she and I get to take youngsters on small rides around the property. I could dream of summer all day long.

Digger nickers at me from behind, bringing me back to my cold and current reality. His eyes are wide, and I swear, my bestie is laughing at me. And this has me upset.

I pin my ears flat and lunge at Digger with teeth ready to bite. But he manages to move away quickly enough to avoid me.

"Whoa, Karma," says Kiyomi. "You're grumpy when you're cold. Come on, I'll bring you in and feed you – that should help warm you up."

Dressed like a nincompoop, I follow my girl. Summer can't come soon enough.

Chapter 62

Kiyomi must brush her hair more than she brushes mine nowadays. On her eyes are funny new colors, like she's rolled around in the mud and forgotten to clean herself. When she places my crown onto my head, her eyes are in line with mine, I no longer need to bend over as much for her. Her arms reach all the way around my neck and cover more of me when we hug. Her clothes must be too small because at times, I can see her bellybutton from the bottom of her shirt. I wish I could find something to cover the girl up.

While her legs seem longer and stronger, mine seem to move slightly slower and feel weaker. And for some reason, I'm tripping more than ever. But the best part of the year is finally here. Summer. Not only is it the best because of all the yummy greens I'll get to eat, but also because Kiyomi will spend more time with me. This year, Kiyomi says that because she's fifteen, same as me, we get to go to a special summer camp together.

There's bustling humans everywhere and high energy among the horses today. The sun hasn't been in the sky for long but, abnormally, there's already a lot of action around here. I can sense that Kiyomi is nearby, even though she hasn't called for me yet. And although it hasn't been long since I saw her last, I'm so excited to be with my girl. So, I walk up to the tie-up area and wait at the gate.

From this point, I can watch what the humans are up to. Four sets of trucks and horse trailers are poised for loading, and the humans throw bags of other stuff into the trailers, too. After watching them scurry around for a while, Kiyomi approaches the gate with a huge smile, a food bowl, and my crown in hand.

"Are you just as excited as me, Karma?" she asks, placing my bowl on the ground before approaching the gate. She's dressed in jeans, cowboy boots and a blue and red flannel shirt. Her hair is long and glistens in the sun, but she still has all that dirt around her eyes. "Let's get you fed and then we can be off to our summer camp."

Digger is still on the other side of the fence. He's acting like a dang ding-dong, pacing back and forth, and calling out to me like I'm miles away. I call back, telling him to hold his horses and hush-up, but he doesn't listen.

"I'm sorry, Digger," Kiyomi says loud enough for all to hear. "It's just going to be me and Karma this trip. He'll be back in three days. Don't worry, it'll go by fast enough."

She turns her attention back to me, rubbing my neck and back. "I hope you'll be okay without your bestie for a few days."

I lift my head and look at Digger, still carrying on. Sure, I'll miss him, but a break might be good for a short while.

Chapter 63

Each horse trailer is at capacity with members of my herd. Legend is on my right, while Major is to my left. Neither of us pays any mind to the other, eating the hay placed in our feed bags. One of them has dang smelly gas, though. And it's really killing the mood of the trip.

On top of my travel companion's flatulence, we're travelling farther than we typically would for our trail rides. Kiyomi did say we were going to a special summer camp, judging by our travel time, I'm assuming its located in an exotic land. Finally, the truck and trailer stop, and the back doors open and offer fresh air and lots of fresh foliage. This trip already promises to be amazing.

"Your turn, Karma," says Kiyomi, approaching me once Major has unloaded from the trailer.

She grabs my lead rope and walks me out of the trailer and into the place we've driven so far to. We're surrounded by grass tall enough to reach my knees, and its vibrant green. Although I'm keen to inspect my surroundings, I can't control myself and lean my neck down to grab a mouthful to nibble on.

"Grabbing some take-out, Karma?" asks Kiyomi with a smile.

We walk together through the grass and toward a row of small cabins. Surrounding each one is rows of thin wires to make temporary fencing. As a backdrop to the cabins are mountains so close, I can see individual boulders. Cascading the stone giants are colossal trees with more foliage beneath them. The sight of this place is making my tummy both giddy and hungry. It would take me a year to eat through all the wild food growing here. But I surely wouldn't mind the opportunity to try.

"We are roughing it out here, Karma," says Kiyomi. "But these are the types of places with the most beautiful scenery. I'm sharing a cabin with Regan. That means, you're sharing a small paddock with her horse, Spirit."

As we continue to walk, pops of color emerge from within the tall grass. Yellow and white daisies seem abundant here, but what really demands my attention are the specks of purple. I lean down and bite at one of the specks as we pass by. My taste buds do a happy dance with the flavor of my favorite mountain flower.

"Here we are," says Kiyomi.

She leads me into the small area of temporary fencing. It's large enough to roam a little with a small watering trough in the corner. There isn't a shelter, but I can tuck in close to the human's cabin if I need to. At least I'll only be in here at night and only for a few days. Once we're safely within the confines of the fencing, Kiyomi removes my crown and walks away.

I follow closely behind her, not wanting to be alone in this strange new place. But instead of turning back toward me, she moves out of my sightline and into the small cabin attached to my pen.

My head lifts and I sing out to her. There's a noise from the cabin that startles me. Kiyomi smiles and leans the top half of her body out through a small, open window of the cabin.

"I'm right here, Karma," she says, as I walk over to her. She reaches her hand out and strokes my neck. "I'm just unpacking. Guess what, we get to sleep next to each other all night for the next three sleeps. Isn't that amazing? We'll be so close, so there's no need to feel afraid. I'll leave the window open all day and night, so you can poke your head in at anytime you want to see me."

Kiyomi's body moves backward and disappears back into the cabin. I push my head through the open window and see she's still in there, humming and rummaging through bags on the floor. I stay in my place for a while before realizing, she isn't going anywhere and that I'm in a safe place. A breeze picks up around me, pushing the tall grass into my legs and tickling me. I forgot that I'm surrounded by fresh grass. I better get busy eating it.

The stars in this place are incredible. There's a heck of a lot of them, and I bet I could make a million wishes on all the little lights in the sky out here. But I feel like I already have everything I could ever want in this life. Perhaps if I were to make one more wish, it would be to see the faces of those who did show me love in the past. Especially, Wyatt. He taught me so much and helped me believe in myself again.

"Karma," whispers Kiyomi. "Karma, come here."

Kiyomi's head is leaning out through the cabin window. Her features are illuminated by the light of the moon and there's a sparkle in her eyes. I walk over to my girl and rest my head on the window ledge of the cabin. She places her small hand onto my forehead and lays back onto her pillow.

"This is going to be the best days of my life, Karma," she says, her eyes heavy. "I can't wait for tomorrow. We're packing lunches and riding out on the trails for five hours. I can't wait. I'm so glad you're here with me. I've never stayed away from home for this long without my parents, and I'm a little nervous."

I tuck my back leg under and stay in place. As Kiyomi drifts off to sleep, my eyes grow heavy, too. After one last look up at the stars, I relax and drift off to sleep with my girl.

I don't know how long I was out for, but I'm hungry. Kiyomi is fast asleep in her bed and the stars are still bright in the sky. I lean my head down and eat the grass at my feet. Spirit, my paddock-mate, is busy grazing on the other side of the cabin closest to Regan's window. But at the rate he's eating, he may have the dang grass all consumed by morning. I'd better catch up. I move farther and eat more, keeping this up until I find myself at the wires making my temporary fence.

Beyond the fence is a cluster of my favorite purple flowers, glistening with dew and full of temptation. If I reach my head over the fence far enough, I could reach them. The temporary fencing pinches my neck a little as I lean over it. My mouth inches close to the flowers, but not close enough. I brave the fences pinching and lean myself further and further, desperate for those purple flowers, until there's a snap. The fence gives way and now, there's an opening. With only thoughts of eating on my mind, I step through the opening and devour the cluster I was after. Once they're in my mouth, I find more ahead. Many, many more.

I walk forward, away from the cabin, and eat another cluster of the purple flowers. I move ahead further and see that they are growing in this place far beyond the limits of my sightline.

Chapter 64

Eating too much of a good thing may be problematic. It's possible I got a little carried away by my taste for the purple mountain flowers. I've eaten too many to count, and my belly is protesting a bit – swirling and twisting, like it's having trouble digesting it all.

The strong scent of water isn't far off. Along drink may ease my belly. With my head low to the ground, I use my nose as a guide to locate the water source. As I walk and the promise of a drink draws nearer and nearer, I pass an abundance of the purple flowers. It's as though they're taunting me now. Dominating the ground, growing strong, knowing I can't eat another bite. I open my mouth, and to satisfy my ego, clutch a cluster of the tasty delights and eat them. That was a dang mistake, my stomach is not happy.

Meandering over pristinely polished rocks, larger than my head and all varying colors, is a clear stream. I knew there was water close. I walk to the stream's edge and lower my head for a drink. The water is cool, refreshing and thankfully, soothing my aching belly.

Shadows form on the other side of the stream, prompted by the sun rising behind the trees. Birds from all directions sing and communicate with one another, alerting the forest to the arrival of morning. I take one more drink from the stream, then turn myself around.

I only see trees and beyond them, rocks packed together to

create the mountain I'm standing on. I clear my nose and draw in a deep breath, taking in the natural elements that create my surroundings. I'm not picking up any scent of Kiyomi, the other horses of my herd or anything else familiar whatsoever.

That means I'm alone. Wait, my herd was just behind me a second ago, weren't they? Where are they now? I run in the direction I've just came from. My heart hammers in my chest and I widen my eyes, looking all over for any sign of predators. How can I alone? I'd never leave my herd by choice, I need them. Yet there's no sign of them and am picking up no scent of them either. How the heck am I all alone?

I'm scared. Not only am I away from my herd, but I'm also away from Kiyomi, too. Although it's risky to stand in one spot with possible predators around, I pause and listen, hoping to hear her singing my name. The only sounds are the birds and a breeze in the trees. The only way I can keep myself safe in this moment is to run.

I push myself to run faster than I've ever done before. Desperation to be with Kiyomi and back in the safety of my herd drives me to keep going. My lungs burn and sweat is forming on my neck, but I don't stop. Dodging trees and losing my footing over uneven ground, I run my fastest.

Then, I find myself in a clearing. I run into the middle of it and stop. Mountains surround me, making me feel small. I clear my nose and pause again, hoping to smell or hear Kiyomi. But I don't.

Something makes a noise behind me, maybe it's a cougar or pack of wolves. Frightened, I run again. I'm not sure if I've gone right or left, north or south, but I'm running as fast as I can, away from whatever has made that noise. After quite a time, my legs ache and force me to slow down. Scaling a rocky path worn out in the side of a large hill, I slip but walk up it, hoping to look around from a higher vantage point.

Once I'm at the top of the hill, I pause and look behind me. Nothing is following me. Whatever I thought to pose a threat has either moved on or wasn't there at all. My chest is heaving and burning, desperate for a break from the running. Moving around in a circle, I search for something familiar. Nothing.

Then, something tickles at the inside of my nose. A smell, but it isn't Kiyomi. I take a step forward and the smell builds a little more than before. After taking another step, the scent intensifies. With nothing else to go on, I follow the smell. I don't know what it is, but I'm too afraid to not find out. The smell is familiar enough.

Chapter 65

The promise of finding someone or something known to me is all that's kept me going. After seeing the moon rise and sink one more time and not sleeping, I'm tempted to give up. But with each step I take, the familiar smell gets stronger and motivates me to keep going.

Although the smell isn't Kiyomi or my herd, it could be someone that can help me get back to them. There are always many humans around my home at Eagle Feather, so it's likely I could be smelling one of them. They could recognize me right away and know exactly how to get me back to my girl.

My sweet darlin, Kiyomi. I can't wait to see her face again. Every morsel of my being needs one of her hugs. I'd give anything to sit with her next to the hay bale at home, eating while she talks to me for hours. I miss her so much; it pains my heart.

Formations within a small hill ahead resemble human-made trails, like the ones Kiyomi and I have been on in the past. Maybe it's a trail she and I have ridden together before? If it is, I can follow it and end up in the parking lot where they often load us horses. If that's the case, someone there will be able to help me find my girl.

With a feeling of hope, I trot toward the trail and once I'm upon it, I follow it precisely. The scent I've been following becomes so strong now. Familiarity surrounds me from all angles. I've been here before.

The trail creeps over the small hill, hugged tightly on both sides by trees. Then, another familiar smell wafts into my nose. It's a horse smell. It isn't Digger, but it's someone I've been close to before. It must be another horse from my herd.

Flutters, like rapidly moving bird's wings, tickle my insides as I become closer to someone and something I recognize. I can't wait for this ordeal to be over. Having Kiyomi's arms around me is all I want in the entire world. Well, maybe a nice heaping bowl of the food she prepares me could be nice too. I'm a dang ding-dong for thinking of food in this moment, that's what got me into this predicament in the first place.

Now there's a smell of wood burning. Above the trees is a tightly swirling plume of smoke climbing into the sky. Smoke like that is created by a contained fire. Those fires are created by humans. There were a bunch of those fires coming from the cabins at the camp Kiyomi and I were at. Have I found my way back there? It's possible I'm not smelling Kiyomi because she's already left for home. It's possible she's no longer at the camp because she's out looking for me. But that's okay, the humans who operate the camp will know how to get me back to her.

An enormous wave of familiarity rushes through my body, making me move faster. The closer I get to the smoke plume, the more excited I become. Help is just a short trot away. I'm almost there.

There's suddenly a break in the trees and the trail ends, opening to cleared land. But the land isn't barren. It's fenced with wooden posts. Tucked within those posts are horses, maybe ten. They sense my presence and look at me.

Each of them runs and they form a small herd, moving toward me at full speed. The familiar horse scent grows stronger as they move closer to me. I want to run with them, too, but I stay in place, knowing they're like me and just want to make sure I'm not an outside threat. Then, they're faces, and features become clearer as they get closer and closer.

That's when I notice the one with the scent I've known from before. It's my old friend, Tex. I've come to the old dude ranch he and I called home so many years ago. The home I had with Ruth and Duke before they sold me at auction. This isn't where I want to be at all.

Chapter 66

After making a fuss and smelling me a million times, the small herd of horses calm and resume normal activity. Perhaps they feel more at ease with my presence because of Tex. He and I had a nice reunion. I smelled him, he smelled me. I licked his neck to say, hello. He did the same. Then, he stayed close to the other side of the fence, aligning with me, and grazed on grass, like I was no big deal.

Although this wasn't the place I expected to end up. Nor is it where I'd like to be, I'm too exhausted to try and figure out how to get from here and back to Kiyomi. Because I've been alone for so many nights, I'm exhausted, having not slept out of fear from predators.

So, instead of thinking, I decide to sleep. With the rest of the herd on the other side of the fence, I tuck my legs under and lower my body to the soft ground. Before too long, I'm lying flat and in a deep sleep.

I have no idea how long I was asleep for. My body needs more, but I can sense a threat.

"What in the heck is going on here?" says a male voice.

My eyes open half-way, but my instincts tell me to get to my feet.

"How in the world did you get here, man?" asks the voice again.

Once I'm on my feet, I turn myself around. Then, as I inhale deeply through my nose, I pick up another scent, aside from Tex, that I've been tracking for the last couple of days. A scent that brought me back here to this ranch.

"I can't believe it," says the male. "Is that really you, Ranger?"

Ranger. A name I haven't heard in years. One I never thought I'd be hearing again in my life. The male lowers to look at my old injury, then stands to look into my eyes again.

"Yip, it is you. How in the heck did you end up here?"

I nicker and take another smell of the human. Then, once I feel less threated by him, I take a good look. This male human is tall with wide shoulders and strong arms. He's wearing blue-jeans and a red plaid shirt with rolled up sleeves. His jawline is sharp and covered in small, prickly hairs. Across his nose are freckles, mimicking stars in the sky, but fewer than what Kiyomi has. Under a baseball cap is wisps of brown hair with flecks of red. There's something about his eyes. Where have I seen these eyes before?

"Ranger," he says. "I can't believe it. How crazy is it that you are here, and all alone?"

He rubs my neck, and it feels nice. Then, he examines my body, walking around from one side of me to the next.

"You don't look hurt or anything. I still don't understand where you came from."

He looks around the place, like a human is going to pop out of the trees and claim me.

"Let's get you into a paddock with some hay and figure out what to do with you," he says.

He doesn't have a halter or lead rope for me, but once he begins walking, I follow next to him. As we walk, he stretches his hand out toward me from time to time and strokes my neck. He shakes his head and stares at me, still in disbelief.

"I can't believe it. I never thought I'd see you again. You really are a rarity."

That word. Only one human has ever called me that. I've figured out who this young man is. It's my old friend. The only other human who has loved me as much as Kiyomi. Somehow, I've found Wyatt.

Chapter 67

Wyatt is a man now. Well, not old in the way Duke was, but he's not the scrawny kid I once knew. He puts me in the same paddock I'd spent so much time in all those years ago. From what I can see, the place, this ranch, hasn't changed much. Except, I smell new horses and more importantly, new mares.

I get excited by this realization. When I first arrived, I must have been too exhausted to notice the herd had newbies. Maybe my wish of knowing the love of a good woman will finally come true. That means I'll need to step up my game because by the look of things, there are several new strapping young men in the herd that'll be competition for me.

Ladies are usually impressed by a well-fed horse – I've been working on that for years and have a robust belly and rump to show for it. Mares like a strong presence for protection – I may need to work out a little and improve on that. From what I can see, I'm the only palomino around – there are some chicks who really dig blondes, and I got a full body of that going for me. I've heard Kiyomi discussing boys with her friend Regan before; they always refer to some as 'hotties' and some as 'notties'. I'd say, I'm one dang magnificent hottie.

Hopefully, I can maintain my full and well-fed body. When I lived in this paddock before, I was fed meager portions of food. But when Wyatt walks over from the hay shed and toward me, he has a wheel-barrel heaving with hay. He stops at my gate before coming through and laying all the hay at my feet. There's so much of it. I'd better quickly eat as much as I can before Ruth or Duke come out of the house and try to take it away, or Wyatt gets in trouble.

"Eat up, my friend," says Wyatt, stroking my neck. "There's plenty more where that came from. Things are different around here. No more feeding the horses based on how useful we humans deem them to be."

With a mouthful of hay, I glance at the main house, then to Wyatt again.

"Don't worry, Ranger," he says. "If you're afraid that Ruth and Duke might come out, they won't. Those two lunatics are long gone. They got what they deserved. Karma finally caught up to them and bit them both in the ass."

I lift my head with wide eyes. He's just said my name. The one my girl calls me. I sing aloud and nicker.

"You happy to hear karma bit those two in the butt?" asks Wyatt, chuckling and smiling.

I sing again, louder this time. Moving away from the hay, I do a small trotting circle within my paddock. I love hearing my new name, Karma. Maybe if I show him how excited I am about that word, he'll figure out that someone I love dearly calls me that, and that we should find her.

"You're a funny guy, Ranger."

Dang it, maybe not.

"Yip, when Duke took off to Arizona, he cleaned out auntie Ruth's bank accounts until she had nothing left. So, she sold some of her horses for quick cash before storming down to find Duke and try and take back some of what he took. When she got down there, though, she decided to stay with him and sell this place. Thankfully, my parents didn't want to see this ranch sold to strangers and bought it. I'm glad we were able to buy some of the horses back. As you might have noticed, we were able to buy back your buddy, Tex. I was quite upset when I learned that Duke had sold you at an auction. He had no right."

I nicker, then get back to eating my hay. While working on chewing a large bite, I admire Wyatt and the herd. They're all grazing peacefully together on lush grass. Each of the horses looks happy and well fed, like me. This herd appears nothing like the ragged, skinny, and tired crew I left so many years ago.

My eyes widen as I catch a glimpse of a blood-bay mare. Her coat glistens in the sun and long raven tresses whips down creating her gorgeous mane. She must notice me staring as she pauses to examine me before turning herself around and only showing me her rump. Which is mighty fine, too, if I do say so myself. A lass like that surely has a gentleman suitor already – but maybe there's a chance for me.

Wyatt continues to ramble on about the ranch and although I'm keen to catch up with my old friend, all I can seem to do is stare at that mare. What is it about being in the presence of ladies that makes me behave like such a ding-dong?

"So, anyway," says Wyatt, leaning on the fence. "Since my parents bought this place, we've been doing all that we can to return it to its once former glory. But my parents are both busy in their careers, so I'm basically in charge of everything around here now. I'm only nineteen, but I'm not interested in going to college or pursuing a career other than working with horses."

I push my mouth back into the hay pile and devour another bite, then another. It sure is nice to be somewhere familiar after being lost in the woods like I was. Wyatt is one of the kindest humans I've ever met, and right now, he's feeding me like a king.

And although I'm awfully grateful to Wyatt for taking me in like he has, there's still a pain in my heart. I keep thinking about how my bestie Digger is doing without me. Now that I'm stuck behind a fence, there's no way for me to get away and try to find Kiyomi and my old home at Eagle Feather. Living my life here with Wyatt would be fine, but it wouldn't be the same. Nothing compares to the bond I have with my girl, Kiyomi. Will I ever see her again?

Chapter 68

There are plenty of stars around here. I've been wishing on as many as I can each night, and always asking for the same thing. Please let Kiyomi find me.

In the past, I've always wished for love from a human. Those wishes never came with the attachment of wanting love from a specific person. I'd only envision the love from a certain soul in the world, not knowing what the human would look like. Now, I only wish for Kiyomi.

I do feel a little guilty thinking only of her. Wyatt has been the kind of loving soul I would have wished for in the past. Heck, he's even better than I could have wished for in the past. That is before I met my girl.

As the sun creeps up beyond the ridge to the east, I wish I knew where Kiyomi was now. What is she doing? What is she thinking? What does she suppose happened to me? My heart aches for all the hurt she must be going through now. Why was I so careless at that camp? Only thinking of my stomach and those dang purple flowers. I'll never eat one of those things again in my entire life. They're nothing but trouble.

"Good morning, Ranger," says Wyatt, approaching my paddock from the barn. He has a bowl of food in his hands, and I nicker to show my appreciation.

I eat once the food is at my feet, then Wyatt walks away, leaving me to dine alone. After Wyatt has fed the other horses, he comes toward me again from the barn. This time, instead of carrying something I'm excited about seeing, he's got a dang saddle with him.

His smile is wide and awfully proud, but my insides flop over onto themselves and I'm not smiling – not even on the inside.

"Thought we'd head out for a ride today, Ranger," he says, resting the saddle on the dry ground next to my paddock.

I nicker, but not with appreciation. I'm hoping I can somehow convince him that using a saddle isn't really my thing. Riding naked without constrictions from straps and bridles is far more appealing to me. Has Wyatt ever ridden naked before?

"It's been so long since I've ridden you, and I'd like to see how well you'll do around here. Never know what kind of habits horses will pick up when they're in new homes."

Wyatt climbs the fence, landing in the dirt with a thud, forcing dust to plume up into the air. First, he grabs a crown and shows it to me. It's not nearly as nice as my green and black beaded one that Kiyomi has for me. This one is brown like the dirt and has no beading at all. Not at all fit for the king I'm accustomed to feeling like.

Nevertheless, I allow him to crown me and stand quietly. After he ties my lead rope to a post, he grabs the saddle and shows it to me. My back aches at the sight of it. I'm not the young chap I was when he and I first saddled up and rode off on the trails. Sure, I could still tolerate a saddle if necessary, but I don't especially want to.

Wyatt lifts the saddle onto my back, and a charge ignites within me. The feeling of the soft leather on my body feels so foreign to me now, and I don't like. I shuffle my body around a little at first, attempting to shake the thing off and onto the ground. But it doesn't budge. Instead, it stays in its place and only irritates me further.

"Easy, Ranger," says Wyatt, looking at me with wide eyes. "It's only a saddle, my friend."

Wyatt moves closer to me and grabs one of the belly straps in his hand. I know what's coming next. He'll pull on it to tighten the saddle onto my back. I don't like it. I whip my head back and, thankfully, Wyatt has tied my lead rope into a slipknot, so with one forceful tug, I'm free from the fence post.

"Ranger, what in the heck are you doing?"

I run away from him as he calls and buck my back legs until, finally, the saddle is off my back and laying on the ground. My chest heaves with labored breaths, both from exertion and anxiety. I'm not sure what has come over me, but for some reason, I do not want that dang thing on my back.

"Dude, what are you getting so riled up about? Haven't you been ridden since leaving here? That seems mighty odd to me."

Wyatt looks at me with concern. He's not mad nor does he appear ready to punish me for the stunt I just pulled. I should be happy to see him this way, but I feel guilty. He's being so nice to me and I just acted like a dang ding-dong.

Chapter 69

Each winter feels harsher than the last, so I'm thrilled that Spring has finally arrived. Since wandering onto Wyatt's ranch, I've watched the season come and go three times. I wouldn't say I'm an old man, but the cold can make me feel that way sometimes.

I often wonder, though, if the pain in my body is from the season at all. These aches only started once I came here and lost Kiyomi. Every single night, I wish on as many stars as I can, hoping to find my girl again. Someday, I hope.

Most nights, when the air seems to bite at my body, I cuddle in close to Tex. He's no Digger, but my bestie within this herd, nonetheless. I sure do love him, and Wyatt. Trouble is, there are parts of my life here that I love very much. But there are parts of my life from Eagle Feather that I miss so dang badly. I don't want to leave Wyatt or Tex. But I still want Kiyomi and Digger back in my life, too.

What the heck is a guy to do? I'm stuck behind this fence, and I have no way of telling Kiyomi where I am. I sing out loudly, as often as I can, hoping she'll hear me from wherever she may be. But I assume she doesn't because she still hasn't shown up.

Nevertheless, there is positivity in each day if I'm willing to see it. I'm fed until I feel full. I have a herd and companionship of my new bestie; Tex. Wyatt is always kind to me and the other horses. We have a large shelter to keep us dry and warm. Nope, not a dang thing I should be complaining about.

"Ranger," shouts Wyatt from the barn.

Although I preferred when my name was Karma, I respond by calling back to him and walking in Wyatt's direction. As I walk, Wyatt isn't alone. Another human stands next to him; one I've never seen around here before, but somehow, I believe I've met them in another place and time. They both watch me cautiously and talk amongst themselves. I can tell they're talking about me by the way they point and stare.

Who is this human? I don't expect it's a client as it isn't the weekend. Is Wyatt thinking about selling me to someone else? Since arriving, I haven't allowed a saddle on my back, or a rider. I will allow him to ride me if he'd just leave the dang saddle out of the equation, but he hasn't.

"His gait is off," says the other human. "Must be from that old injury you were telling me about. And when he walks, his right foot turns inward slightly, like a pigeon toe."

The other human is a woman. She's much older than Wyatt, but also much smaller than him. She has dark hair with grey swimming through it, and it's pulled back. Her glasses are large and sit low on her nose. I flare my nostrils to examine her scent – it's one I've smelled before, I'm sure.

"Would his gait being off make him sore enough to not allow a saddle?" asks Wyatt.

"It shouldn't," says the woman. "I'll get a better idea after I examine him."

"Hey, Ranger," says Wyatt with a weak smile once I'm at the gate.

He opens it and quickly places my crown onto my head before leading me and the woman into the warmth of the barn. There's a nice bowl of food waiting for me, so I eat it up as the humans look me over.

"Will this set up do all right, Lori?" asks Wyatt, moving to the side and making way for the woman.

"This will do just fine," she says. "Hello, Ranger."

Lori smiles at me and looks into my eyes. I study hers, too; they're a deep brown, but have a light within them that I like. There's such a familiarity about them, too.

"Have I worked on this horse before?" she asks.

"Possibly," says Wyatt. "My aunt and uncle may have had you out before?"

"No," says Lori. "That's not it. I've never met your aunt or uncle. So odd, I feel like I've worked on this horse before, but in another place."

"Well...," says Wyatt, just as his phone begins to ring. He pulls it from his jeans pocket and looks at the screen. "I'm sorry, but I need to take this call."

"Go ahead," says Lori. She places her hands on my neck, pauses, then gently glides them down. Then, she moves her hands to the top of my back and glides them across my spine. She's giving me a great rubbing down; it's so relaxing.

"What technique are you using?" asks Wyatt, walking back into the barn and putting his phone away.

"For now, I'm just massaging and palpating him," says Lori. "I'm trying to find any obvious injury or misalignment before I go deeper."

"You know," says Wyatt. "I'm studying all kinds of therapies for horses. I hope to make this place a rehabilitation facility someday. Along with the dude ranch."

"That's wonderful," says Lori. "I could give you some great information, if you'd like?"

"Sure," says Wyatt.

Lori moves her hands down my legs and up again. Nothing she's doing makes me jump or uncomfortable, so I stand still and let her continue.

"How long has it been since you've ridden him?" asks Lori.

"Well, I've been trying for three years now," says Wyatt.

"Interesting," says Lori, pulling her hands away from my body and looking at Wyatt. "I don't know what to tell you."

"You didn't find anything wrong?"

"No, physiologically, this horse is sound and should be able to ride just fine."

"I wonder what he's doing then."

"Has anything major changed for him? Did a horse he was close with leave the ranch? Was there another human handling him before who has now left? Anything major happen?"

"Well, not in the last three years, but before that, maybe."

"I think this horse is depressed. It seems to me he has lost his zest for life and riding."

"That's so sad. I certainly don't want that for him, he's such a rarity of a horse; kind and loving. Is there anything I can do?"

"Figure out what's made him depressed and find a way to fix it for him."

"All right, I'll do my best."

"It's so odd, why can't I get over the feeling that I've seen this horse before?" says Lori before she and Wyatt walk away.

Chapter 70

Since Lori left, Wyatt hasn't said much to me. In fact, each time he feeds or grooms me, there's a long and sullen look on his face. I can tell he's disappointed by our relationship. I don't want to let him down, but I can't help feeling the way I do. Even still, after all this time has passed, I miss Kiyomi.

Wyatt works near the barn as the afternoon sun beats down on his back. Leaves appear to pop on dainty branches, perhaps with anticipation of basking in the glow. Mixed grasses of green and brown adorn the ground, offering us horses a sweet treat. Birds serenade us as they return home to our ranch following their winter retreats.

All else is quiet, until the sound of an engine comes from down the driveway. The other horses and I lift our heads and perk our ears to listen to whatever is approaching our home. Wyatt must hear it, too, as he stops working and focuses on the engine sound getting louder.

My heart rattles within my chest. I don't know why, I'm not afraid of the things with engines that make this sound. But as the vehicle encroaches nearer to our ranch, my heart hammers harder against my ribs. My stomach flops a little, too, which is odd because it was fine only a second before.

A small blue car emerges on the driveway and for some reason, the sight of it makes me want to sing. I can't explain why, exactly; I don't think I've ever seen this car before. Instead of the car driving the length of the driveway, it stops, but not in front of the house like most vehicles coming here would. In fact, the driver of the car slams on the brakes in front of our pasture, opens the door and runs around to the fence.

A thin human with long, golden hair climbs over the fence and moves into our pasture. This is highly unusual because strangers don't typically do this sort of thing. Wyatt notices it, too, and runs toward the car and human with a worried look on his face.

We all watch the thin human closely, waiting to see what will happen next.

"Hey," shouts Wyatt, running quickly toward the human. "What do you think you're doing? Get away from my horses!"

My gaze moves from Wyatt, then back to the other human. My heart is pounding so hard, it hurts.

"Karma," sings the thin human from near the fence.

Holy heck. My eyes grow wide, and an intense pressure swells my chest. I take a quick breath and lift my head before singing loudly to the point of it burning my throat.

"Karma," sings the human again, her words sputtering from her mouth like she's choking on them. "Karma, come here."

A surge of energy pushes throughout my body, and I run. I haven't moved this fast in three years, and I worry if I don't move faster, I might not make it to her in time.

"Hey," shouts Wyatt again, getting closer to the thin human girl. "Get out of there."

Instead of listening, the thin girl runs away from Wyatt, and toward me. I run so fast, my feet thunder against the ground. After pushing myself beyond my limits, I'm finally standing in front of the girl.

Her eyes are a vibrant green, mostly because she's crying. I search her face and examine the freckles blanketing her nose;

they mimic shapes made by the stars in the sky. Her long, strawberry blonde hair moves in the wind and hangs low down her back. It's her. Then, she hums a tune I haven't heard in years, but one that instantly fills my heart with love. It's my girl, older than before, but it's her. Kiyomi has found me.

Chapter 71

Kiyomi's arms wrap tightly around my neck. Her tears soak my hair, and her heart is thumping hard within her chest. Wyatt has caught up to us and instead of reacting, he simply stares. He looks both concerned and bewildered; unsure of how to handle this intruder on our ranch.

"Hello?" Wyatt finally says.

Kiyomi ignores him. She embraces me tighter, fighting to catch her breath between sobs. My insides are alight with many sensations – immense love, gratitude, relief, but also guilt. I've been wishing for Kiyomi to find me again every day since arriving here. But Wyatt loves me, too, and I don't want to disappoint him. How can I be so lucky to have two humans who both love me so much? More importantly, how could I possibly choose only one?

"You stole my horse," says Kiyomi. Her teeth are clenched, and she looks at Wyatt with anger in her eyes.

"Whoa, whoa, whoa," says Wyatt, waving his arms at Kiyomi. "I did not steal Ranger."

Kiyomi moves to stand in front of me, like she's protecting me from Wyatt. I'll have to figure out a way to let her know that he's a good guy. There's a look of confusion on Wyatt's face, but something else, too. He seems dumbfounded somehow. Sure, it could just be because of Kiyomi's accusations, but I can't help feeling it's something more.

"His name isn't Ranger, it's Karma," she says.

I lift my head and sing for them when she says my name. There's something harmonious about the way she annunciates my name. It's unique only to her, and it grips me from within and holds tight.

"See, his name is Karma," she says, looking at me and smiling.

I nicker for Kiyomi. Then, I do the same for Wyatt. I'm not going to lie, it feels dang good to have humans fighting over me, to be such a wanted man.

"Listen, I don't know who you are or how you ended up here," says Wyatt, removing his ballcap and stepping closer to Kiyomi. "But you're on private property, and quite frankly, you're behaving like a lunatic."

"You think this is lunacy?" asks Kiyomi. "This is only a shred of the lunacy I've felt over the last three years. I've been searching for Karma – my horse. I've placed missing posts on all outlets of social media, in every Vet office from here to kingdom come. Surely, if you're truly a horse person, you would have come across something. You must have known I was looking for him. Unless you didn't want me to find him because you stole him."

"Look around, this is a dude ranch. We're in the middle of nowhere. We have limited access to the internet. Besides, I'm not the kind of guy to spend time on social media, and the Vet always comes to us."

Kiyomi takes a deep breath, like she's trying to regain her composure. I stand still, probably looking like a dang ding-dong without a clue.

"Can we just take a quick pause here?" asks Wyatt, holding his hands up in the air like he's calling a truce.

"No way," says Kiyomi, with a fury I've never seen in her

before.

She turns her back to Wyatt and looks into my eyes. One of her hands grips tightly onto my mane, while the other holds my withers. She takes a deep breath, then gracefully hoists herself up onto my naked back with one swift motion.

"What in the heck are you doing?" shouts Wyatt with wide eyes. "You'll kill yourself up there."

I stay still for Kiyomi as she sits on my back. A charge exchanges between us, a jolt of energy, uniting us to become one.

"Ranger hasn't allowed a rider onto his back in three years," says Wyatt. "He'll buck you off."

Kiyomi looks at Wyatt and flashes a quick smile before squeezing her legs gently around my belly. I move ahead, still hesitant of the situation, but I can feel Kiyomi prompting me to move forward, and she'd like it to be faster than a walk.

I trot at first and she finds her seat. Then, before too long, we're galloping through the pasture.

"Where are you going?" shouts Wyatt from behind us. "What in the world is happening? What about your car?"

Kiyomi and I ignore him and just ride.

Chapter 72

I'm sorely out of shape. It's been far too long since I've had the kind of exercise needed to keep up a gallop with Kiyomi. My chest is heaving, and sweat is forming on my back. I really need to get more workouts in.

Once we reach the fence line and find the gate, Kiyomi slides off my back. She rushes to unlatch the gate and swings it open. Then, she grips my mane again to climb back onto my back. But something inside me resists letting her on. Shuffling my feet, I move my backside away from her body, making it more difficult for her to climb up.

It isn't her. I want to be with her. But as we approach the open range beyond this ranch, the one I spent too much time lost in, I freeze. If Kiyomi and I run off together into the wilderness, we could find ourselves in trouble.

"Come on, Karma," she says with a smile. "Let's get out of here. I'm going to take you home now."

I nicker and shift my back end to the side, not giving her a clear way onto my back. We do this little dance together long enough for Wyatt to ride up on his quad.

"Are you trying to let all of my horses go?" shouts Wyatt, rushing to close the gate Kiyomi just opened. I've never seen Wyatt with so much heat in his voice or body. He's never shown me an angry side of himself. In this moment, he's dang mad.

"I'm calling the police."

"Good," says Kiyomi, placing one hand on her hip while

resting the other on me. "I'm calling the police, too. You stole my horse."

"I didn't steal your horse," says Wyatt. "He wandered onto this ranch three years ago, alone and hungry. Horses never go off on their own unless things are really bad. Even then, they'll endure a lot of pain and suffering before they'd ever take off from a home. If he was your horse, you must have neglected him something awful."

Kiyomi pushes her body into mine and starts sobbing again. Her arms wrap around my neck and pain radiates from her to me.

"I love this horse more than I love myself," she says. "I don't know why he wandered off and left me."

I nicker and arch my neck around, hugging my girl back. Then, I look at Wyatt with softness, hoping to communicate with him. She never treated me badly. My home was incredible at Eagle Feather, and I always had things better than good. I was the dang ding-dong in the situation, wandering off alone and creating this mess. Thankfully, it seems like he has heard me somehow. His body relaxes and eyes soften as he watches Kiyomi clutch to me with desperation.

"He obviously knows you well," says Wyatt with a calmer voice than before. "And he obviously loves you, too. Can we start over? Let's make coffee and sit down and talk about this?"

Kiyomi turns and looks at Wyatt. I can feel she's settled down a little.

"I'm not leaving him for another second," she says. "I can't let him leave my sight ever again."

"Okay," says Wyatt. "You two stay here. I'll go back to the house and bring us coffee to drink out here."

"Fine," says Kiyomi.

"You're not going to open that gate again?" asks Wyatt. "Can

I trust you?"

Kiyomi sighs heavily. "I won't open the gate again."

Wyatt nods his head and smiles before leaving us.

Kiyomi holds her cup of coffee but doesn't drink it. Instead, she watches Wyatt closely.

"I can't believe he let you ride him bareback like that," says Wyatt, smirking and sitting in the grass near Kiyomi and me. "I've been trying to saddle him for years."

"We always ride bareback," says Kiyomi. "I think it's easier on him. You know how his back sways deeper than it should, and with his old leg injury, riding without a saddle helps him move more freely."

I can tell there's still tension between the two of them. I step between them and lower my head to eat grass. I'm close to Wyatt on one side, so he reaches his hand over and rubs my forehead. I allow it and notice Kiyomi, still standing as if on guard, watching us.

"How did you know to come up here?" asks Wyatt.

"Lori," says Kiyomi. "She worked with Karma and me years ago and knew that I was searching for him. I ran into her at a horsemanship clinic, and she said she thought she'd seen Karma here. I left immediately and came straight here."

"Right, Lori," says Wyatt. "She was here last week. Funny, she did keep saying she thought she'd worked on Ranger before. But we didn't exactly get too far into it."

"Karma," says Kiyomi. "His name is, Karma."

"Fine," says Wyatt, his eyebrows raising.

"He seems to like you," says Kiyomi. "He looks well."

"Oh, yeah," says Wyatt. "This guy and I actually go way back."

Wyatt explains how I lived here before being sold to Vickie at auction. As they chat, I graze on the grass between them. With me so relaxed, Kiyomi seems more relaxed, too. She even sits down in the grass across from Wyatt and takes a sip from her coffee cup. As they sit, I move my eyes back and forth to watch them. Funny, from this position, my gaze keeps returning to the freckles on their faces. It's odd but, somehow, they appear to have a similar cluster on their noses, almost mirror image.

"I promise," says Wyatt with sincerity, "I didn't steal your horse. Heck, I was extremely shocked he ended up here. The only reason I didn't try and find out where he came from was because I worried that he wasn't in a good home and that was why he came back here."

Kiyomi looks from Wyatt to me, then down at her hands.

"What happened, anyway? How'd you lose him?" asks Wyatt.

Tears stream from Kiyomi's eyes as she reaches her hand out to touch me. "We were at summer camp together. Somehow, he broke through the temporary fencing during the night while I was asleep. We searched all over for him."

"I'm sorry, that must have been the worst feeling in the world. If I had known you were looking for him, I would have contacted you, honest. I just happen to love this guy, and I didn't want to let him go. You know? I am sorry."

I nicker and look at Kiyomi, hoping she understands that Wyatt is telling the truth. Her eyes lock with mine and she pauses for quite a time, like she's searching her heart for the truth.

"I believe you," says Kiyomi.

"Good," says Wyatt. "What's next in all of this?"

"I can't leave him," says Kiyomi.

"Well," says Wyatt. "I can't just let you take him just because you say he's yours. No offence, but you were acting kinda crazy when you first got here. Besides, it's not as if you can load him up into your small car and take him home anyway."

Kiyomi smiles and it eases me to see her and Wyatt at peace.

"I can't leave him," she repeats, this time, her eyes well up with tears.

"Fine," says Wyatt. "Take one of the guest cabins, and we can take some time to figure this all out."

I nicker and nuzzle into Wyatt, then back over to Kiyomi. She nods and looks back at Wyatt.

"I'm warning you," she says. "Don't you dare try and mess with me. I may be small and scrawny, but don't be fooled. I'm tough and could kick your ass if you try messing with me in any way."

Wyatt smiles and nods. "Understood. I promise, my intentions are good."

Chapter 73

Kiyomi disappears into the small cabin Wyatt has offered her. I feel a little anxious, not wanting to lose sight of her so soon. But instead of staying inside, she walks back out through the door with her arms full of heavy quilts and pillows. She carries them across the property before laying them on the grass next to the fence opposite me. Although I could roam off into the pasture and graze with my herd, I stay in position next to my girl.

She tucks herself into the makeshift blanket bed until only her head is visible. The sun nestles down beyond the mountains to the west, making way for the moon's next shift. The night air is warm, so Kiyomi shouldn't get cold laying on the ground.

"I can't believe I found you, sweet boy," she says. "I've been searching for you. Not a day has gone by that I didn't miss you and wish to find you."

I nicker, then lower my head to bite at the grass near my feet.

"You seem like you've been well taken care of here," she says.

I have been well taken care of here. Wyatt is a good man, and if I had to choose between the two of you, it would break my heart.

"Remember the first time you and I rode together? It was on the moonlit ride, and I made a wish for you to be my horse forever."

I remember. I made the same wish.

"I love you so much, Karma."

I love her so much, too. Kiyomi's eyes close and her breathing softens. I'll stay here and watch over my girl through the night and make sure she's safe.

"Good morning, boy," whispers Wyatt, laying a bowl of food at my feet.

I lean down and eat it. Wyatt stays in place and looks over at Kiyomi, still sleeping on the ground next to the fence.

"She slept here all night, hey?" asks Wyatt. "She sure is a spitfire; crazy even. But also, beautiful. Anyway, never mind."

I nicker, then eat more of my bowl of food.

"What'll we do, boy?" asks Wyatt, rubbing my back as I eat. "I can tell this girl loves you more than anything. The thing is, I love you, too."

I love you, too, Wyatt. I nicker again, then sing out. This stirs Kiyomi and she opens her eyes.

"Karma?" she asks, sleepily and disoriented. "Karma?"

Her eyes open fully as she pulls the blankets off from her body and stands. She looks at Wyatt, then to me and stares.

"So, I didn't dream it?" she says, walking over to me. "I was afraid I had dreamt it all. I was afraid that Karma was still lost to me."

"You're not dreaming," says Wyatt. "He and I are very real."

Kiyomi strokes my neck and leans in close.

"How'd you sleep out here?" asks Wyatt.

"Fine, actually," says Kiyomi, giving him a sideway glance.

I finish eating my bowl and lift my head before resting it on the fence between them both. Each of them rubs my neck. Yip, I could get used to this. A silence lingers between them. Not only that, but the mood also feels awkward and indifferent. I sigh loudly, waiting to see what will happen next. Finally, Wyatt makes a move.

"So, where do we go from here?" asks Wyatt.

"I can't leave him," says Kiyomi.

"How old are you?" asks Wyatt. "Are you legally allowed to be away from home?"

"I'm eighteen," says Kiyomi, rolling her eyes at Wyatt. "How old are you? You barely have facial hair."

"I'm twenty-two."

"And you, what, own this place? Or are you the ranch hand?"

"My parents own it, and I manage it."

"I'll need to figure out where I'll be boarding Karma, and how to get him there," says Kiyomi. "I'm starting college in the fall, so I'll want him to live closer to me there."

"So, you're planning to just take him away from me? After him being here for three years. I'm not sure I want you to do that."

"He's my horse!"

"Prove it!"

Wyatt's teeth clench and his cheeks are red. I can tell he's worked up, which isn't something I've seen too often. Kiyomi, always one to wear her emotions on her sleeve, has tears in her eyes. Her forehead scrunches tightly, like it hurts her to think.

"I'm sorry," says Wyatt. "I didn't mean to make you upset. It's just, I can tell you really love this guy. But I need you to understand that I do, too."

Kiyomi nods her head and uses her sleeve to wipe the tears from her eyes. Then, she looks over at Wyatt and stares for a moment, like she's searching his eyes for answers.

"I don't want to take him away from you," she says. "I can tell he loves you and that you've been good to him. But I can't leave him again. I never want to let him out of my sight. I'll sleep here on the ground next to him each night if I must."

"Let's take a little time to figure this all out. Why don't you stay, if you can, in that guest cabin? But if you do stay, you'll need to help me with chores."

"Sounds fair," says Kiyomi. "What do you need me to do?"

"Catch the other horses and bring them in. Then, they'll need to be fed. There's a board in the barn with a picture next to a card listing what each horse is fed each day."

"I can handle that."

"All right. I must do some maintenance on a few of the guest cabins."

"Fine. I'll feed the horses."

"Fine."

Watching these two interact is entertaining. They're behaving like ding-dongs. I can tell each of them wants to dislike the other but can't for unknown reasons. They're reminding me of horses a little. Get close for the sake of a common good, but don't get too close to my territory or what's mine. I just hope they don't start biting each other. Especially on the rear-end, that'd get weird. Although, things between them are already weird enough.

Chapter 74

After a full morning of chores, Wyatt offered to make he and Kiyomi something to eat.

"I'm not going inside your house," Kiyomi says.

"Why?" Wyatt says.

"Because I'm still not sure if you're an axe murderer or lunatic," she says.

"I see," he says, grinning with amusement.

"I'll eat, but I want to be outside, near Karma."

"Fine. I'll bring sandwiches out."

Wyatt walks off toward the house, leaving Kiyomi and me alone. She climbs the fence so she and I can be close and at eye level.

"What should I do next, Karma?" she asks. "Nicker if Wyatt is a good person."

I nicker, immediately, and even nod my head a little to help get my opinion across.

"Okay," she says, smiling. "Oh, look what I found in my car..."

Kiyomi reaches into her jeans pocket and retrieves a small object. Her fingers stay clutched around it as she reaches her hand out and toward my face. My nostrils flare and I pick up a familiar scent that has me feeling giddy. I nicker as Kiyomi opens her hand and reveals a horse treat within it. My lips grab it quickly before I chew, allowing the nostalgic flavors to roll over my tongue. Once that's gone, I nudge at my girl for more.

She giggles, then rubs between my ears. "You've always loved your treats, Karma. I've missed you so much."

Her head moves until each of our foreheads are touching. We stay this way for a while, like our minds are exchanging information. I've missed this darlin so much, too.

"I hope you like salami," says Wyatt, interrupting as he approaches Kiyomi and me with sandwiches in his hands.

"My favorite, actually," says Kiyomi.

She jumps down from the fence and stands next to Wyatt. Then, she takes a sandwich from him and bites into it aggressively.

"I suppose it's time we talk about what to do next," says Wyatt. "I understand you and Karma are bonded. I hope you can understand that he and I are bonded, too."

Kiyomi sighs as she chews. She looks at me, then to the sky, like she's searching.

"What is it you do on this ranch, again?" she asks.

"Well, it's a dude ranch on weekends – mostly in summer. But I'm thinking of taking it in a new direction. I'd like to work on horses, bodywork mostly, like Lori does."

"I want a job here, on weekends."

"What?"

"Karma is obviously happy here, and I can tell he loves you. Don't get me wrong, he still loves me most, obviously, but I can tell he loves you a little less than me."

Wyatt laughs and looks at Kiyomi. "Okay."

"I'm meant to start college next week, but only a two-hour drive from here. Your place is closer to my school than his old home at Eagle Feather."

"What are you taking at college?"

"I'm becoming a certified equine therapist. I'd like to help humans and horses dealing with trauma. Someday, I plan to have a place called Karma Ranch & Sanctuary. A place where people and animals seeking help can come together and heal in unison. But, also, I'd like to write books in my spare time. So, I'll be taking English and writing classes, too."

"Will you have spare time when doing all of that?"

"I'll make time."

"What kind of books do you want to write?"

"I'd like to write about horses, and other animals, and the bonds they have with humans. Since first meeting Karma, I've felt so connected to him. He knows me so well, and I seem to instinctively know what he needs. Also, he helps me with stress, anxiety, sadness – I don't know how exactly, but he does, and I'd like to share that with others who may need it."

Wyatt finishes his sandwich and wipes his hands on the front of his black t-shirt. He adjusts his ballcap then folds his hands together and leans into the fence.

"I can't pay you much," he says.

"What?" she says.

"If you were to have a job here on weekends, I couldn't pay you much. I'm still trying to re-build this place after my aunt and uncle ran it into the ground. There's not much money left over, which is why I don't have any help around here already."

"Don't pay me. I'll work weekends in exchange for Karma's board."

"So, you're leaving him here?"

"I don't know what else to do at this point. I can't bring him with me to college, nor can I afford to pay full board for him someplace else."

"I'd keep taking good care of him," says Wyatt. "And now that I know he doesn't like being ridden with a saddle, I'll take him out bareback when you're not here. If you're okay with that."

"That'd be fine, but I'd better stay a few more days and teach you how."

"Sure," says Wyatt with a smirk.

Chapter 75

Kiyomi has slept next to me on the ground for the past three nights. Once the sun tucks itself away at the end of the day, Kiyomi does the same within her stack of blankets on the grass. She tells me things about what I've missed in the years we've been apart until falling asleep.

During the day, she teaches Wyatt how to ride me bareback. Little does Kiyomi realize just how knowledgeable Wyatt is with horses and all the experience he has riding. But I can tell he doesn't mind spending the time with her, learning her secrets about me and whatnot.

"I don't want to leave you, Karma," says Kiyomi, tears forming in her eyes.

I'm grazing on grass in the pasture when she crouches down next to me and kisses my forehead. My eyes blink softly at her loving touch. I sigh heavily, take another bite of grass, then lift my head.

Wyatt is on the other side of the fence, standing next to Kiyomi's car. She's fiddling with the hem of her white t-shirt and has a worried look on her face. A pained energy radiates from her, and it pains me, too.

"I don't want to leave you, sweet boy," she says, leaning in for a hug. "I promise, I'll be back in five sleeps, on Friday. So, after you've gazed at the stars and moon five times, I'll be back."

She pulls away from me and wipes tears from her eyes with the back of her hand. Her long hair glistens in the late afternoon sun, as if she's glowing. Then, she turns her body and walks away from me.

I'm not keen to be too far apart, so I follow closely behind her. Too close as my nose accidently nudges her back from behind.

She giggles, then turns her body to walk backward. "You're a silly boy. But I sure do love you."

I nicker and keep pace with her walk until we reach the fence, and I can follow her no further. With a quick movement, Kiyomi tucks her body through the bottom two rungs of the wood fence and steps onto the grass on the opposite side to me. She leans her head over the top rung and kisses my forehead again. Then, she turns away.

"I don't want to leave him," says Kiyomi.

"I understand," says Wyatt, opening the car door for her.

"I'll be back in five days," she says. "Ready to work, of course. But I'm going to miss him so much in that time. Maybe I should put off college for the first semester and be with him instead."

"Is that really a logical idea?" asks Wyatt.

"No," says Kiyomi, tears slipping down her freckled nose. "Logic doesn't apply when you love someone so deeply."

"True – why don't you call each night and check in with me?" asks Wyatt with a smile. His cheeks flush red and he shoves his hands into his jean pockets. He looks down and watches rocks bounce off the edge of his boots. "I mean check in on Karma. That's what I meant to say."

Kiyomi's cheeks flush red, too, and she smiles. When she turns to walk away from Wyatt, she trips and laughs like she's partly choking. The pair of them seem like dang ding-dongs to me.

"I'll definitely do that," says Kiyomi. "I'll call every night."

"Good… great," says Wyatt, closing the car door for Kiyomi once she is safely in the driver's seat.

The car engine ignites before the wheels begin to move. Kiyomi looks at me through the open car window. She's smiling, but I can tell she's having a hard time. I nicker, then sing out, watching her with wide eyes as her car slowly moves along the driveway toward the exit of this place.

"I won't be gone long," says Kiyomi. "Karma… I love you."

Hearing her say my name that way stirs my soul. I lift my head and sing back to her, as loud as I can. Then, I run until I'm keeping pace with Kiyomi's car. She smiles and laughs, then leans her head out of the open car window a little.

"Karma," she sings.

I sing back. Tears fill her eyes, but she drives on anyway.

"I'll see you soon, sweet boy," she says before her car disappears over a ridge within the driveway.

I've reached the edge of the fence line and can follow no further. I lift my head and sing out after her again, but she doesn't respond. She said she would be back in five moons, but I miss her terribly already.

Chapter 76

Time is going so slowly. Why did it go super-fast when Kiyomi was here, but it seems to drag on now when she's not? She told me to count five nights of stars and moons, but it's only been three so far. Each night, I wish on a star for Kiyomi to be back here with me quickly and to never leave again.

At least I'm still here with Wyatt. Next to Kiyomi, he's my favorite human in the entire world. It would have broken my heart to leave him behind and go off with Kiyomi if it came to that. Now that he knows I prefer to be ridden barback, we go out each day after chores are done, and I love it. But even though I have Wyatt, I can't help still wanting my girl.

I hear my name sung out from near the barn. I lift my head and sing loudly in response. Then, I turn myself toward the barn and trot in that direction. That's Kiyomi's voice. But I've only counted three moons, there should be two more before she comes to see me.

"Karma," she sings again.

I sing back and pick up my pace to a gallop. When I set my sights on the area near the barn, I only see one human – Wyatt. That's weird, I've never heard his voice sound like Kiyomi's before.

Wyatt steps close to the fence with a big smile and leans his upper body onto the top rung. He's on the opposite side to me and waits.

"Karma," sings Kiyomi again.

Where in the heck is her dang voice coming from? Am I losing my mind? Is she calling me from somewhere other than where Wyatt is? What kind of game are these two playing? Maybe she's playing hide and seek with me, the way we did in the trees while living at Eagle Feather.

I stop running and spin myself around in a complete circle. As I do, I search in all directions, focusing on the trees, and try to locate Kiyomi. But I don't see that girl anywhere.

"Karma," shouts Wyatt. "Come over here, buddy. Yip, come on now."

I focus my sights on Wyatt again and trot. When I get closer to him, I notice he's smiling like a ding-dong and looking at the phone in his hand.

"You should see him," Wyatt says to his phone. "He's looking all around for you. I think we've got him confused."

I reach the fence and stop close to Wyatt. My eyes are wide, and I flare my nostrils with each inhale. He hasn't brought me anything to eat, nor does he have my crown like he's preparing to take me for a ride. What in the heck is this boy playing at? And where is my girl's voice coming from? Wyatt turns his phone around, so the screen is facing my direction.

"Hello, Karma," says Kiyomi, smiling at me from the phone's screen. "I miss you, sweet boy."

How did she get into there? I press my nose onto the phone and smell it. Her scent isn't on the thing, only Wyatt's. But how did she fit inside something so small? And why is Wyatt carrying her around in his hand?

"Karma," Kiyomi says, laughing. "You have an awfully large nose from this angle."

"I think he's trying to figure out how to get at you within the phone," says Wyatt.

"Awe. Only two more sleeps, Karma," says Kiyomi. "Then I'll be there with you again."

I nicker and pull my head back to look at her. I wish she weren't in that tiny phone and here with me instead. It would be the best if she were here with me and Wyatt all the time.

"He looks good," Kiyomi says to Wyatt.

"He is good, but I can tell he misses you," says Wyatt. "So, how's school going?"

"It's going well," says Kiyomi. "I have my own dorm room, which is nice. I prefer to have my own space."

"I like having my own space, too," says Wyatt. "Well, a little company is nice sometimes, too. Depending on, uh, who it is, you know? I… I'm, well, I'm looking forward to, uh, seeing you this weekend."

"Yes, yeah… I… I'm looking forward to it, too," says Kiyomi.

Wyatt shifts his body to lean into the fence. The phone is now facing him only, and I can hardly see Kiyomi's face. That's mighty rude if you ask me. I lean my head over the fence and rest it on Wyatt's shoulder. This way, I can see my girl's face again.

"Karmas not finished talking to you I guess," says Wyatt, laughing. He reaches his free hand up to my neck and rubs it.

"Karma is lucky to have you," says Kiyomi. "You're so good to him. I feel lucky that he's with you while I'm at school, too."

"Like I said," says Wyatt. "I love him and am happy to have him here."

"Is there anything you need from town before I head up there on Friday?" asks Kiyomi.

"Actually," says Wyatt, walking away from me and toward the barn. "Could you stop at the feed store for me?"

“Sure,” says Kiyomi.

Wyatt shifts away from the fence and slowly strolls toward the house. He keeps talking as he moves away from me, so I call out to him. But he ignores me. So, I call out again, and again. Still no response from him nor does he turn back. In fact, it seems like Kiyomi is ignoring me, too. The pair of them seem to have forgotten that I am the priority around here and are focusing entirely too much on each other. What a pair of dang ding-dongs.

Chapter 77

"Karma," sings Kiyomi loudly. "Karma, come here."

I lift my head and sing back to her. Then, I look at the barn where her voice is coming from. The last two nights, each time Kiyomi has called my name, it's been from Wyatt's phone. This time she's physically here.

"Karma, come here," she sings again.

I run as fast as I can toward her. Every few steps, I kick my back legs and whip my mane. I'm so dang excited to see the darlin.

"Hey, sweet boy," she says once I'm stopped next to her. Kiyomi stretches her hand toward me and resting within her palm is a treat. I lunge for it and gobble it up quickly. The sweet taste of it rushes across my tongue and makes my insides do a happy dance.

"I missed you, Karma," says Kiyomi, rubbing my neck and reaching into her pocket for another treat. "See, I told you I'd be back in five moons."

I nicker and eat the next treat.

"Shall we go for a ride?" asks Kiyomi, showing me that she's holding my crown and lead rope in the other hand.

I nicker and lower my head. She climbs over the fence to stand next to me before placing my crown and fixing my lead rope into reins. Then, she turns her head toward the barn and smiles.

"Wyatt," she shouts. "You almost ready to go?"

"On my way," says Wyatt.

Saddled and walking next to Wyatt is Tex. I didn't know those two were coming along, too. I want alone time with Kiyomi.

Kiyomi encourages me to get near the fence. Once she has me standing parallel to it, she climbs up to the top rung, still holding my reins, then sits on my back. Wyatt opens the closest gate and Kiyomi and I walk through it.

"Should we stick close to the house, or do you want to ride in an arena?" asks Wyatt.

Kiyomi looks at him as though he has two heads on his shoulders. Then, she makes a grunting sound and turns me around to face him.

"Are you concerned about my riding ability?" asks Kiyomi. "You know, I've been riding horses since I was five. You do the math."

"I'm sure you're a fine rider, but I was just trying to be polite, because you're bareback. Wouldn't you feel uncomfortable being out on a trail ride without a saddle or reins?"

"I've been on hundreds of trail rides. And for most of those, I've ridden bareback."

"Okay, I won't ask about it ever again."

"Try to keep up," says Kiyomi, smiling before encouraging me to walk forward.

Tex and Wyatt move in close behind us, all their dang equipment making noise with each step they take. I feel Kiyomi settle in on my back, and once we've gone a short distance, I feel the familiar oneness we'd always shared before. Her hands and body make the slightest movements, gentle commands, and I understand exactly what she wants me to do.

We walk past the pasture where the other horses are and

approach a ridge. Spanning out beyond is a great expanse of wilderness and it's beautiful. My heart flutters within my chest as I remember being lost in those woods.

"It's beautiful out here," says Kiyomi. "There must be miles and miles of trail to ride with your dude ranch guests."

"Yes," says Wyatt. "There's incredible country to see out here. If only I could get the guests to come back."

Kiyomi leads me to a worn path. We walk beneath a canopy of trees with sunlight trickling down through their branches. Near my feet and hugging the trail is long grass and wildflowers wilting from the cooler fall nights. The path is large enough for Tex and me to ride side by side, keeping Wyatt and Kiyomi close to one another, too.

"So, no guests again this weekend?" asks Kiyomi.

"Nope," says Wyatt.

"And no social media presence for the ranch at all? What about a website?"

"We're an old-fashioned outfit. We've never had a website nor anything on social media. I wouldn't even know where to begin with all of that."

"Well, the world seems to work via the internet and social media these days. Anytime anyone is looking for something they either Google it or search up social links."

"Okay," says Wyatt. He removes his hat from his head and scratches his shaggy locks with his fingers. I notice Kiyomi staring at him as he does, and for some reason, she fidgets and runs a hand through her long hair, as though she's grooming herself.

"I could help you with all of that if you want. Especially since I won't have much work to do this weekend without guests."

"All right."

Kiyomi and Wyatt talk and talk as we walk the trail through the woods. Soon, we approach a small creek.

"Should we let the horses have a rest and drink?" asks Kiyomi.

"Sure," says Wyatt.

They both move to the ground and let Tex and me drink from the creek and graze on grass. The day is growing hotter with the sun's rays bursting from a cloudless blue sky. Kiyomi takes off her jacket and lays it down on the ground. Wyatt does the same, removing his jacket, and lays it neatly next to Kiyomi's.

As I graze, Kiyomi walks along the creek, looking into it like it's a marvel. Wyatt sits on his jacket and rests. After Kiyomi has walked a short distance from Wyatt, I notice him fiddling with Kiyomi's jacket. Then, he pops something from within her pocket into his mouth.

My eyes widen and stare in disbelief, knowing exactly what he's just eaten. I nicker then call, keeping my sights on him.

"What are you getting on about, Karma?" asks Kiyomi, walking back over to us with a handful of small rocks.

Then, she looks at Wyatt who's still chewing, but has an awful look on his face.

"Are you okay?" she asks him.

He doesn't respond, only nods his head but with a scrunched forehead and worry in his eyes. Then, with his mouth still full, he asks, "What kind of granola bites did you have in your pocket and just how old are they?"

"I don't have granola bites in my pocket," says Kiyomi, looking at him quizzically.

"What was in your pocket then?" he asks.

"I have a pocket full of horse treats," says Kiyomi, now

looking amused. "Don't you know what those look like? Wyatt, did you just eat one of Karma's cookies?"

I nicker and step toward them. Then, I nicker again, hoping Kiyomi will understand that I'm saying I saw Wyatt eat one of my dang cookies and I'm not okay with that. Wyatt stands to his feet, takes a few steps away from Kiyomi, then bends over at the waist. He spits aggressively into the grass before moving over to the creek to rinse his mouth out with water.

Kiyomi laughs and before long, Wyatt is laughing, too. My eyes are still wide, my heart is hammering in my chest and I'm sure as heck not laughing. What kind of nerve does Wyatt have not only eating one of my cookies, but then spitting it out like its garbage. If I wouldn't get in trouble for it, I'd bite him right in the butt for doing that. No one messes with my treats.

Chapter 78

Seeing Kiyomi's face on Wyatt's phone each night when she's away helps the time pass a little easier. The only trouble is Wyatt only gives me a few seconds to see my girl before he dominates the dang conversation, and it really ticks me off.

Kiyomi's plan for increasing the dude ranch's social media presence has worked. We've been hosting guests for trail riding more and more. Even through these past winter months and over Christmas, our cabins were at half capacity. Now that the warmth of spring has melted the snow and encouraged the grass to grow, the ranch is gearing up for a busy summer season. The best part is, Kiyomi will now be here fulltime. I'm excited to spend every day with my girl.

"Karma," sings Kiyomi from near the barn.

I lift my head to look at her and sing back. She has a bowl of food and my crown in her hands, which means we must be going out for a ride.

"Karma, come here," she sings again.

I take off running in her direction, my legs loaded with excitement. Singing and whipping my mane as I move.

"Good boy," she says, opening the gate and allowing me to pass through to the other side of the fence. Once I'm next to her, I stand still and allow her to place my crown onto my head. Then, to reward my patience and loyalty, she gives me four treats all at once.

"Boop," she says, as her pointer finger gently taps the end of my nose, a game she taught me so many years ago. Then, she leads me to a wooden tie-up space with a bowl of food waiting for me on the ground. “Let’s get you fed.”

I dive into the food as Kiyomi ties my lead rope to a post. Then, as I’m eating, her phone rings from within her pocket. She smiles and pulls the phone out before answering it.

“Hello,” she says with a giant smile.

“Hello,” is said by a female voice from within the phone.

I lift my head and look at Kiyomi, particles of food slip from of my mouth as I chew. I recognize that voice.

“How are you doing?” Kiyomi asks.

“I’m good,” says the other female voice. “Just at the barn feeding my boy.”

“I’m feeding my boy, too,” says Kiyomi. “Let’s see what happens if we point our phones at each of them. I wonder what they’d do?”

“All right,” says the female voice.

Even though I’m still eating and nowhere near done, Kiyomi grabs hold of my crown and gently motions for me to lift my head. I sigh heavily, a little frustrated that she’d interrupt my meal, but do her bidding anyway. Then, she points her phone’s screen at my face and holds it there.

“Who’s that, Karma?” Kiyomi asks.

I can’t believe what I’m seeing on the phone’s screen. How in the holy heck did he get into there? It was difficult to fathom Kiyomi being inside a phone, even though she’s quite small, but him? He’s one of the biggest dang dudes I’ve ever met in my life. How does he even fit all that hair into there? Is that really even him?

My nostrils flare and clear, trying to pick up his scent, hoping I’ll find a familiar smell. But I’m not smelling anything out of the ordinary. I nicker, and it forces his ears to pick up. With wide eyes, he nickers back. Hearing him makes me nicker again. He nickers again, too. Kiyomi and the other female laugh as we do. A bubble of excitement swirls within my insides and demands to be released through my mouth in an epic song. My face moves closer to the phone, and I sing loud and proud. This pushes him to nod his head and call out in his unique and obnoxious tone that could only come from him. It must be him.

"Is it nice to see your bestie again, Karma?" asks Kiyomi, rubbing my neck. "You do recognize him, don't you?"

I nicker, a response to Kiyomi's question. I can't believe it. I never thought I'd see him again. It's my bestie, Digger.

"They seem to remember each other by sound," says the other female voice.

"Besties are difficult to forget," says Kiyomi. "No matter how long you've been apart."

Kiyomi releases the hold on my crown then moves the phone for the screen to face her instead. Why do she and Wyatt always do that to me? They think they should decide when I'm done speaking to whoever is on the other end of the phone. I haven't seen Digger in four years. I have a lot to catch him up on. Perhaps I should be getting my own dang phone.

"So, Megan," says Kiyomi to the female with Digger. "Did you decide whether or not you'll be coming up here this summer?"

"Yes," says Megan. "That's why I was calling. I'm coming to help you and Wyatt with the dude ranch this summer. And… I'm going to bring Digger with me, too."

"Yeah," shouts Kiyomi, startling me for a beat. "It'll be so awesome to have you here, not just for the help, but to hang out with you all summer."

“I’m super excited, too,” says Megan. “We should be there mid-afternoon Friday. It’ll be neat to see how Digger and Karma react to seeing one another again.”

“It will,” says Kiyomi. “Okay, drive safe and I’ll see you Friday.”

“See you Friday,” says Megan.

Kiyomi pushes her phone back into her pocket then leans her face close to mine. She’s smiling wide and rubbing my face with her hands.

“Did you hear that, Karma? Digger is coming to spend the summer with us. You get to see your bestie again.”

Chapter 79

I can smell the guy even before seeing him. A truck and horse trailer pull up in the driveway, and I lift my head to smell. Not only do I get a whiff of his musky scent, but I also get a hint of nostalgia, too. Everything is pointing to Digger being close.

I take off running along the fence that lines the driveway, moving closer and closer to the smell. I lift my head and sing out as I run. Then, I spot Digger's nose through the window of the horse trailer before he sings back to me.

The truck and trailer move further and further up the road and toward the barn. I turn myself around and run along the fence line again, keeping pace with Digger within the trailer. He calls to me again, and I respond before the truck and trailer stop in front of the smaller paddocks on the other side of the road near the barn.

Kiyomi and Wyatt come out of the barn, both smiling and waving. Then, Megan, climbs out of the driver's seat of the truck and hugs Kiyomi. I stand close to the gate and watch. Digger's face peaks out of the window and he watches me, too.

Megan walks around to the back of the trailer and opens the door. She steps inside and moments later, walks out with Digger on a lead rope. Instead of being cool and staying next to Megan, Digger pulls his head, trying to walk in my direction.

"Sorry, Digger," says Megan. "You need to quarantine before you can see Karma or the rest of the herd."

Digger nickers and calls out. I nicker and call out, then pace the fence moving back and forth. Within seconds, Digger is pulling Megan in my direction. Wyatt moves in to hold the lead rope, too, but Digger is too strong and determined. He pulls the two humans toward me, so Kiyomi tries to help, but even with all three, they can't hold him back. I'm flattered, obviously, but I don't want Digger to get in trouble or hurt a human just to get to me.

I lean my head over the fence, but the humans get a better grip on Digger and pull him away and toward the gate for the small paddock. Once he's inside, they remove his crown and leave him alone.

Digger runs and paces the fence. I run and pace the fence. The humans laugh and look at us like we're a couple of dang ding-dongs. But I can't help it, and, Digger can't either. So, we keep pacing and calling out to each other; a couple of old friends reunited at last.

My legs and lungs are burning, but it's not stopping me. Digger hasn't worn himself out either. The sun has set, and a full moon offers the perfect lighting to see my surroundings clearly. Since Digger arrived, he and I haven't stopped running and calling to each other. Its dang frustrating that the humans are keeping us apart.

"Enough!" shouts Kiyomi, coming out of her cabin in her pajamas. "You two are driving me crazy."

With sleepy eyes and messy hair, Kiyomi moves over to the gate where I'm pacing and opens the latch. I try to keep my composure and stay at her side like I should, but I'm just too dang excited. I push past Kiyomi and move over to the gate where Digger is in his paddock.

The moment we're close enough, we sniff at each other's

necks and both squeal with excitement. Kiyomi pushes past me and opens the gate before stepping inside to push Digger back off the gate. I follow her, and finally, find myself next to my bestie.

We smell each other again, then I groom his neck and Digger groom's mine. It's funny, I swear I can hear music playing around us. The stars in the sky twinkle, adding sparkle to the moment; not like we need more sparkle.

"You've landed yourself in Digger's quarantine, Karma," says Kiyomi. "I hope you're happy with yourselves. Now, the two of you need to shut up so the rest of us can get some sleep."

Kiyomi leaves and goes back to her cabin. Digger and I groom each other for a few minutes longer before stopping. Then, like my bestie can read my mind, he moves over to one of the fence posts, turns himself around and starts scratching his butt on it. I follow and do the same thing on the fence post two over from Digger. I've really missed this dude.

Chapter 80

It's been raining non-stop for several days. The ground is so wet, I feel as though I'm walking on ice. My back is soaked through and I'm shivering so Kiyomi has put a blanket on me. I don't like the way they feel, too restricting, but more embarrassing is that the blanket has pink flowers all over it. I'm a progressive man and all, but I don't like flowers unless they're for eating.

Digger and I left quarantine last week, so I can show him around the place a bit more. We don't have a poo pile quite as impressive as Eagle Feather's, but I showed him ours anyway. I remember how much he loved the thing in our old home.

Kiyomi and Wyatt are in a bad mood today. They aren't pleased with all the rain falling. Not only because it makes things difficult for horses and humans, but also because they were expecting the ranch to be full of guests this weekend and each one canceled. Since there is little work without guests, they gave Megan the weekend off and she decided to visit home. Digger stayed, though, and Kiyomi and Wyatt agreed to babysit him. Although, aside from feeding, I'm really the one watching out for the guy.

As the rain continues to soak everything through, Kiyomi and Wyatt do chores in the barn. Both have the same gloomy appearance as the sky. I'm not sure they should be quite as upset as they are, though. They get to be inside while it rains and neither of them is stuck wearing a blanket with pink flowers on it.

Hoping I can cheer them up somehow, I walk toward the gate within the fence closest to the barn and call out to them. Music is playing in the background, it's a man singing along to guitars, drums, and a fiddle, so they don't hear me. Kiyomi is lifting feed bags from a pallet and placing them in a pile along the far wall. Have they considered that feeding me that feed might help them feel better?

As Kiyomi lifts one of the bags, the bottom falls open, spilling the feed from inside onto the floor. My ears perk up and I pause in case they need me to come and help clean up the mess.

"Damn!" shouts Kiyomi, throwing the ripped feedbag onto the floor and placing her hands onto her hips. "Stupid bags are so flimsy."

"You sure it's the bag's fault?" asks Wyatt, smirking and looking away.

"What did you just say to me?" asks Kiyomi.

I've always known Wyatt to be a smart man, but in this moment, that was a dang stupid comment to make. Hopefully he'll survive after saying it.

"I said," says Wyatt, turning to look at Kiyomi. "Are you sure it's the bag's fault? You aren't exactly delicate when you're stacking them."

"Maybe you should stack the damn bags yourself," says Kiyomi.

"Whoa, I'm just kidding," says Wyatt, smirking and moving to lift one of the bags. "Geez."

"Why do I get the sense you aren't kidding?" asks Kiyomi.

She bends over and picks up a handful of the spilled feed. Then, she lifts her hand into the air and throws the stuff at Wyatt. He laughs and ducks, then picks up some feed and throws it at Kiyomi, too.

What in the heck are those two ding-dongs doing? Why are they throwing perfectly good food around? I nicker and lean my head over the fence. Then, I nicker again, trying to prompt them into throwing that food into my mouth instead of at each other.

"You asked for it now," says Wyatt. He picks up another handful of the feed and quickly runs to stand in front of Kiyomi, backing her into a corner. She laughs nervously as he takes the feed and drops it over her head. She squeals with laughter and squirms from her position. Then, she runs around him and rushes to grab more feed off the floor. Wyatt is on to her plans, so he takes off running through the back part of the barn, and Kiyomi runs after him.

They run, laugh, and dodge each other for several minutes before Wyatt turns toward Kiyomi, lifts her up and throws her over his shoulder. Then, still carrying her, he runs outside, allowing the rain to soak them both.

"Wyatt!" Kiyomi says through laughter. "Put me down! I'm soaked!"

I nicker and pace the gate. Maybe I should join in. It looks like the two of them are playing a super fun game. Surely, they must need a third.

"You started it!" says Wyatt, smiling and turning around in circles.

"Put me down!" says Kiyomi.

Wyatt does as he's asked and places Kiyomi onto the ground to stand on her feet. They laugh and Kiyomi uses her fist to whack Wyatt in the chest. Then, they pause and stare at each other. Neither of them is smiling anymore and both have stopped laughing. Each one looks into the other's eyes, and it appears they're both breathing heavily.

Then, Wyatt clasps Kiyomi's face into his hands and presses

his lips into hers. Kiyomi wraps her arms around him, and they stay with their lips smooshed together for quite a long time.

What kind of game are they playing now?

Chapter 81

Kiyomi and Wyatt play their new lip smooshing game all the dang time. I thought it was just something to do when it was raining, but they're smooshing their lips together a heck of a lot. Not only that, but they also always have their hands twisted together like one giant knot. Even when we're out riding on the trails, they move Wyatt's horse and I close together so they can twist their fingers and clasp hands. It's a safety risk if you ask me, and they should stop doing it.

They kept that silly game going even after the summer ended and Kiyomi went back to college. The worst part about it all is that whenever Kiyomi comes home on the weekends, she always stops to smoosh lips with Wyatt before she even comes to see me. That's just dang rude.

Even now, a year later, as they stand together and continue to play their game, it's like she doesn't notice me patiently waiting for her. I've let her know where I'm standing by pacing back and forth. Heck, she's even ignoring all my best lyrics. I've been singing them loudly for her since she stepped out of the car.

Finally, they step apart and turn toward me. As they walk to approach, they make a knot with their hands and smile like ding-dongs. I'm beginning to worry these two might be sick in the head.

"Karma," sings Kiyomi.

I don't sing back. I've been singing and singing for that girl for so long, I'm too offended to answer her back now.

"Karma," she sings again.

I stand and stare at her. Can't she see I'm standing right here? I've been standing here all along.

"Hey, sweet boy," she says, approaching the gate.

She pulls her hand away from Wyatt's and reaches into her pocket. Then, she holds her hand out and offers me treats. I take them and I guess I forgive her now. As I chew, she uses her pointer finger and gently pushes it into my nose before saying, "boop." I lean in close to her face and tap my nose onto hers.

"Do you want a horse treat, too?" Kiyomi asks Wyatt, smirking and holding one out toward him.

No, he does not. Those are my dang treats. I move my head and snatch the cookie from Kiyomi's hand before Wyatt has a chance to take it.

"Ha, ha," says Wyatt. "No, thank you."

Kiyomi climbs over the fence and stands close to me. My eyes soften as she rubs my neck with her hands.

"This is my last weekend before school is over," says Kiyomi. "What should we do to make the most of it, huh Karma?"

Wyatt climbs over the fence and stands next to Kiyomi. Then, he rubs my neck, too, which makes me relax even more. I really do love these two, even if they don't have their priorities, meaning me, straight.

"That's right," says Wyatt. "Last week of school for you, and then you'll be done. I can't believe you're graduating. Time flew by so fast. Any ideas on what you'd like to do next?"

"Well," says Kiyomi. "I'm excited to get going with my career. But I guess that means I won't be able to work here anymore."

"Right," says Wyatt, looking at Kiyomi and pursing his lips.

He looks nervous, and I can feel anxious energy radiating off him.

"I can still manage your social media, though," says Kiyomi, her voice shifting to a whisper. Oddly, nervous energy is now radiating off her, too. "And I hope we'll still see each other as much as possible."

Wyatt sighs heavily and steps toward Kiyomi, not taking his eyes off her for a second.

"I'm not sure that's going to work out for me," says Wyatt.

Kiyomi's face drops and I feel pain in her heart. "Oh, what do you mean by that?" she asks.

"I mean, seeing you as much as possible isn't going to work for me."

"What will work for you then?"

"Kiyomi," says Wyatt, pulling her face into his hands and pushing his lips into hers for a moment. "I'm deeply in love with you."

Kiyomi's face lights up and the pain in her heart shifts to immense joy. "I am deeply in love with you, Wyatt."

Wyatt steps back and gets down onto the ground. He has one knee on the grass while the other is bent. He must be trying to give Kiyomi a leg up so she can jump onto my back. Just in case they need my help, I shift my body to stand in between the two of them so Kiyomi can climb on.

"Karma," says Wyatt laughing, rubbing at my backside as a gesture for me to move out of their way. "I'm kinda in the middle of a big moment here."

Getting ready to ride with Kiyomi is always a big moment for me, too. Instead of climbing onto my back, though, Kiyomi steps around me so she and Wyatt are facing again.

"It's fitting that he would be here and right in the middle of us for this," says Wyatt. "After all, he's the one who technically brought us together."

Kiyomi doesn't speak. She keeps staring at Wyatt and breaths heavily.

"Kiyomi," says Wyatt. From his pocket, he pulls out a small gold ring with a sparkling stone on it. I inspect the stone and it reminds me of one of my wishing stars.

"Kiyomi," he continues. "This ranch doesn't work without you. I don't work without you. Will you marry me?"

Kiyomi's eyes flood with tears and she smiles. Then, she holds her hand out toward Wyatt. I lower my head and smell it just in case she's trying to give him another one of my treats, but she's not.

"Yes," she says. "I will marry you."

Wyatt slides the golden ring onto her finger, then stands. He lifts her into his arms, and they smoosh lips again. I suppose I might need to get used to watching them carry on like this for the rest of my life.

Chapter 82

There's something oddly entertaining about that thing. As the afternoon sun sets beyond a cluster of birch trees, all full of fall foliage in colors of red, orange, and yellow, the artificial color of green flaps among them in the wind. Kiyomi told me the green things are called balloons. They've been tangled in that same tree since Wyatt and Kiyomi's wedding two years ago. Each time someone points out the deflated things in the branches, Wyatt and Kiyomi always say they'll climb up there and take them down. But they don't. Secretly, they must want to keep them there as a memento of the amazing day.

Digger would enjoy watching the deflated balloons with me, too. When he isn't here visiting along with Megan, I miss him a heck of a lot. But they always seem to come back and visit from time to time. And when they do, we always get up to our old shenanigans and being besties.

"Karma," shouts Kiyomi from near the barn.

I lift my head and sing loudly before turning my body around and looking for her. There she is, in the same spot she calls me from each day since the wedding.

"Karma, come here," she says again.

I lift my head and sing again before running toward her and the barn. She's smiling and I see the same gleam in her eye that I did when we first met all those years ago when she was a scrawny kid. Did she understand then, as a child, that she made my wishes come true?

"Hello, sweet boy," she says, opening the gate and letting me walk through. I stand close to her and remain still while she places my crown onto my head. Then, I take a treat from her outstretched hand. She rubs my neck and leads me toward the barn where there's a bowl of food waiting.

"Well," says Kiyomi. "We have a new horse arriving today, Karma."

I nicker and look up, and food falls from my mouth as I chew.

"Wyatt should be here with her any minute. Yes, it's a mare. But she isn't coming alone. She has a colt only days old with her. The poor things didn't have a great home, so they're coming to live with us."

Kiyomi rubs my neck, then sits on the ground next to me as I eat. Something we've done together thousands of times, but still, I love it just as much as I did the first time. I lower my face close to her and she lifts her hand. Pointing her index finger, she gently taps the end of my nose with it and says, "boop." Then she smiles as I push my nose onto her nose, playing our game.

"I'll need you to be the sweet and welcoming horse you always are to the newcomers, Karma. Show them around and make sure mama and her little boy are safe and watched over."

I nicker again. I can do that. Funny, now that I'm of a certain age, I've come to really like the youngsters Kiyomi works with around here. I didn't think I could ever like being around babies after spending so much time living with them at the Vet clinic. Now, I've grown to like them.

The sound of Wyatt's truck grows louder beyond the barn doors. Kiyomi stands up from her spot next to me and walks back outside. I gobble up my food, not keen to share it with anyone new. I'm happy to show the new gal around, but sharing my food is an entirely different story.

"Hey," says Kiyomi, approaching the truck as Wyatt exits it. "You guys have a nice drive this morning?"

"Yip," says Wyatt. "She's still fast asleep in the back."

"Worn out," says Kiyomi. "Well, let's have a look at the newcomers, shall we?"

Kiyomi and Wyatt mumble a bunch as they walk to the back of the horse trailer. I stand still and watch through the open door of the barn.

"Awe," says Kiyomi. "How adorable are you?"

Footsteps echo from the horse trailer before landing on the dirt. Then, a song is sung by the voice of an angel. I've never heard this singing before, so I know it's coming from the new mare. I lift my head and sing back. Then, the new horse sings again. Once she's through, the small voice of a young horse tries to mimic the melody of its mother. I lift my head and sing again.

"All right," says Kiyomi. "Give us a second, Karma."

"Should we put them in this front paddock?" asks Wyatt.

"Yeah," says Kiyomi.

They lead horses around the other side of the trailer, making it so I can't check out the newcomers. A gate opens, then, closes again. Finally, Kiyomi comes back into the barn and gets me.

"You can't get too close yet, but I'll let you take a look at the new mare and colt," she says. "I know how excited you get meeting new horses, but just try and be cool. I need you to show them around their new home here on Karma Ranch."

Kiyomi leads me out of the barn and to the left. There's a powerful jolt within my belly the first time I lay eyes on her. Standing within the paddock closest to the barn is a horse with beautifully muscular legs. She has a vibrant red mane, like the heat of fire, and a white body with red patches. Her eyes are slender and framed by long lashes akin to butterfly wings. I have never laid eyes on such a magnificent creature in all my life, and I've been around. Ding… dong, well hello there, darlin.

"This is, Rhoda," says Kiyomi, leaning in close to me. "Isn't she beautiful?"

I nicker and sing aloud, still in utter shock by this fine lady before me. Then, a colt only days old, pops out from behind her and looks at me. My heart flutters, and I have a strong urge to watch over the little fella and teach him stuff.

"We don't have a name for the colt yet but isn't he adorable?" asks Kiyomi.

I nicker and whip my head, hoping Rhoda will notice my wavy-haired mane. Chicks can't resist my beautiful locks.

"Looks like he's smitten," says Wyatt, walking over to the truck and trailer.

"He is," says Kiyomi. "But I'm impressed by how calm he's being around her, too."

"Must be trying to impress her," says Wyatt. "Act cool and all."

"Right."

Wyatt opens the door to the truck, then walks back over toward Kiyomi and me. "Look who decided to wake up."

Kiyomi turns to look and smiles. "Hello, my beautiful girl. Did you have a nice time with Daddy?"

Wyatt is holding the small human filly that Kiyomi delivered a year ago. They call her their daughter. In my opinion, she is made up of the best parts of both Kiyomi and Wyatt.

"Kaka," she says. Drool drips from her sparsely toothed mouth, and she waves her hand toward me when she says it. She giggles and scrunches her dainty nose – dotted with light freckles that mimic the stars in the sky.

She began calling me kaka only a few weeks ago. I'm sure it must mean something awesome, even if Wyatt and Kiyomi always laugh whenever she says it. But heck, that little darlin can call me whatever she likes.

"You want to ride, kaka?" asks Kiyomi, smiling and giggling. "Okay, kaka, let's go for a ride."

Wyatt holds their daughter in one hand, then seamlessly gives Kiyomi a leg up and onto my back with the other. Then, he lifts their small one up and nestles her directly in front of Kiyomi. The little darlin's hands tangle into my mane and grip tightly. For something so small, I can tell she has strong hands, just like her mama.

I don't know how I got so dang lucky. The only thing I've ever wanted in this life was love. And now, heck, I'm surrounded by it. Even through the times life was not perfect, I tried to love others anyway. Seems to me the more love I was willing to give, in the end, more love ended up coming to me. I'm not sure how to describe it, exactly.

Perhaps, simply put, it's just horse karma.

The End

CPSIA information can be obtained
at www.ICGtesting.com
Printed in the USA
LVHW112036270323
742731LV00020BA/489